A TASTE *of* HONEY

DARREN COLEMAN

A TASTE *of* HONEY

Amistad

An Imprint of HarperCollins*Publishers*

HarperCollins books may be purchased for educational, business, or sales promotional use. For information please write: Special Markets Department, Harper-Collins Publishers, 10 East 53rd Street, New York, NY 10022.

FIRST EDITION

Designed by Chris Welch

Library of Congress Cataloging-in-Publication Data has been applied for.

ISBN: 978-0-06-085193-4
ISBN-10: 0-06-085193-7

07 08 09 10 11 DT/RRD 10 9 8 7 6 5 4 3 2 1

This book is dedicated to my good friend
and fellow author Joy King.

Your friendship means the world. Thanks for the push.

Also to my friend Lynn Thomas;

you may have lost your mother, but the beauty of her spirit
lives through you. You've dedicated yourself to being a beautiful
person and to helping others in their tough times. We all get
by with a little help from our friends. God bless you.

A TASTE *of*
HONEY

1

June 1992

FROM HAILEY TO HONEY

This nervousness was different from what I felt the day when I'd let J.D. stick his hands inside my panties while we rode the Metro bus home from school down Georgia Avenue through the heart of the nation's capital. J.D. had been my first boyfriend and for as much as I could at that point in my life, I loved him. I'd been willing to let him explore my body bit by bit until the day when we went all the way on the top bunk in his bedroom. He was my first. I was his third, but his inexperience left me with no real clue as to why sex was so damned important. Even after a year of sexing every chance we got I was still looking for the fireworks, wondering why J.D. could never last for more than two minutes. I'd actually wondered what I was doing wrong.

At the hands of the man standing a few feet away from me, finally I was feeling something. Just watching Manny take his shirt off I could feel my temperature rising. I truly had knots in my stomach as my heart fluttered like a butterfly on speed.

"Fine-ass" Manny, as me and my girlfriends called him, lived with Cheron in the apartment across the hall. Cheron was like a glamour girl to me, which made it understandable why she barely spoke to any of us young girls who routinely camped out in front of the building. She moved in a rush it seemed whenever she went out in her red Camry coupe. Stealing glimpses of her was like a major event, since she was always dressed in the latest fashion, rocking seven-hundred-dollar purses, diamonds in her ears and on her wrist. It was easy to see why she'd landed a guy like Manny. She was beautiful, hip, and fly. If for no other reason than the fact that she was always so well put together, she was like a hero to me. Even still, one glance at him and you knew that he could have had any girl he wanted, including Cheron. He looked like he'd crawled out the pages of a magazine with his bronze skin, chiseled chest, and curly hair.

I figured he was at least twenty, too old for me to be looking at him the way I did but I couldn't help myself. None of my friends could. Usually, I'd come home from school and he'd be home out front wiping down his car, which was a brand-new Benz. Sometimes he'd be sitting on his porch reading a *Final Call* or a *Vibe* magazine while listening to music through the screen door. The entire year that they'd lived there, all he did was smile at me until the day he saw me in a miniskirt I'd borrowed from my best friend, Rorrie.

That was the day he'd looked down at me from his balcony as I headed up the short walk to the door and asked, "Shorty, what's your name?"

A part of me was so shocked that he'd actually spoken to me that I nearly ignored him and headed into the building, up the steps and into my apartment. The other part of me was hoping that this man had really graced me with his voice, so I answered in a near whisper, "Hailey."

"Hailey," he said as he took a huge gulp from a Styrofoam cup he'd placed on the porch next to his chair. "What time your mother come home from work?"

"She'll be here about six," I answered, wondering why he wanted to know.

He nodded and a slight grin appeared on his face. "Come up here for a second," he commanded as if I'd truly known him or had some type of relationship with him. He'd beckoned me to his apartment and there was not a hint of doubt in his voice that I'd come.

I'd climbed those stairs nervously and now here I was. From the moment I walked through the door it had felt like I'd stepped into the Twilight Zone. Briefly I had admired their apartment. It wasn't plain like ours. I thought the black carpet and white leather couches looked rich. The walls were painted in oranges, reds, and yellows, and they even had a big-screen television that was showing videos on BET, with a stereo on top of it that was blasting Jodeci's latest, "Feenin'."

Manny had sat me on that couch long enough to break down for me what was about to happen. "Hailey, I see how you and your friends look at me. I also know you're still in high school. I was going to wait until you graduated, but looking at you I can tell that you're ready to become a woman. I've also seen your little boyfriend sneak in and out of your house so I know you ain't no virgin."

His words were so silky-smooth but it didn't even matter. The entire time I only watched his face as he spoke, the sounds that came out of it were irrelevant until he leaned in and kissed me for the first time.

Fifteen minutes later the room was spinning as my clothes

came flying off. I knew I had to be crazy up in the bed that they slept in, but where he led, I was willing to follow.

I wasn't a freak, a whore, or even a sex fiend like so many of the girls I knew, but I had given in to Manny so easily that I didn't understand it. He'd pulled the curtains in the room so that it had darkened to the point where I could only see shadows of him. He told me to relax and I tried. His kisses felt good on my neck and his massaging of my breast had my body on fire. Then he did something that was unexpected.

With my legs pinned up by his hands he put his mouth on me and ate me. Rorrie had talked about it, but I had no idea that it would feel this good. I felt relaxed and tense at the same time. His warm tongue sent shockwaves through my body and I felt an unfamiliar urge to explode. I didn't know what was happening other than I knew Manny was taking good care of me.

He did this for five more minutes and then he stopped, to my dismay. At this point I opened my eyes and saw him sliding up toward me; I knew he was about to enter me. I reached down to feel him, but he moved my hand away and replaced it with his. Obviously he was trying to keep me from being scared by his size, because I felt the pressure from the second he began entering me. He was stretching me but my wetness, surprisingly, allowed him to glide right in once he made it through the initial pains.

What happened next blew my mind. Not twenty strokes and he began to pant like a wounded bear. I didn't realize it but my hands were on his back and I moved with him. He tensed up and I kept moving as he screamed out. A few seconds later and he collapsed beside me.

There was silence for a few moments until he said, "Hailey,

I'm sorry. I can't believe I came so fast. I never do that, but damn, you got something special right there. I mean that."

I didn't know what to say. I was used to it. J.D. had always blasted quickly. "It's fine," I said.

"No, it's not," he said. "A man is supposed to represent and take care of your needs too. Did you like when I ate you?"

I smiled on the inside. "Yes."

"Well, I'm supposed to make you feel even better during the sex but I couldn't help myself. I just felt so good. Unbelievable actually."

I chuckled and asked, "Seriously?"

"Hailey, you just don't know. I've been with a lot of women, but that right there that you have is golden. When I went down on you it was the sweetest sex I ever tasted." I was smiling at him but he couldn't see me. "Matter of fact your mama shouldn't even have named you Hailey. She shoulda' named you Honey, 'cause that's what you have between your legs . . . a big ol' pot of honey." Then he shot me a smile that I didn't even know he had and I felt myself melting a bit.

Manny got hard again and I let him climb on top so that he could do me again. He tried but didn't last any longer the second go-round. I wasn't angry and didn't know enough to be disappointed but I immediately decided to head home to shower and finish my homework. Thirty minutes later I heard a knock at the door. I looked out the peephole and saw Manny.

I looked at the clock and it said a quarter till six. My mother would be home in fifteen minutes. There was no way I was letting him in but still, I opened it. "Hey," I said. "What's up?"

He extended his hand to me and said, "Listen. This is our little secret you know that right?"

I nodded yes and said, "For sure."

"Good," he replied but went on. "I just wanted to tell you again how much I enjoyed you." Then he placed his hand on mine and I felt the paper. "You deserve this." He'd handed me a bunch of bills folded up.

I looked down and saw that it was nothing but hundred-dollar bills. "Manny, you don't have to give me money."

"Don't be crazy. I know you can use it. And plus, it was worth it. Any guy you give that loving to, needs to pay," he said smiling. He winked at me and asked, "I'll see you after school tomorrow?"

"Okay, maybe," I said before closing the door.

In my room, my heart went crazy when I counted out the eight hundred dollars that he'd given me. Puzzled, I jumped up and pulled my skirt and panties off then I went to the mirror. I stood on a chair and examined my vagina, trying to figure out what in the world made it so special that Manny of all people would pay me to have sex.

I tossed and turned all night long, thinking about the next day and what would happen. I imagined "fine-ass" Manny losing control over my loving again and giving me more money. I had never had more than a few hundred dollars at one time, and my grandmother had to die for me to get that. I imagined Manny would be waiting on his balcony at home for me while I stopped off at Union Station after school to do some shopping.

Finally I drifted off to sleep with a smile on my face, looking forward to what would happen the next time I gave Manny a taste.

It felt so good to be able to buy whatever I wanted for the first time, but as I walked through the mall I was troubled by the fact that I couldn't spend any of this money on my mother. If I did, she'd wonder where it had come from. Then as I walked past a stand that sold umbrellas something caught my eye. The stand had wallets on it. I bought one and strolled right into one of my mother's favorite stores.

My mother loved church, but skipped some Sundays because she didn't have anything to wear, which I never understood. I knew that she had always taken pride in her appearance. I'd listen to her stories about how she'd had it going on back in her day. She was beautiful and I was thankful that I looked so much like her, but I didn't see the sense of style that she always bragged about. In fact, I thought my mother was extremely plain and almost nerdy.

I decided to use almost half of the money I had to change that. I was able to buy her four outfits and two pairs of shoes and still I had some left over. For myself I copped three pairs of jeans, some shorts, a few tops from Gap, some new Air Jordans, and some new panties and bras from Victoria's Secret.

As I strolled out of the mall looking like a young celebrity, arms full of bags, I heard a guy calling for my attention. I ignored him and continued up the platform toward the subway. By the time I reached the top of the escalator, there he was.

"You didn't hear me calling you?" he asked once he was at my side.

"I heard you, but I don't know you," I said, continuing to walk.

He smiled and then he said, "Yeah, but I'm trying to change that."

"Yeah, well I'm not interested."

Still walking he continued, "It's like that. Your loss, especially since I see you like to shop."

I stopped and looked him in the eye. "Why is that?" Young and green, I had taken his bait and he had me on the hook now, which made us even. To be honest, I had no idea how much I would love being able to shop until today. It was my first time going from store to store without my mother and spending money that wasn't for Christmas.

"I like to shop too and I don't mind spending on my girl especially if she treats me good."

I nodded. "Well, I ain't your girl and I don't want to be." I finished with "So how is that gonna benefit me?"

The truth was that I wasn't even allowed to have the boyfriend I did. In fact, J.D. didn't even have my phone number and I'd only snuck him in a couple times during the whole year. I was a month away from my fifteenth birthday and it had long been established that I'd be sixteen before I could have a boyfriend.

"Let me get your number and I'll break it down for you when I come pick you up." I stared at his face. He was tall and handsome. His teeth were messed up though, and his eyes looked a little beady, but his haircut was perfect and for some reason I was feeling his baby mustache. He was nowhere close to Manny's league but he had a certain cockiness about him that was appealing. I could tell he had a little money, because the thick chain with diamonds in the charm gave it away.

The fresh jeans he had on, plus he was rocking the same Jordans that I'd just bought, had me feeling his style. "I don't have a number." The look on his face turned to a smirk. "I don't give out my home number."

He reached into his pocket and pulled out a card. As he dug for the card he showed a huge wad of cash—on purpose, I was sure. He handed the card to me and said, "I own this tattoo parlor. You call me and maybe you can come past there and we can talk about what you like and about what I like. Maybe I'll hook you up with a tat on the house."

At the risk of sounding young and dumb I shook the bags in my hand at him and in my most self-assured voice I said, "You see what I like."

He nodded. "I'm good with that. My name is Tank. What's yours?"

I almost said "Hailey" but caught myself. I wasn't sure if I'd ever call him but if I did I wasn't going to do it as Hailey. So without having to think much further I replied, "Honey. My name is Honey."

2

KHALIL

She wasn't my real mother but that didn't make it hurt any less watching the ending unfold before my eyes. My father was begging her not to leave. Not to leave us. Though I was standing right there in the hallway, I might as well have been invisible.

"Kevin, I can't do this anymore. I can't," Frannie replied to his pleading.

"Frannie, what about Khalil? What about him? He needs you. You're the only mother he's ever known." He tried everything else, now I was the pawn. True, I wanted her to stay but I had no idea how much weight I would carry with my father's girlfriend.

Yet, now I was waiting for something. It was the first time my name had ever been brought up in an argument. What he'd said had been true. My mother had been a drug addict and neither of us had seen her in almost ten years. I was about to turn thirteen and Frannie had been around since I was six.

"I'll always be there for Khalil, but I can't do this anymore."

Then my father said the unthinkable.

"The hell you will. If you leave here then you'll never see him again." Hearing this sent a slice of anguish through my insides. I didn't know why he'd said something like that. "I mean it. You won't be taking my son around any other men."

Frannie paused and I could tell from her voice's trailing off and quaking that she was near tears. "Kevin, that's your decision and I'll have to respect it." Then she looked over at me standing there. She shook her head slowly in what appeared to be disgust before she said, "Khalil, I love you. I always will and I'll try to see you as much as I can as long as your father . . ."

Cutting her off, my father stepped into our line of view. "Bitch, you don't love him. If you did, you wouldn't leave *us.*"

At the top of her voice she yelled as tears began to pour: "I'm not leaving him. I'm leaving you, Kevin. I'm leaving you."

As cold as ice he walked past her and opened the door and replied, "It's the same thing. Now go."

She wiped her face and grabbed her bags and headed out the door. "I'll call you to arrange to come and get my things."

"Don't bother. Anything you left will be in the Dumpster by the morning."

She yelled something from the hall as my father slammed the door. He ran to the kitchen, found a bottle of liquor, and drank straight from it. Then he took a seat on the couch and called me to him. "Khalil, listen," he said in his deep, raspy voice. "I'm sorry you had to see that, but that's the way love goes. I did everything for Frannie and this is how she repaid me. She don't care about me and she damned sure don't care about you."

I was dumbfounded as I stood there watching my father drinking white liquor as if it were water. "Dad, I can't see her anymore?" I asked.

He was silent, sensing my pain. Then he nodded. "If she calls to see you, sure you can. But don't hold your breath. She don't care about nobody but herself and you'll see how easy she forgets you. We're better off, believe that. You're my son, not hers and if you sit around waiting on her, you'll see exactly what that means."

I did. Over the next few months I learned how to make do without a woman in the house. I kept waiting on Frannie to come by or to call to at least let me know that she cared about me, but she did neither.

She let me down and slowly but surely I began to hate her just as much as my father did. Without her presence though I had no one to project the ill feelings on so I bottled it all up, until Tina came.

3

HONEY

By the time I left the mall I realized that I wouldn't make it home in time to be able to spend time with Manny. When I climbed out of the cab he was standing on his balcony waiting, looking at his watch. It was after six and my mother was already home. I looked up and smiled at him. He didn't smile back, which made me uncomfortable. *Was he angry?* I climbed the steps, hands full of bags, and prepared to put my keys in the door when Manny's swung open.

"Hey, what happened to you today?" he whispered.

I held the bags up in the air. "It took me longer than I thought."

He nodded. "Looks like you burned the mall up," he said, still sounding like he had a slight attitude. "Listen, I want you to come over in a few minutes."

"What about Cheron?"

"Don't worry about that. I'll be on the balcony once she's gone so all you gotta do is come out front. If you see me out there then everything's good. Hurry up though."

I frowned. He could tell I wasn't sure about it. But that was all wiped away when he said, "Here, catch." Then he tossed a bunch of bills folded up and wound tight in a rubber band. "I'll see you in about twenty minutes."

Mama couldn't believe her eyes as she looked at the things I'd purchased for her. She'd bought the story about me finding the wallet but had asked, "Baby, are you sure there wasn't any identification in the wallet?"

I told her a story about me finding it on the floor of the Metro bus. She couldn't argue with that. She did complain about me spending all of it. "You always need to save something. Even if it's a gift from above, you need to save some and give some back." She laughed as she tried on the sandals that she'd been wanting. "Child, these things are nice. Nine West are my favorites."

"I know, Mama."

Five minutes later she was in her room trying on her outfits. Once I heard her on the phone bragging to one of her friends I decided to leave. "I'm going out for a minute, Mama."

"Okay, sweetie. Don't be too long. I'm going to fry some chicken and make you some mac and cheese."

I tucked my money inside of my pillow and pulled out the Victoria's Secret bag that I'd hidden at the bottom of the Foot Locker bag. I washed up quickly then took my clothes off so that I could put on one of the new pairs of panties and a bra. I loved the feel of the new bra. It was one of the new push-up ones. I was already a 32C and growing, but the new bra gave me a little extra confidence.

I put my clothes back on and headed out the door into the humidity just long enough to find Manny up on the balcony. He was doing curls with his dumbbells, looking fine as ever. I looked up and he waved as he said, "Come on."

The routine was the same. He ate me out and got me soaked only to get in and bust quickly. "Dammit," he shouted. "I don't know what's up." He was mumbling to himself. "It ain't like I haven't had some good . . ."

"Is it something I'm doing wrong?" I asked. "For all that you're doing for me I want you to enjoy yourself."

He laughed and sat down on the bed. "Naw, precious. It ain't you . . ." He caught himself. "No it *is* you, but not because of anything you're doing wrong. I can only keep it real with you, you have got to have the best pussy I have ever had."

I cringed when I heard the word *pussy.* It sounded so crude. "Is that why . . ."

"Yeah. That's why I keep coming so fast. I can't help it. As soon as I start to stroke it, it feels so hot, wet, and there's something else that I can't describe but it feels incredible. I'm telling you, Hailey, your shit is the bomb."

"That wasn't what I was going to ask. I was asking if that was why you keep giving me money?"

He shrugged his shoulders. "I guess. But I give you money because I have a lot of it. And, plus if I'm nice to you, then you'll be nice to me. This is our secret, I wouldn't want this to get out."

"Because I'm underage, right?"

"Shorty, I don't know how old you are. As a matter of fact if you say you're eighteen then I gotta believe you. You are eighteen right?"

The look on his face told me that I needed to go along. "Yep, eighteen."

"Good." He smiled before he leaned in and kissed me. Quickly he was all over me and hard again. Just as he started to get into a rhythm where it seemed like he'd finally gained control of his problem I decided to see exactly how much I could affect him.

I began to moan loudly as I humped him back and then I cried out, "It's yours, Manny."

"Oh shit," he yelled back. "Ohhhhhh, shit." His body began to buck wildly and he came again. He'd gone almost two minutes this time.

My eyes were closed as I was in some weird afterglow, feeling ultra-relaxed. Inside I was proud of what was appearing to be my superpowers. I was ready to get up and get dressed when I felt my hair being pulled as if someone was trying to literally separate my head from my shoulders. The pain came sharply and when my eyes opened and I realized it was Cheron my heart skipped a beat. The look on her face told me that I was dead.

"You have got the wrong one you little ho," she barked.

I didn't know what to do. Here I was, ass-naked in her bed and she was already in jeans and sneakers with a handful of my pony-tail. I tried to yank away but her grip was too firm. She threw a series of punches that I was able to block with my forearms. This only angered her more as she was yelling and trying to hit me. I wondered what was taking Manny so long to intervene. When he grabbed her I noticed that he had on a pair of shorts by this point.

"Hailey, put your clothes on and go on home," he said as he was pulling his chick out of the room. If getting dressed had been an Olympic sport, I would have set the world record. He'd barely pulled her into the kitchen when I went scurrying past them and out the door.

———

Even in the safety of my home I was still nervous waiting to see if Cheron was going to come for me, or worse, to tell my mother. That would have been a disaster, because I was certain that she was convinced her baby girl was still a virgin. I sat on the couch for the rest of the evening, prepared to run interference for any knock at the door. I drifted off promising myself that I'd never go near Manny again if Cheron showed any willingness to give me a second chance.

I woke up at seven in the morning relieved that the night had come and gone without incident. I watched with my eyes half-shut, feigning sleep as my mother was leaving for work at the Walter Reed Army Medical Center. I took my time leaving for school. It was the last week of classes and most people were skipping anyway. I was going because I had an exam and plus I wanted to show off my new clothes. Most of all, I didn't want to be sitting around in the event that Cheron came knocking.

I stared at myself in the mirror as I prepared to leave out the door. I looked super-cute in the snug Bebe T-shirt and black miniskirt, not to mention the fresh new Jordans. On top of all that there was something about wearing new underwear that made you feel good and it was my second day in Vickie's.

I hadn't made it up the walk when I heard Manny's voice behind me. "Yo, Hailey, you alright?" He was on the balcony.

I ignored him and kept on walking toward the corner where I usually met my girlfriends. I got halfway there and Manny came running up behind me. "What's up with you, girl?"

I paused only long enough to say, "Manny, this was a bad idea in the first place. I was up all night waiting for Cheron to come to my house and tell my mother."

"Oh, you don't have to worry about that; she knows better."

"Well, I don't believe that. She was mad as hell," I responded.

"Trust me. She and I had a talk and she understands. Matter of fact she's going to move out for a while until she and I decide what we're going to do, so we can do our thing as much as we want."

"That's just it, Manny. I'm not really trying to do it anymore. It's not even me. I thought about it last night and it just ain't right me taking money for sex. That's what prostitutes do and I'm *not* a prostitute. I think I just need to chill."

"Chill? C'mon now. You can't get me hooked like this and then quit on me."

"I *can't*?" I asked.

"Well, I don't want you to. And don't tell me that you don't like all the shopping you'll be doing." I had no reply. "Nothing has to change. Just call it me taking care of you. I took care of Cheron. It's no different. And that's another thing. I checked her about her going off like that. She won't be saying nothing to your moms."

I breathed a sigh of relief. "Good."

"Hey, baby, why don't you come on back and spend the day with me," he said, grabbing my arm gently.

I made an attempt to pull away. "Nah, I got a final today." I didn't notice but Rorrie was walking down from the corner. I was sure part of it was nosiness. I hadn't breathed a word to her about Manny.

When he saw Rorrie he let my arm go and said, "I'll be waiting on you this afternoon, alright?"

I didn't respond but headed for the corner. It felt good to be desired by him, but I was beginning to feel unsure about the whole thing. I had no idea where it was heading but a big part of me was excited about having an older man who was so interested in me and about the possibility that the money might continue to roll in for doing something that most girls were doing for free.

The whole day was going great until J.D. came to my table during lunch while I was trying to get in some last-minute studying for my biology exam. "So, where you been, Hailey? I've been calling you but I'm not getting no answer."

"I been busy, J.D. Trying to get ready for my finals."

"Too busy for your man?" J.D. stood over me. I looked up at him. He was only five foot five, an inch taller than me. He was trying to appear imposing but it wasn't working. He had a baby face and the softest eyes ever. A lot of people said that we looked like brother and sister, mainly because we shared a Hershey-chocolate complexion, high cheekbones, and similar Chinese eyes. The only difference was that mine were hazel and his were dark brown. We both had fine hair and he always talked about how pretty our imaginary child would be. *Imaginary,* because I never really gave a thought to having a child with him or anyone, at least not for a very long time. Rorrie and I both wanted to go to college to become doctors. I also loved fashion. Everyone always told me that I was pretty enough to do some modeling as well, almost forcing the thought to enter my mind, but more than the modeling I dreamed of having my own boutique.

"J.D., please. I have to study. I don't have time for this."

"What about today after school. Can I come over for a little while?"

"For what?"

"What you mean 'for what'? It's been a while since you gave me some. You don't want me to be looking nowhere else do you?"

When he said that, something came over me. I folded my book and looked up at him. When I looked into his eyes and saw that he was dead-serious, I knew one thing was certain. It was over between he and I. The craziest part of it was that I suddenly felt sorry for him. I grabbed my books and stood up before I responded, "J.D., you can do what you want. I don't know what makes you think that I was gonna keep having sex with you for free."

"Huh?" he said as the look on his face turned to one of astonishment.

"You heard me. What am I getting out of the deal? You come over, eat our food, climb on top of me and come in a minute. What's in it for me?" He didn't say anything, so I delivered the death blows. "Exactly, nothing at all," I yelled. "I'm through with that. If you're a minute man then it's gonna cost you. And since I know your stacks ain't like that, J.D., you ain't got to call."

I began to walk off and he followed behind. "So, Hailey what you saying? It's over."

"Yeah."

"But, I love you."

"I'm sorry."

"What can I do?" he begged.

"Nothing that you're capable of," I said as I turned the corner. He stopped with the last comment. As I made my way toward my biology class I walked with a new confidence. I knew I'd crushed J.D., but oddly, I didn't feel bad about it. Manny had definitely provided me with a new way of thinking. Why should anyone get it for free, especially if they weren't pleasing me? In this situation I already knew for certain that J.D. didn't have any money. Half the time he begged me for half of what I had.

I aced my test, found Rorrie, and headed for the bus stop so we could ride home. We took our seat in the back as usual and Rorrie started immediately. "So what was up this morning? I waited all day thinking you were going to say something about 'fine-ass' Manny. You didn't tell me you talked to him."

"Oh, it wasn't nothing. He was asking me about Cheron and if I've seen her around."

"It looked like it was more than that. You sure you ain't holding out on me?"

I looked her in the face and burst out laughing. I couldn't hold it in anymore. For the rest of the ride I told her everything about Manny and I. She was so shocked that I finally had to say, "Girl, close your mouth before you catch a fly."

We laughed as we climbed off the bus. "Girl, you wasn't scared when Cheron walked up in there?"

"Hell no. I told Manny you better control this chick before I go off."

"Daaaaannnnngggggggg." Rorrie was mesmerized. "Now he done thrown her out."

"Yep. I'm heading over there right now."

She shook her head in disbelief. "Well call me later and give me the details."

"I will," I said, watching Rorrie as we parted ways at the corner. I walked hurriedly down the block to my building. When I got there Manny wasn't on the balcony so I stood on the walk for about five minutes, waiting. When he never showed, I knocked on the door for the next few minutes. When Cheron answered I backed away slowly. She didn't say a word but the look on her face said everything. Manny walked up behind her and slammed the door shut. I heard yelling and I turned and went to my apartment. It was the first time I'd ever been lied to by a man and it hurt. Not because I was in love, but because I trusted him.

It took me a few minutes to calm down once I got inside my apartment. I called my mother at work and she informed me that she was going to work a double shift. "There's five dollars on my dresser, go to the carryout and get yourself something," she said. "I've gotta run. I'll be home a little after midnight."

It was strange but I was actually looking forward to her company, maybe her safety. I went into my room and lay across the bed, imagining Manny in the apartment and how much sex and money he'd probably given Cheron. After I'd acted as if I was actually *with* him and broken things off with J.D. I was feeling like a fool. As my pride began to get the best of me, my mind began to wander. Before I knew it I had picked up the phone.

"Hello," he said.

"Hey, Tank. This is Honey."

4

KHALIL

To keep it real, I didn't like Tina the first time I saw her. She wasn't attractive. She was loud and she always smelled like smoke and beer. I thought my father was crazy to even bring her around and I remember being shocked that he could have ever been so desperate and lonely as to fall for someone like her. I could go on and on about the ways that her coming into our home ruined my life. How she turned my father from a weekend drinker to a drunk. How she introduced him to drugs and eventually got him hooked. But that wasn't the worst of it. The worst part was the people she began to bring around as my father lost control of himself and our home.

As far as apartments in New York City went, we had a nice one until the changes Tina brought with her. We lived uptown in a rent-controlled building equipped with a security door and a real lobby. From day one I could tell Tina was scheming on how she was going to move in. My father did nothing to stop her. Before long it seemed as though it was Tina's name on the lease. Her friends began to come and go but her sister, Tenille, hung around so much that it felt like she lived there too. Tenille was younger than Tina; I imagined her to be about thirty. She was so reckless when it came to my well-being that she would smoke marijuana right in front of me. It didn't matter if I was trying to finish my homework or watching television, she just didn't care.

Coming in the house one night from visiting my birth grandmother on my mom's side, in my limited wisdom I decided it was time to talk to my father about how I felt about how our lives had changed.

As we walked up 124th Street I asked, "Dad, do you think Frannie will come back?"

He looked down at me. "What made you ask about her? Have you seen her?"

"No."

"Well, why you ask me about her? I told you when she left that she didn't give a damn about us. She haven't been around to check on you just like I told you she wouldn't."

"Yeah, well I sure miss her, especially because I don't like Tina that much."

All of a sudden he paused in his tracks. "What did you say?"

Knowing I'd put my foot in my mouth I wanted to retract. "Nothing. I ain't say nothing."

I thought he was about to hit me. Instead he grabbed my shoulders and said, "Listen up. When you get older you'll understand, but right now you don't. Women, you can't depend on them. They use you up, they emotional and unstable. Look at your mother." His voice was cracking as he preached to me. "I told her that we didn't need to have a kid, but she insisted that she was going to do it, with or without me. Then what did she do? I'll tell you what, she got hooked on crack and left you with me. Don't get me wrong, I love you son. I know I don't say it, but I do. But sometimes I got to live for me."

He started walking again and I trailed him. He looked back to make sure I was close enough to hear him. "Tina makes me happy. That's all you need to know. You don't gotta understand and you ain't got to like it, but that's how it is."

I was silent for the rest of our walk home. When we got to the front door he said, "Khalil, let me hold that money your grand-mother gave you. I'll give it back to you this weekend." I realized just that quickly why he'd taken me over there for a visit in the first place. It wasn't about me. It never was.

I handed the twenty to him knowing I'd never see it again. It was ten o'clock when we walked into the house. I headed straight to my room and closed the door. I buried my face in my pillow and started to cry. Even though my father told me to hate women because they'd never be there for you when it counted, the reality was that I hated him.

An hour later I was awakened by the sound of music blasting in the living room. Staring up at the ceiling I tried to drift back to sleep but my full bladder wouldn't let me, so I got up and headed for the bathroom. On my way back I stepped out into the living room to see who was having the party, and was hit right in the face by the smell of marijuana. This didn't shock me at all when I saw who was sitting there. What shocked me though was when I realized what Tenille was doing, or rather, had done. I recognized the other woman from up the hall. I'd heard my father call her Jasmine before when he spoke to her in passing. I always thought Jasmine was a pretty woman, tall and thin. She lived with an-other woman, who wasn't as pretty and who never spoke.

Tenille was sitting on the couch with nothing but her bra on, which was hanging halfway off of her shoulders. All the while Jasmine was on her knees in front of Tenille and at first I thought she was kissing only her thighs. Tenille's screams were so loud though that curiosity caused me to take a closer look to figure out what had caused her to react in such a dramatic way.

I was mesmerized as Jasmine kept her head buried between Tenille's thighs. I'd heard of women being gay and I'd even seen magazines before, with two women doing things to each other, but seeing it in person was blowing my thirteen-year-old mind. My closer inspection revealed that Jasmine was kissing and licking Tenille between her legs like it was nobody's business.

Neither of them noticed me as I stood back quietly amazed at the spectacle. I was in a trance as I watched for twenty minutes while they took turns kissing each other until Jasmine noticed me. "Hey, we got company," she said, pulling away from Tenille.

Tenille looked up and yelled, "Get your ass back in that room." Her tone scared me and I took off and headed for my room, closing the door.

I pulled my covers up over my head, confused, scared, and even angry that my father had allowed our home to become a place where strangers did drugs and had gay sex in the living room.

My hands wouldn't stop trembling as I clutched my pillow tight and tried to forget what I'd just seen. The images kept flashing through my mind as I fought myself to relax. As I lay there I kept thinking of Jasmine's naked body, which made me feel nervous inside. The apartment eventually went silent and I drifted off to sleep.

It must have been four in the morning when I felt someone touching me. Immediately I remembered how Frannie would come in my room and sit on my bed and read to me until I fell asleep. I called her name out in my state of half-sleep. "Frannie?"

"Shhhhhh," she said. I opened my eyes and realized that it was Tenille sitting there. My heart began to beat like a kick drum when I realized she was rubbing on my chest.

"Please don't hurt me," I whispered. Then as my eyes adjusted to the small amount of light that crept into the room I noticed that she was naked.

"I'm not going to hurt you, Khalil. Just relax and let me take care of you."

Take care of me? "I'm okay," I said, voice cracking.

"Shhhhhhh," she said again. "Don't be scared," she said as she stuck her hand down into my underwear. She kept repeating herself over and over again while she rubbed me.

My breathing was heavy at first out of fear but as she continued to rub me something began to happen to my young body. Without warning she began to yank on my underwear. I tried to grab them but felt her strength as she gripped my wrist and squeezed so hard that it hurt. At this point she pulled them off.

"Khalil, this is going to feel good. I promise."

I don't want to do this. Please stop. I wanted to scream out, but a part of me was actually starting to enjoy the sensations. I looked into Tenille's face. She was nowhere near as bad as Tina in the looks department but she looked nothing like the women who I'd had crushes on either.

I tried to block out what was happening but when she climbed on top of me there was no way to ignore her actions. Out of nowhere I felt my penis enveloped in warmth and wetness. Tenille moaned out the same way she had earlier with Jasmine. I was having sex. Although I knew that one day I would, I always imagined it would be with a girl my age that I liked. My friends and I talked about it sometimes but none of them had ever been able to describe what I was feeling.

At that moment I hated Tenille. Even with the sensations that she was sending through my body, I hated her so much that I escaped her and what we were doing. I thought back to Frannie and how she cared about me. I began to imagine that it was her here doing this to me instead. Just like that, a calm came over me.

My breathing was getting heavier and Tenille was rising and landing on me at a more rapid pace. When she began to speak to me, "Fuck me. C'mon you lil' bastard," something inside of me broke.

I felt so good but so dirty at the same time. I closed my eyes as I broke from the inside out. I grunted and my belly began to sting and tingle at the same time. It was like nothing I ever imagined as it felt like my entire insides were on fire. Tenille began to cry out and I opened my eyes as I watched her cringe and gyrate until she collapsed on top of me.

As I tried to comprehend what had just happened she started trying to lick my ears and face. When she reached my mouth and stuck her tongue into what felt like my throat my stomach churned; I jerked away from her as I leaned over the bed and threw up.

Tenille got up off the bed, carefully avoiding the mess, and headed for my door. "You'd better clean that up," she said as she reached for a pile of her clothing at my door.

I looked up at her and gave her a nasty look that I'm sure she missed. She dressed quickly and left without a care as if she'd come in my room and done nothing more than say good night. I felt violated and though I had never looked at Tenille as someone who was supposed to care for me, she was an adult. By virtue of that fact alone I expected more. Adults were supposed to look out for children, not rape them or use them as Tenille had done me.

I wiped my mouth on my pillow and cried like a baby, upset at what my life had become. I had no idea at that moment what she'd actually done to me, because if I did, surely I would have cried harder.

5

HONEY

The day I saw Cheron was back in the house with Manny I started hanging out with Tank, but because of my mother I never even thought about letting him drive onto my block. I always went to wherever he was. Tank was different from Manny even though they were both the same age, twenty-one. Tank didn't seem as intense as Manny and he always wanted to hang out and have fun. On top of that, instead of offering me money to do whatever I pleased, we shopped at the malls together. We spent so much time at Tyson's II, Montgomery Mall, and Mazza Gallery it almost felt like we lived there.

Tank was so generous that I was having trouble stashing all of the clothes and shoes that he was buying me. He even gave me the money to get a two-way pager that only he had the number to. What amazed me was that he was doing all of this without getting any. I knew it was just a matter of time though and when I looked around my room at all the gifts, I was willing to give in whenever he asked. If Manny didn't live across the hall I might have forgotten all about him, though strangely, all I saw for the entire time since

I'd started seeing Tank was his and Cheron's door. There hadn't been a trace of him coming, going, or sitting on the balcony.

This routine of me meeting Tank in the morning, hanging out all day, and then him dropping me off at the corner went on for three weeks before he finally asked me to spend the night with him. I told him I'd try but it might be hard to pull off because of my mother and the tight leash she kept me on. I told him that she'd be out of town for a training class sometime in the next week or two and that I could tell her I planned to stay at Rorrie's house and sneak out for the night since security was lax on her end. He agreed to wait until I could pull that off but in the meantime the shopping continued as it was until one day I decided to try my hand.

"Tank, I appreciate all the clothes but sometimes I like to shop with my girls. Do you think that you could just give me the money instead?"

He'd laughed. "What's wrong, you don't like shopping with me?"

"It's not that but a girl likes to keep a little change in her pocket so that she can feel independent. Plus, I need to buy some girl things from time to time and it really isn't all that comfortable to do that with someone else. Get it?"

He nodded. "Honey, I don't got a problem with that."

"Cool." With that I leaned across the seat and gave him a soft, lingering kiss. We were headed back toward my neighborhood after having lunch at his favorite restaurant, Ruth's Chris Steak House. I had gotten full of the steak and lobster tails and didn't feel like the trek up the block. I knew my mother would still be at work so I directed Tank to my building for the first time.

When we stopped in front of my building in his all-black Acura coupe I knew all eyes were on us, but the windows were too dark to peer in. I was set to get out when he said, "Honey, hold on for a minute."

He reached into his pocket and pulled out a wad of cash. I was expecting him to peel something off. Instead he handed the whole thing to me. I said, "Thanks," as if I had been expecting it. Inside I was ecstatic.

"It's all good, but do you think I can come in for a second? You said your mom won't be home till six, right?"

It was only four so I shrugged my shoulders thinking that I might as well get it over with. "Yeah, but only for a minute."

"Okay," he replied, all smiles.

We climbed out and I nervously had him follow quickly inside. "Hold on for a minute," I said and left him at the door. I ran into my room and did a quick inspection. I stuffed the money he gave me into the toe of one of an old pair of rubber boots that I kept in the back of my closet. Then I put my diary away as well as the R. Kelly scrapbook. I didn't want to seem like a stupid young girl. But when it came to R. Kelly, I was just so into him and his new CD, *12 Play.* Secretly I wanted to marry him but at fifteen I was smart enough to know that was simply a fantasy. There was nothing that a teenage girl could do to get the attention of a superstar like him.

Then I took off my skirt and the sleeveless linen top that I had on. Then I called Tank into my room as I pulled the curtains closed. When he walked in I was standing there dressed only in my panties, bra, and the sandals that I'd worn. The look on his face confirmed what I already knew.

He moved toward me and kissed me long and hard. When he pulled away he said, "Honey, you are so damned beautiful. I can't believe you want me."

I was puzzled. "Why would you say that? Any girl would like you Tank."

He shook his head. "Well a lot of girls do, but you ... you're just different. I know most girls like me because of my money, but you could get any man you want with money."

I smiled at his compliment. "You think so?" I smiled, hoping and truthfully believing he was right.

"Shit yeah. You fine as hell, got a super-sexy body, you dress real fly and your conversation is good. Plus you know how to make a man feel important. When we out, I see all the dudes checking you out. I know they be wishing they could have you." I was speechless. "But they can't afford you," he said, laughing. "You just look like money." Then he kissed me again as his comments lingered in my mind.

He didn't have a condom but I let him do it anyway. Unlike Manny, Tank didn't go down on me first. His piece wasn't as big as Manny's either but it was okay. I did the same movements with him that I did with Manny which seemed to be getting Tank really excited.

He started humping really fast which I took as a sign that he was ready to come so I said, "Don't come in me."

"Ohhhh, ohhh ... shit." Then he jumped up. "Turn over. I want to hit it from the back," he commanded. I did and within seconds he was back inside. I had a clear view of the clock on my nightstand. He'd been at it for three minutes already, which was a record for me, when he grunted like a donkey and pulled out, squirting all over my back.

I jumped up and ran to get some toilet tissue as he fell onto his back. I cleaned up and brought him some. As he wiped off he shook his head in disbelief. "Honey, I'm in love with you," he said out of the blue. I didn't know what to say. "Did you hear me?" he asked.

"Yeah, I heard you, but I don't believe you. I think it was just the sex."

"No, no," Tank said emphatically. "The sex was great, I mean better than great, but it's more than that. I never wanted to give anyone my all like I do with you."

I was getting uncomfortable with the love talk. I liked him, but I was more caught up with the things he was giving me and the power that I seemed to possess over him. "We gonna have to talk later," I said, pointing to the clock.

"All right, we will." I rushed him out the door and made sure there were no traces of him in the house.

Once he left, Rorrie came by and we laughed at him and his generosity. We didn't intend to be malicious it was just the fact that we knew he'd probably been such a dog in the past. Aside from the fact that he wasn't drop-dead gorgeous, he had all the other trappings of a lady-killer.

I ended up giving Rorrie a hundred dollars so that she could buy an outfit for the Tevin Campbell and Mary J. Blige concert that Tank was taking us to the upcoming weekend.

"Thanks sis," she said. "Or should I call you Honey."

"You better call me Honey, 'cause you know it's sweet."

"Hell, I only know what you tell me. But from the looks of things, it must be." She slapped me a high five as we sat Indian-style on the bed.

Tank persisted with the I-love-you talk for two weeks and kept trying to have sex with me without a condom. The second time I let him do it he blasted inside of me and I suspected that he was trying to get me pregnant. His excuse was that it was just too good to pull out.

I decided to put him on ice and stopped calling him and returning his calls. By this time I had over two thousand dollars saved and a shoe box full of telephone numbers that other guys had given me. Rorrie and I been sitting out front laughing about guys when we saw Manny's Benz pull up. I hadn't seen him coming or going in over a month, Cheron either. I was a little nervous that she might jump out and start something. I'd lied to Rorrie about my reaction so I knew I'd have to jump bad if she did.

I was relieved when Manny got out alone. I'd forgotten how good he looked as he made his way around the car. He walked toward us, staring me right in the eye.

"Hi, ladies," he said.

"Hey," we both said.

He kept it moving and walked straight into the building.

"Daaaaaamn, that man is fine," Rorrie said once he was inside the building. "What's up with you keeping it all short with him?"

"I'm not gonna press him," I said. All the while I was hoping he'd noticed how good I was looking in the tight yellow jeans I was wearing and the sequined Guess tank top.

My heart did a cartwheel, a backflip, and a somersault when he came to the balcony and yelled out my name. "Hailey, come here for a minute."

"Girl, let me go see what he want. You want to go chill up in my crib?"

"Nah, I'm gonna run home for a minute. I might want to come back and spend the night with you."

"Cool, I'll catch up with you later," I said to my best friend.

"Call me," she said.

——————

Ten minutes later Manny and I were sitting on the couch as he told me what had been going on. He'd gotten locked up and so had Cheron. It turned out that he had three apartments besides this one that he used to stash drugs. Manny was a drug dealer and Cheron wasn't even his main girlfriend. In fact, he had a wife, which made my heart sink a bit when he admitted it. Cheron knew about his wife, which was apparently the only reason why she'd gotten over what had happened between us. She'd known all along that she would never be the only one.

I didn't know why he was telling me all of his business all of a sudden. "I just wanted you to know because I'm planning on moving to Atlanta in a couple of weeks. My wife is pregnant and I need to think about my future. I never planned on staying in this game too long."

As he talked I could see the fear on his face. "So are you going to jail?" I asked.

"No. My lawyer is great and the charges against me were dropped. Cheron, unfortunately though, she might have to do a little time if things don't work out. She got caught red-handed. She's a trooper though. She didn't drop dime on me and I love her for that. It's all about loyalty, Hailey." I was impressed with her and how she had his respect.

For the first time we actually talked about life. I didn't know much about him before this point but listening to him I got to know that he was truly intelligent and a caring person as well. What shocked me was when he apologized to me. "Hailey, I feel like I took advantage of you and I'm sorry."

"No need to apologize. We both got something out of the deal." I smiled. "I'm not mad at all."

He nodded. "You learn fast, I see. Well at least I taught you something, but I'd like to warn you though. Stay clear of guys like me. Street niggas like me. Most of 'em won't be as nice as me and they'll ruin your life and not even look back. Fortunately for Cheron, I'm going to look out for her. I posted her bail and I'm planning on paying for her lawyer. She may not get anything but probation, but still she'll end up with a record."

"Well, let me ask you this. If you weren't afraid of her snitching on you would you have looked out for her?"

"You know what the good thing is?" he asked. "She was smart enough to put herself in a position where we didn't have to find out. Always use *this* as well as this," he said pointing at his head first then his crotch. "In the opposite order you're headed for disaster."

We talked for a little while longer and he asked me about college. I told him that I wanted to go away somewhere, maybe California or New York. He suggested Spelman or Clark. I knew why.

I was about to leave when he asked me if he could make love to me one last time. The next time he came by this apartment, he said, he'd be moving. Who could resist him, so I said, "Okay, but it's gonna cost you. I don't do charity cases." Then I smiled.

"I wouldn't have it any other way." He laughed. This time we got in the shower together and he took his time. Once we were in the bed he was so passionate that he almost took my breath away. I was surprised that he lasted five minutes this time.

When we finished he went into a spiel about how it was still unbelievable to him how I could make him erupt so quickly. Fifteen, twenty minutes, he claimed he always took with other women.

I slipped my jeans on without putting back on my panties and bra. I held them in my hands as I was just going in the house to shower again. Manny kissed me at the door as if he knew it'd be the last time he'd lay eyes on me. "If you are ever in Atlanta, look me up," he said.

I nodded. "I will." He opened the door and when I turned to walk out, Tank was standing in the hallway, waiting like a guard dog.

"This is how you repay me, Honey? You bitch," he growled.

"What are you doing here?" I said.

"Your girl Rorrie told me you was in here fucking this nigga."

My head began to spin. "Rorrie? What?"

"Yeah, she been trying to creep with me for weeks, ever since the concert I took y'all too. I shoulda' gone ahead and tapped it since I see how you rolling." Tank had moved up on me. His eyes were ferocious and he looked unstable. I thought he was going to hit me so I backed up.

He must have sensed that I was going to run so he reached and grabbed me by the throat. I gasped and tried to pry his hand loose to keep him from choking me. Again, Manny had to come to my rescue. He slid around my body and pushed Tank into the wall. "Main man, you need to chill."

Tank immediately began to throw punches. His were wild but the ones Manny threw in return were precise. He knocked Tank to the ground with the second punch and told me to get back inside.

I glanced over as Manny reached down to punch Tank some more, but then it happened. Amid the barrage of blows, Tank reached into his pocket and pulled out a knife. Almost simultaneously I heard Manny's cries then a thud. I slammed the door before Tank could get to me.

He began to kick the door. "Honey, I love you. Please, open up. I love you," he yelled out as I began to cry. He'd gone mad.

"I'm calling the police," I yelled. "Get out of here."

The next twenty minutes I barely remember. I heard sirens then a knock at the door. Paramedics, police, a stretcher, a sheet over Manny's body. All followed by confession. He'd died because of me.

It seemed as if my mother hated me once she found out what had happened. She didn't look me in the eye from that day forward. She was furious when the police advised us to move, since they hadn't yet apprehended Tank, but my mother wasn't having it. "I have a job right up the road. I don't have the time or money to move because her hot ass can't keep her legs closed," she told the detective.

Instead she shipped me out to her sister's home in Columbia, Maryland. Denise was four years older than my mother and even more religious. Still I had no choice.

Ironically, going from the hood to the *nice* neighborhood turned out to be hell for me. I went to a new school with a bunch of white kids that I had nothing in common with and I stood out like a sore thumb. I tried to forget the life I'd left behind in the city, the best friend who'd betrayed me, and the murderer who'd flipped my life inside out.

After being a loner for the first month of school, eventually I tried to fit in with the uppity kids, but my interests had changed so much in the last year that I couldn't connect with most of the girls I met. I missed the money and the clothes. I often thought about Manny and the things he'd shared with me. Within two weeks I began sneaking out to hang out with guys I'd met at

Columbia Mall. None of them captured my interest. They simply didn't have enough money. That was until I met this one kid with rich parents who had his own credit card. I gave the kid a sample and in no time flat he'd maxed the card out taking me to all of my favorite stores.

One evening after I came in two hours after my silly ten P.M. curfew, my aunt was sitting in the living room talking to a man she introduced as a detective.

"You're late again," she bitched.

"I know I had to stop off and . . ."

"I am so sick of your excuses." She'd cut me off. "Come here and sit down."

My aunt looked as if she'd been crying. The detective began to speak. According to him they'd apprehended Tank. This made me happy as I immediately thought of my return home. Then the detective went on to say that he'd been caught while flee-ing the scene of another murder. As they'd suspected he might, Tank had come looking for me again. Of course I was nowhere around, but my mother was.

6

KHALIL

After a while I got used to Tenille's abuse. I actually came to not only expect it but almost enjoy it. She had begun to convince me that she was the only one in the house that loved me. It just so happened that the only attention that anyone paid me came in the middle of the night.

Deep inside I knew it wasn't right. It just didn't feel natural. Oftentimes she hurt me by being so rough. Sitting on my face, nearly smothering me at times. "Boy you need to get stronger," she'd say. "Give me fifty push-ups."

I did them every day until fifty became too easy, then I did a hundred. I did get stronger and angrier every day at my life, which proved to be a dangerous combination. I attended Powell Middle School on 129th Street, in the heart of Harlem. With my home life a wreck, I began to act out in school, bullying other kids and being insubordinate.

This morning I hadn't been feeling well and for no reason in particular, I decided to stick my foot out and trip a passerby as we headed to the cafeteria for an assembly. Some rapper-turned-activist by the name of Chuck D was coming by our school to give a speech to what they called the at-risk youth. I was quickly becoming one of them.

When the student I'd tripped fell on his face and busted his bottom lip, the only thing I was going to be permitted to see was the principal's office. I got there and it was overcrowded as usual. Being the last to enter, I wound up having to take a seat in the back with the nurse. After an hour of sitting, waiting to see the principal, I began rocking back and forth in my seat as I fought the all-too-familiar feeling.

"Son, what's your deal? Do you need to use the bathroom? You've been rocking in that chair for thirty minutes," the nurse said.

I ignored her and tried to stop rocking but started again a few minutes later. Again she started. "What is your problem?"

Finally I spat, "I do have to go, but I don't want to."

"Why not? Do you need privacy?" I assumed she meant to take a dump.

"No," I responded. "I just don't want to. Lately every time I try to go it hurts."

"What do you mean it hurts?" She frowned and looked down the nose of her glasses at me.

"It hurts like hell ... I mean it feels like I'm shooting razor blades out of my hole."

Her face showed shock. She asked me my name first then she started with a bunch of questions.

Have you been having sex? Are you sure? Your symptoms say such and such. If you have had sex, then it's your partner's fault. They have done this to you; they gave you a disease. If you don't tell the truth I can't help you. You should know that in some cases where venereal disease occurs that it's possible to develop septicemia and die.

None of it scared me until she said, "Khalil, that feeling you have it's going to get worse and worse if you don't tell the truth."

I put my head down and continued to fight the urge to urinate until I could bear it no longer. I went into the bathroom and braved the pain as indeed it was getting worse every time. I stood on my toes and grimaced as I was almost dizzy from the pain.

I had begun to sweat from the ordeal. When I came out of the bathroom I sat back down and began to tell my story.

Then she left the office for about three minutes and came back in with the guidance counselor. Ten minutes later we were on our way to Harlem Hospital.

The antibiotics coupled with the IV they administered at the hospital had kicked in and after a few hours I was able to use the bathroom without pain. This would be the only bright spot of the day.

I would later learn that the police and child protective services had shown up at my house, finding my father both drunk and high. Tenille was there and when they announced the charges and put the cuffs on her he attacked her and wound up getting locked up too. The only one who didn't get arrested was Tina.

I was taken to a youth center on the East Side for the night, where they had a dormitory for children waiting to be placed into foster care. My case worker sat with me until midnight and assured me she'd be back first thing in the morning to take me to school.

The next morning I learned I wouldn't be going back home. My father was being charged with neglect. It turned out that to protect herself, Tina had ratted my father out and given the authorities drugs that he had in the apartment as well as a hand-gun that he kept in his closet.

I didn't shed a tear even though I was torn apart inside. Everything was happening so fast. Even though my world had been rough, it was all I knew.

A week later, after I'd been temporarily assigned to live in a group home, I was on the train headed to Brooklyn. Once I'd gotten word that my grandmother had told the case workers that she was too sick to take care of me, I'd made it my business to find out from my social worker where Frannie lived. I'd asked if I could send a card to her so she wouldn't worry about me, to which she'd given me the okay. I had no intention of sending a letter or a card. I was going to show up in person. It had been almost ten months since I'd seen her and it felt like ten years.

I walked up Third Avenue toward the address that I had written on a piece of paper. I was scared I'd come to the wrong neighborhood, because all of the houses looked like rich people lived in them. Still, when I came to the address in my hand I knocked on the door. It was then I realized that it was an apartment building and not a house. I didn't have an apartment number so I looked at the buzzer and found no names that looked familiar.

I waited for someone to walk out of the building and I walked in. I began knocking on each door. I was on the second floor, third door, when Frannie opened it. "Khalil," she said, looking more surprised than happy. "How did you get here?"

"Hey Frannie," I said. I was set to tell her how I'd skipped lunch so that I'd have money for the train ride and that I'd come because I wanted her to take care of me now that my father was doing twelve months in jail, but instead, I burst into tears. She looked out into the hallway, almost as if she was trying to make sure no one was around, and reached for me and embraced me. Feeling her and smelling her again after all this time was too much.

I cried in her arms for what seemed like thirty minutes in between telling her bits of my story. She cried almost the entire time as she begged for my forgiveness. She couldn't believe what had happened.

Then her husband came home.

Our reunion was short-lived and together they drove me back uptown to the group home. As she walked me back in she assured me that she would do everything she could to gain custody of me. The only thing about it was that I didn't believe her when she said it.

That was the last time I ever heard from Frannie and the last time I ever believed that anyone would do something to help me. My childhood ended that day as I watched their Cherokee drive down Malcolm X Boulevard. From that day on I knew that life was about survival and it was every man, woman, and child for themselves.

7

July 2006

HONEY

I snatched the phone off of the counter as it began to vibrate. "Yes," I answered.

"Priest apologizes for the delay but we are now en route."

"Okay," I said, and hung up the phone.

I'd rushed to make sure that I was ready for him when he arrived; now I had time to spare. I decided to take a drink from one of the bottles of wine that he'd had sent up. I stepped out onto the balcony of the penthouse suite. I had an ocean-view suite at the Shore Club, one of South Beach's poshest hotels, while I was in town working for two days. Priest had come down for the African American Film Festival and to hang out with a few of his fellow athlete friends at Alonzo Mourning's annual fund-raising party weekend.

He always sprung for the best, I think to make up for what he lacked in personality; nevertheless the luxury was nice and I didn't *hate* hanging out with him as I did with some of my other clients. The fun part had been all the shopping I'd done earlier; now it was time for business.

Moments like this always gave me pause. As I stared out into the Atlantic Ocean I thought about my life and how it had all changed so drastically. I thought about my mother and how she'd died at the hands of that maniac, who I'd hate forever but whose name I never dared speak.

I especially thought about Manny, and the unborn child he left behind because of me, almost every single day.

When the wind blew behind me, it didn't matter whether it was a breeze coming off the Atlantic like tonight's or a gust shooting up from behind on Michigan Avenue in Chicago. Manny was with me and often I could almost hear his half-apology for the journey he'd sent me on. *Hey Honey, do you like who you've become? I'm sorry for my part in turning you out to a life of materialism and sex for hire. But at least you're still here.*

True, I was still here but I sometimes felt like I should use the word *barely.* I walked around with a hole inside of my spirit that I tried to fill with cash, Birkin bags, and a host of Oprah's favorite things. It was strange: even though I knew that what I was doing would ultimately prove futile, I couldn't stop. The temporary rush of pleasure I felt when I traded a piece of me for fortune, in what I always felt was a lopsided exchange, was the only surefire method I'd ever come up with for dulling my pain.

Instead of turning myself around when my mother was killed, I got progressively worse. I didn't make it through my senior year of high school before my aunt grew tired of me staying out all weekend and bringing home fur coats that cost more than her car. On New Year's Day of my senior year she put me out. I didn't graduate high school, but when I officially quit, my GPA had been a 3.85, which in itself was a tragedy, when I look back on it.

I left Aunt Denise's house and immediately moved in with

Gerry Monroe, a rich white man who I'd met at a bar in downtown Baltimore. I refused to sleep with Gerry the first time he'd taken me to dinner. At that point I wasn't pressed for money and I wasn't sure if I could sleep with a white guy, but I knew he was loaded so I kept in touch with him until I did wind up needing him. Of course I never had to ask to move into his five-bedroom home. All I had to do was tell him of my situation with my aunt and he begged me to come and stay until I got on my feet.

The longer I refused him the more desperate he became to keep me around. I eventually left him, but not until he'd purchased me a brand-new BMW, in my name of course, and I'd secured enough money to pay my rent for six months. All of this and he never so much as smelled the promised land between my thighs. I almost felt sorry for him, but I didn't.

I stopped being amazed a long time ago at how much money men, and sometimes women, were willing to part with just for the fantasy of having the unattainable. More often than not I became that fantasy. No matter how famous or rich a person was. All you had to do was tell them *no,* and it drove them to do the most insane things.

One investment banker even took me along on his honeymoon to Spain with him. My room was two doors down from his and his wife's. I wound up meeting her when he'd booked us both hot-stone massages at the same time in the spa. She was nice I thought. For him though she was either *too* nice or not nice enough. I never bothered to figure it out. The three grand per day I was paid to lounge around was what it was all about for me.

As a young girl I'd always felt cute, but as the years went on my looks became my business. I ate right, worked out religiously, and spent thousands of dollars of other people's money to make sure that my body was flawless and that my face was always Cover Girl–worthy. My breasts naturally sat up like two grapefruits, my ass looked like I ran track for a living, I had legs for days, and my skin had been pampered by the finest creams and lotions money could buy.

I had capped teeth like most of the Hollywood celebrities and my hair never needed much work since it was jet-black and fine like silk. It meant nothing to me that I could have worked as a video ho-fessional if I chose, but the idea of sitting on a set waiting on the "man next to the man" to notice you so that you could possibly get screwed by a rapper or some R&B fag didn't appeal to me at all. To top it off most of those girls made five hundred for an entire day, which was a joke to me.

I lived by the motto "Use what you got to get what you need." A bunch of women all over the globe had it all wrong. They were using what they had to give others what they needed. Never that for me.

My cell phone rang. "Hello, this is Honey."

"Honey, we've arrived."

"I'm in 2024."

"Thank you."

Priest played point guard for New Jersey. Usually I hated ballplayers. Too cocky, too ignorant, and they all thought you should want to have a baby with them. I had a strong preference for quiet money, but I made an exception for Priest.

When the knock came at the door I was dressed in a robe, a corset, and five-inch heels. I opened it and he was standing there, tall, in jeans, a white T-shirt, and a platinum chain hanging down to his belly. "Hey, Honey," he greeted me with a kiss on the cheek.

I noticed that he had a small entourage with him. One thick-bodied guy who looked like a bodyguard, and two women—one white, one black. They were both dressed and looked like a couple of typical groupies in that they, like most groupies, never real-ized that going half-dressed could be done with style and class. "Honey, I brought a few friends with me. This is my man, Big George. That's Jan and she's Reese," he said as he'd fingered each of his cohorts. "They're going to hit the club with us. I thought we'd have a couple of drinks and get loose before we roll."

"Oh, okay." I was pissed. I wasn't into crowds and didn't like my face seen by a bunch of random folks but I tried to stay professional. And I definitely didn't like the look of the big guy. He began eyeing me like a smothered pork chop the second he stepped through the door. The more I looked at him the more uncomfortable I became. Truthfully, I couldn't tell if it was the cliché beady-eyes thing he had going on or if it was the he-looks-like-a-serial-killer thing he had going on.

Priest leaned in and said, "As good as you're looking, Ma, I'd rather stay here with you but they can't get in the party without me. And they flew all the way in from L.A."

"I'm fine. I'm with you," I said. "But I'm going to need them to step out while I get dressed."

"Honey, they okay. They with me, baby." The look on my face gave him a response and he quickly said, "Can I at least take them out to the pool. C'mon, I did pay a couple Gs for the room."

I excused them out onto the balcony to drink while I dressed in a raspberry-colored Cavalli dress and a pair of matching rhinestone Chanel sandals. When I stepped out of the room to alert Priest that I was ready he smiled as he stared at me. I caught the shade from the two women. I was used to it, plus they looked like they were high already.

We headed down to Washington Avenue to a brand-new club called The Point. When we arrived the line was wrapped around the building and the police had blocked off the street. Big George was driving the Denali we were in and we were able to get through the barricade and have him drop us off at the front door while he parked right on the street. We were whisked through a VIP entrance and up a side stairway that was made of marble. We had a section reserved for us, a plush couch and a table in front of it with a flat-screen television mounted to it and two three-hundred-dollar bottles of Veuve Clicquot champagne in the buckets of ice. Priest seemed fascinated that ESPN was on. The VIP had white carpet on the floor, which I thought was crazy, except for the walkways and the bar area, which were wood. The lighting, the artwork, and the furniture all rivaled that of the finest homes I'd ever seen.

"This club is hot, right, Honey?" he'd asked for the fifth time in ten minutes. He was drunk from the drinks at the room and seemed to be playing me really close. I didn't mind him hugging me and giving the appearance of us being together, but he was practically smothering me.

Under his lanky arms all I could do was sit and observe. This section of the club took up an entire floor except for the railing where you could look down on the stage, dance floor, and bar on the general-admission folks. The music had the entire club vibrating as Dem Franchize Boyz's *Lean Wit' It, Rock Wit' It* pounded through the speakers. I'd been in some of the world's nicest clubs, but this one topped them all.

I hadn't realized that there were live performances scheduled for the night, by Yung Joc and Lil' Wayne. We'd arrived relatively early but in South Beach the clubs fill early and it was important to Priest that he make a decent entrance. He'd just signed a new contract, his name was ringing, and he needed to be seen.

What I didn't realize was who he wanted to be seen by. As another group came up the steps into VIP a small commotion was created by the groupies, both male and female, who found a way to make it up there. Big George tapped Priest when he realized who it was.

His ex had just walked in among the entourage of the boxer Nate Montgomery. Nate was from D.C. and I'd followed his career and rooted for him, growing up in the area. Now he lived in Miami and had recently regained the championship after a several-year hiatus. While stealing a few glimpses of the champ, I overheard Priest and Big George talking about her. It was obvious that Priest felt some kind of way about her. So much so that his whole mood had changed.

I could tell that Priest hadn't been planning to start any trouble but he desperately wanted her to see him with me. When I saw her I realized why. She was drop-dead gorgeous and just her coming in with Nate had made him jealous.

For the next half hour Priest dragged me across the floor to the rail and back, trying to get her attention. I was convinced he had when she and I made our first eye contact. She'd cut her eyes at me and I'd smirked at her, playing the role. I knew what Priest wanted so I planned to give it to him. I was paid well and there was a reason why. If he needed to feel like the man then he would, as long as he was paying for it. Even though I found his insecurity extremely annoying.

As we stood by the rail I said to Priest, "Do you want me to go over there and put a bug in her ear?"

"Say what?" he shot back.

"You know, go kick off some drama. Act as if I'm the insecure new girlfriend. If she thinks you have me, she's gonna want you back. Or at the least wanna fuck you." I played on his tremendous ego as my respect for him waned more each second.

He grinned then he stopped grinning and asked, "You for real?"

I shrugged my shoulders. "If you want me to be."

"How much is that gonna cost me?" he asked. I was glad he knew what time it was. Everything extra cost extra.

"How much you got on you?"

"You'll have to do more than that to get this," he said tapping his pocket.

"How about if I take you in the corner over there afterward and let you make love to me right here in this club?"

His glassy eyes were now wide open as he broke into a slight grin. "Yeah, that'd be nice." Then he blurted out, "Two more Gs."

I shook my head. "We might ruin this dress. It cost fifteen hundred by itself. This is a public display and I'll be the one to wind up looking like a whore. You ... you'll just look like the man. Let's make it six," I said, knowing he'd probably agree to five. I knew how much money he made per game and how much he could afford to blow, so I always pushed him.

"Deal," he said, shocking me. "Go do your thing and I'll meet you in the corner."

I stuck my hand out and watched him peel a knot of hundreds. At thirty years old he was a complete fool. I'd seen him spend money like water and wondered how many years it'd be before he was destitute.

A minute later I walked right up on his ex, Miranda, and told her flat-out that Priest wanted her to be jealous. She replied that he was a nut. "Get away from him while you can."

I explained to her that I wasn't attached to him and wasn't thinking about getting into a relationship. I stopped short of letting her know that this was strictly business. Looking back I saw that Priest and Big George were all gazing in our direction. "Do me a favor. Can you point in my face and curse me out? I'm going to point back then I'm going to walk off. You do that and I'll meet you in the ladies' room and drop like five hundred dollars on you. How does that sound?"

She nodded. "Cool."

"But I'm going to need about ten minutes, because he wants me to have sex with him in the corner first."

"F'ing pig," she said. "You're going to do it."

I tapped my purse and then she nodded in understanding.

I rode him hard and fast. I felt nasty as Big George stood with his back to us wishing that he could stare or join in I'm sure. I blocked it all out, even where we were as I went into my zone.

As far as the sex went, it was all an act for me. My performances were all Oscar-worthy even though I'd yet to fully enjoy sex with any man. Manny, of course, had come the closest to pleasing me and that was more from what he did orally. I did however know how to fake it like a porn star and I got paid to play, so I played on.

That's exactly what I did and had Priest crying out and filling the condom with his sperm in a couple of minutes. He loved the dirty talk and couldn't handle me riding him controlling the rhythm.

Priest had gotten so excited when he'd seen Miranda taking a peep at us. What he didn't realize was that she was merely waiting on the five hundred I was dropping to satisfy my inexplicable urge to humiliate him as I got more money out of him.

I kept my word and met her in the ladies' room for the exchange. "Thanks," she said.

"It's nothing."

"I got to tell you. You did get me a little horny. I might even give him a call."

I told Priest that she'd confronted me in the ladies' room and mentioned calling him. Everyone was happy. Until he saw her kissing on Nate and another woman a few minutes later while he was heading out of the men's room. It was like he'd been sent into a rage as he began to rant uncontrollably until we left the club ten minutes later.

We left the club and went back to a condo in Coral Gables. I could have calmed him down I believed but he insisted on bringing the Bobbsey Twins along. The two of them had spent the entire time getting higher and higher on the drugs that Big George had on hand. He'd offered me some as we drove toward his condo and I'd looked at him as if he, his momma, and his mamma's momma were crazy.

"Priest, you should know better than that. Plus your two groupies are doing enough drugs for all of us. You'd better slow them down before one of them winds up in the hospital and you wind up on the front page."

"Don't worry about them. They're only here for the show. Who cares what happens to them?" I shook my head in disgust. "What?" he asked.

"Nothing," I responded. He was a pig.

Not that I'd never gotten high, because I'd dabbled, but I never took drugs that I didn't watch the person with everything to lose take and I didn't witness Priest using anything but liquor.

Once we made it to the condo more partying and more drug abuse by the girls took place. I sexed Priest once more and then I walked around the place looking for somewhere to relax as the party continued without me. Unnoticed by the men who were now enjoying the girls who were so high that they could barely speak, I moved to one of empty bedrooms and saw that it had a balcony on it. I stepped out onto it and sat on the thick patio chair. The champagne and the breeze must have kicked in and I dozed off. When the sunlight began to hit my face it proved to be my alarm. I got up and was prepared to catch a cab back to my room, knowing that it was early.

I reentered the condo and began to walk around. I didn't see anyone and was shocked that Priest had left me as if I were some nameless groupie. When I made it to the living room it looked like a real party had broken out as the furniture was disheveled and the pillows were thrown about.

Angry at being left behind, I stepped out onto the street and headed toward the bagel shop that sat on the corner. I would get a bagel, some coffee, and get back to my room so I could quickly pack for my flight back to D.C. Priest had gotten his money's worth from me and if I never saw him again I couldn't have cared less. When I stepped inside the Einstein Bros Bagels everyone's eyes were on the television that was in the corner as they buzzed about the story.

"That's a damned shame," one of the customers said.

"What happened?" I asked the girl on the register as I paid for my coffee.

"The police found some girl's body an hour ago. It wasn't too far from here."

The family had just been notified and they are on their way from Los Angeles, the newscaster said. I took a look at the screen, at the photo they plastered on the screen. *The deceased had been identified as Janice Sears. The police suspect a drug overdose but won't have anything concrete until an autopsy is performed. She is believed to have been accompanied on the trip to Miami by a friend, whom authorities are trying to locate at this time.*

My mouth dropped open when I recognized the girls. One Bobbsey was dead and the other one missing.

8

KHALIL

She caught my eye when I noticed her standing by the window as we waited for the announcement to call for boarding. The entire time she seemed to be frantically debating on the phone with someone. I had to admit that I studied her simply because she was so beautiful that she could have been a movie star. I didn't see a wedding ring so I figured that it was probably a boyfriend that she'd been arguing with. Once we'd boarded and I'd taken my seat I was surprised that she was in fact traveling alone and that like me, she was seated in first class.

When she walked past me with her carry-on I was a little disappointed, but then she quickly came back and said, "Excuse me." The empty window seat next to me belonged to her. She scooted by me and made no effort to keep her rear end from my view. She had the word *Juicy* stitched across her ass. Though I recognized the brand, I loved the double meaning. In the two seconds it took for her to pass me I immediately wondered if what was in those pants was, in fact, *juicy*.

"How you doin'?" I asked once she had gotten seated.

"I'm fine," she said and then turned her head toward the window. She made it clear that she didn't want to be bothered, and I wasn't the type to push. I was flipping the pages of a magazine and was resigned to letting her be invisible. I was looking forward to us getting into the air so I could put on my iPod and completely zone out. If I had to sit next to a beautiful woman that I couldn't at least chat with then I'd completely ignore her. It wasn't like I wanted anything other than conversation from her.

Thirty minutes after the takeoff we began to experience some turbulence. I pulled my headphones off in order to hear the flight attendant's announcement. Up to that point, I hadn't even noticed that she'd opened her eyes but I heard her sniffling and when I looked over she had tears in her eyes.

"You all right? You aren't scared are you, because I fly all the time and this is totally normal," I said, attempting to comfort her.

"I'm fine," she said for the second time, without expression. "I just have a lot on my mind. Really I'm okay."

"Well, how about you let me get you a drink?" She paused for a few moments then nodded her head. "Cognac okay?" She nodded again. "A Coke to chase it?"

"No, straight," she replied. I smiled, as I knew this was how the conversation would get started.

I asked for six of the mini-sized bottles of Hennessy and placed them in the pocket in front of me. She downed the first one as if it was a bottle of water. The second, she sipped slower. I didn't say anything, to let on that I wasn't trying to do more than just be a kind stranger. My head began to bob as I put my headphones back on.

"What you listening to?" she asked.

"Ne-Yo."

"How is it?"

"Not bad. I really like a couple of the songs."

She was sitting there next to me but she had a faraway look in her eyes, which were an amazing hazel. "I thought about getting it. Maybe I will."

"So, listen. I know I'm a complete stranger but I'm a really good listener. You might not get the opportunity to tell another stranger what's weighing heavy on your mind."

"You are a stranger. But I wouldn't want to dump my worries on my worst enemy right now."

"Well, if you're sure you don't want to talk then I might as well introduce myself to you. I'm Khalil. Khalil Graves."

"My name is Honey. Just Honey." She almost smiled.

"Well it's a pleasure meeting you. Were you in Miami for the film festival or for a vacation?"

She turned so that she faced me as she leaned back toward the window a bit. "What makes you think I don't live in Miami?"

"I don't know. The accent probably. You sound more like you're from . . ."

"Get it right." She laughed.

"Virginia?" She frowned. "D.C." She nodded. "So is that where you live?"

"I live just above the line in Chevy Chase. What about you?"

"I live a couple blocks east of Capitol Hill. You never answered my question. If you were here for the festival."

"Oh, not really. I was here for a meeting. And you?"

"I was actually a judge for the film fest."

"So you're in the film industry."

"Sort of. I'm a cinematographer by trade but I just finished shooting my first film that I've directed, it's called *Shades*. It's an indie but I have really high hopes for it. Right now it's in post-production. Before that I'd mostly been doing music videos for the last few years."

"Anyone I might have heard of in it?" she asked. I was used to that tone. She wanted to know if I was a legitimate filmmaker.

"Actually yes. You've heard of Shawn Simmons?"

"Of course."

"What about Nate Montgomery?"

"The boxer?"

"Yeah."

"Of course I've heard of him."

"Well he's in it too."

She chuckled and then said, "I just saw him in the club last night."

"Oh okay. He'd invited me to The Point last night. So you went?"

"Unfortunately."

We downed another couple bottles and the conversation began to flow freely and we didn't stop talking for the next hour and a half. When we landed she said, "You know, Khalil, I feel a little better than I did when I boarded."

"Well it was nice talking to you and meeting you." We climbed off of the plane and headed toward the baggage claim. We walked together almost like a couple and stood next to each other once we reached the luggage carousel. From looking at her presentation I wasn't surprised when she stepped toward the conveyer belt to take the Louis Vuitton luggage. I was surprised at the size of the two huge pieces. She had a ton of stuff.

"Honey, let me help you with that," I said as I grabbed the first of two fifty-pound pieces. "How long were you in South Beach for, a couple of weeks?" I said sarcastically.

"One of those was nearly empty when I went. I filled it up, courtesy of Bal Harbour Shops." She smiled.

My luggage came and I said, "Is your ride here or did you drive?"

"Oh, I'll just catch a cab."

I started to part ways then. I knew that my girlfriend wouldn't approve of what I did next but I told myself that it was harmless.

"Well consider today to be your lucky day. I drive an SUV so I can give you a ride home. That way you don't have to ruin some poor cabbie's shocks with your ton of luggage."

"Are you sure? I catch a cab home from the airport all the time."

"Absolutely. Come on. As a matter of fact, let me wheel one of those for you."

We pulled out of the garage in my Cadillac EXT and hit 395 headed for Chevy Chase. It was blazing and humid so I turned on the air but she still put her window down. "I need some air, maybe the liquor," she said.

"No problem."

"So, Khalil. Do you love what you do?"

"I did love it at one point. I still like it."

"If you don't love it anymore, why do you do it?"

"It pays the bills and it's a stepping stone to greater things. Plus I've made a lot of connections to help me with my future in directing."

She nodded as she stared straight ahead. "So do you make a lot of money doing what you do?"

I laughed. "I do all right for myself. Why do you ask? You thinking of getting into the profession?"

"No reason. I hope I didn't offend."

"Not at all."

Then she turned to me and asked, "So do you have a wife, a girlfriend?"

It amazed me that we'd talked for the last couple of hours but this hadn't come up. I looked over into her beautiful face and realized that I probably hadn't brought it up for a reason. And although I had never cared enough about any woman not to cheat on her, my situation now was different.

My life had been in turmoil. An abusive situation, to foster care, to more abuse had been my journey. Through it all I'd learned to travel light and look out for myself. No matter where I was mentally the only constant was that school at first, then work, had been my refuge and I'd stayed out of trouble as best I could. I kept my grades up and in the fall of my senior year I'd applied to both Howard University's and NYU's film schools. I'd been accepted into Howard and thus landed in the nation's capital.

On my own it had been a free-for-all. I'd left the poor, beaten, and battered Khalil behind and introduced everyone to a new me. The one who didn't care about anyone other than himself, and what I found amazed me. Women loved it. The nonchalant attitude seemed to be an enigma, even a challenge that they stepped up to the plate to meet, one after the other.

I crushed them all. Even the nice ones, for reasons I couldn't really understand at the time. That was until I met the girl who I believed was the one.

Now here I was, riding along with a stranger, playing the role of the Good Samaritan. In all actuality, I was captivated by her charms. Still, I felt compelled to answer her truthfully once I re-played her question in my head.

"So do you have a wife, a girlfriend?"

"Yes, I have someone I've been seeing."

She nodded. I expected the conversation to turn cold from that point. Honey didn't seem like the type to date anyone who'd try to make her play second string. She was far too stunning for that. I imagined that my dropping her off would be the last I'd see or hear of her. Instead she stayed the same. "Well, she's a lucky girl, whoever she is."

"Thanks."

We pulled up onto her street and as she directed me to her house she gasped then yelled out, "Oh my God."

"What?" I said back as I watched her slide down in her seat.

"Keep driving," she said in a whisper. "Just keep driving." My heart began to pound, because I didn't know what was hap-pening. I looked over and saw a huge man walking down some steps but that was it. "Make a left at the corner and just keep going."

"Okay. But what's going on?"

"Please, just drive."

I did as she asked. "So where are we going?"

"I don't know. I need to think," she said, sounding nervous as a spy whose cover had been blown.

"Do you want me to take you to my place?"

"What about your girlfriend?"

"She's out of town. She sort of lives out of town. She's doing a residency in Richmond."

"Okay, please then. That'll be fine. It'll gimme some time to think this through."

I turned the radio down a little and said, "You're gonna have to tell me what's going on though."

She began to tear up again and then she said, "Okay, I will."

We pulled up in front of my house a few minutes later. I was glad that I didn't see any of my neighbors as we walked to the door. She breathed a sigh of relief as the cool air hit her in the face. I motioned toward the living room and she walked in and took a seat on the couch while I offered her a drink. I carried my bags upstairs and when I came back downstairs she was looking at a picture in a frame that sat on the end table.

"Is this your girlfriend in the picture?"

"Yes."

There was an uncomfortable silence. I didn't think it was possible but she suddenly seemed to be even more agitated than she was before. Then out of the blue she said, "I'll tell you everything, but there's something that I need you to do first."

I nodded in agreement without even knowing what she was about to ask. "Okay."

"Take me upstairs and make love to me." With that she stood up and moved toward me. "Now."

9

HONEY

I was like a leaf blowing in a hurricane, completely at the mercy of life's brutal winds. Through no fault of my own, I'd been sucked into a potential scandal that could rock the sports world even more than Kobe's romp with the desk clerk. Though I hadn't seen Priest disposing of the body, I had seen her pumping herself full of drugs that he provided. Now I'd just spotted Priest's bodyguard, Big George, in front of my home. How he learned my address and beat me home I'd never figure. What I did know was his being at my home couldn't have meant anything good for me. I'd warned him about giving the girls drugs and I guess now he wanted to dispose of any witnesses.

My mind was already spinning, fighting to keep from taking me over the edge amid the possibility that my life could be in danger when I picked up the picture and saw *her* face. I'd never forget her smile, even if it were thirty years that had passed instead of thirteen. I couldn't figure out why all of a sudden this was happening. My stomach was turning as the anger and pain all came rushing back. I knew all along that our paths would cross again and I wondered what would happen. Would I want to kill her?

Never could I have imagined this scenario. This man standing before me. This beautiful young brother was *her* man. Rorrie, the bitch who'd been the cause of all my pain, was his girlfriend. Her conniving had cost my mother and Manny their lives and destroyed mine in the process. Meanwhile, she'd gone on living her life as if nothing had ever happened. Now as I looked at Khalil, it was clear to me. He'd been delivered to me for a reason. I knew that the time had come to have my revenge.

"Where is all this coming from?" he asked in response to my request that he make love to me.

"Does it matter? Khalil, I've seen the way you've been looking at me all day. I know you want me."

He bit his bottom lip and took a deep breath and began to shake his head no. "Honey . . . I mean, you're beautiful, but I can't do this."

"Why, because you love her? Or because she loves you?"

When he didn't answer right away I looked at him with a slight smirk. I walked past him and toward the steps. I could feel his eyes locked on my ass as I hit the steps. I unzipped my top and dropped it on the steps as I ascended them.

"Honey?" he said as he began to follow me. "Where are you going?"

At the top of the steps I casually stepped out of the bottom to my suit and continued my search for the bedroom. The first room I saw was nearly empty. The second had a computer desk that took up the entire wall. I could hear Khalil calling my name from the base of the steps. I headed for the last room, certain that it was the room in which I would send Rorrie's life crumbling to pieces. I reached behind me and unclasped my bra and dropped it onto the parquet floor of his hallway.

"Honey," he called out as I heard him climbing the stairs. "Oh shit," he yelled out. "What are you doing, girl?"

I'd found his bedroom and dropped my panties on the floor in front of the bed. When he hit the door of his room he saw me there on the bed, naked. He locked eyes with me and walked over to the bed.

"Why?" he asked. His eyes showed conflict. He must have loved Rorrie. But typical of a man, he'd made a series of bad judgments that had landed him in this situation. Thinking that he could handle things, that he could be a knight in shining armor without it leading to this. Perhaps things were out of his control from the second he saw me. It really didn't matter now. I was in control of him. What I was about to give him usually cost thousands, but this time it was free. He was staring at me with hunger in his eyes. The shades and curtains were closed in the room, only allowing for a pinch of sunlight to invade. Still there was enough for him to see every detail and every curve. The distinct contrast of my skin and my areolae, my deep-chocolate nipples sitting up off of my breast.

I sat up on my knees and grabbed his face in my hands as I pulled his mouth to mine. "Just know this," I said in a whisper. "Once you make love to me, your life will never be the same. I can promise you that. Once you get inside of this, you'll forget all about her," I spoke softly into his ear. "I promise that I'll have you coming so fast and hard you won't be able to think of anything else, ever."

His eyes were closed and I began to kiss his face and neck. When I heard him moan I knew that he was a goner. This was routine for me, all about giving him pleasure. It was just a means to an end for me. I'd never been emotionally connected to any partner even if I found them attractive, which was almost always. Even still, I seldom took on any client that I didn't find attractive. I'd believed that intellect and power were very sexy when used properly between lovers. With maturation, I'd come to learn that being attractive didn't always equate to physical looks.

Still in all the years I'd been having sex, I'd been with only a selected few outside of business. And in those situations the cards were always on the table beforehand. But this moment with Khalil was different. He began to do that which I had never allowed anyone since Manny to do, which was kissing me in the mouth. It felt strange but good. I began to lose track of myself and what I was trying to do.

I felt flush as I fought to regain my control. *This was about Rorrie,* I said to myself as I pushed his lips away and grabbed his shoulders. There was still the conflicted look on his face. He was disappointed in himself for wanting me so bad. He was so easy to read. The desire he was feeling for me was his weakness.

"Lay down," I demanded. I reached for his pants and unbuckled them. When I pulled on the sides and slid them off I was pleasantly surprised by the size of his tool and the fact that he wore no underwear. I motioned for his shirt and he leaned up enough to yank it off. I gazed upon his totally naked body. He was definitely handsome from head to toe and I reasoned that most any woman would fall for him.

I straddled him and began to kiss his neck and shoulders. All the while he could feel the thin strip of hair above my vagina rubbing against his penis. I slid down to his chest and began to softly pinch and lick his nipples. I looked into his eyes and saw that he was mesmerized. My hand was now stroking him, gently, professionally.

His skin tasted clean, yet manly. Without my permission his body's natural aroma invaded my nostrils and sent an unfamiliar rush through me once again. My grip was firmly on his manhood and I noticed that he was lifting up from the mattress. I was shocked when the words slipped from his mouth. "Honey, you gotta stop. I can't do this. Rorrie is my fiancée." He tried to rise up from the bed.

I don't know what came over me but I felt an almost out-of-body experience. My desire to take him, to break what he shared with my enemy overtook my sensibilities. Anger and passion for what I wanted swept over me and I smacked him across the face. Hard.

He was stunned and his eyes were wide-open as I quickly mounted him. His thickness shot up into my center in an instant. Before he could even understand what had happened I had both of my hands on his chest as I fucked him. He was silent for a few moments as he stared deep into my eyes.

I bounced and grinded, preparing to do to him that which I'd done to every man that I'd experienced. I knew that it was just a matter of time before he lost control. The look on my face had turned into a sinister grin.

He began to pant and I began to count down. I looked at the clock and then back at him. One minute. I could feel my wetness just about to envelop him. There was incredible friction. This was the first man that I'd been with unprotected in ten years. I'd had a couple of condoms break and fortunately for me I hadn't paid a price, but this was different. I was being extremely reckless but I didn't care. The only thing I cared about was taking his mind and getting him to lose any feelings that he had for Rorrie.

It would be in that moment that I would go out of my way to let her know that her pain was at my hands.

His breathing grew heavier and I poured it on. I clenched my vaginal walls on him and bounced harder. I saw a different look on his face. He looked almost angry as we were now fucking. He didn't want to succumb to my will to make him explode. I rode him harder and realized it was time to *talk* him over the edge.

For the next couple of minutes I spoke the words that I knew would drive him to his climax. "That's right, Khalil. Tear this pussy up. How does it feel," I growled. "You're so big, Daddy. Mmmmmmm. Fill me up."

He reached and grabbed my ass cheeks and continued to bang from underneath me. I looked at the clock, three minutes. I was growing impatient on the surface as I began to wonder if he was enjoying the feelings.

Suddenly he reached up and grabbed the back of my head and pulled my face to his. His tongue began to dance inside of my mouth and for the first time I felt stimulated by more than my own power. I felt his weight shift and him pushing me onto my back.

In a few swift motions he was on top of me with my legs in the air. He began to slide masterfully in and out of me until I began to feel something that I couldn't explain.

He settled into a rhythm and I honestly began to lose track of time and space. My muscles were clamping down on his shaft without warning. The room began to grow dark then light again and I tried to look over at the clock but the numbers were blurry. I couldn't hear him breathing anymore over my own breath. The only thing I could hear was the smacking sound of our bodies colliding. When he spoke his voice seared my insides and commanded a reaction.

"Honey, this pussy . . ."

"Yes, tell me."

"It's so . . ."

"Tell me," I moaned.

"It feels so . . . good . . . I'm . . ."

That was all I heard before I felt a powerful thrust from him that felt like he was trying to knock me through the mattress down to the floor below us. With it I felt like my heart exploded and was emptying through my womanhood. I screamed out as I lost control. I had never felt anything like this. My eyes closed tight and it felt as though my body was a river flowing toward the edge of a waterfall.

All the sensations that I had ever imagined I'd feel when this moment happened were pulsating and erupting from my center. "Ahhhhhh, ooohhhhh," was all I could get out, followed by a grunt and a spasm as my body shook and trembled through its first orgasm.

I hadn't realized that Khalil had stopped moving and was now on top of me lying still in his own pleasure-induced fog. The room was quiet as my breathing slowly returned to normal. I looked over at the clock and couldn't believe it. Twenty minutes had passed since I'd climbed on top of him.

We woke an hour and a half later when his phone rang. I was on my side and he leaned over the bed away from me. I could hear her voice coming through the line.

"Yeah, baby. I'm fine. My flight got in around three or four." (He was explaining why he didn't call.) "I'm just trying to catch up on some rest. Can I call you when I get up?"

I sat there listening, eyes halfway open. Lying in her spot, I was sure, listening to him lie. "What time will you be in on Friday? Okay, good. I'll call you when I get up."

I don't know why but I felt a tingle in my heart when I heard him mumble, ". . . Love you . . . too."

The rage returned and when he hung the phone up it was time for me to go. I'd have him take me to a hotel until I could figure out what was going on with Priest. I decided that I wouldn't give him my number when he asked, though I'd have his.

"You awake?" he asked.

"Kind of," I responded. Then I asked, "Could you get me something to drink and a facecloth?"

"Sure." He got up naked and went to the hall closet and brought back a thick washcloth. "What would you like to drink?" he asked as I walked past him into the bathroom.

"Surprise me, but give me some ice with it and if you have anything to snack on . . . that'd be great."

He marched off down to the kitchen. I sprinted to his cell. Flipped it open and looked at his call log. There she was, *Rorrie 202-555-4851*. I burned it into my memory in case I'd need it later to wreak havoc. Then I dialed my number long enough to make my phone ring and hung up. Then back to his call log to delete the call.

When he walked back into the room I was walking out of the bathroom like I'd been in there the entire time.

"Khalil, I need to go."

"I thought we were going to talk and now I think we really need to."

"There's nothing to talk about. You have your life and I have mine. It was great meeting you and maybe our paths will cross again."

He was silent. Then I gathered my clothes and dressed. I watched as his eyes betrayed him again. He wanted me, yet he didn't want to make a move. I had him drop me off at the Grand Hyatt and just like I'd expected when we pulled up he asked me, "Honey, can I get your number? Just to check on you?"

As badly as I wanted to say yes, I shook my head. "I don't think so."

He reached into his pocket and pulled out a business card and extended it to me. I ignored him and said, "Thanks for everything . . ." I paused and continued, "Oh I almost forgot. I'm sorry for slapping you like that." Then I added with a smile, "But aren't you glad I did?"

The look on his face told me what I already knew. The pleasure had been all his. I felt his eyes again as I walked toward the entrance. Five days at best and he'd be climbing the walls trying to find me. By then I'd hopefully have this situation with Priest all straightened out and be able to concentrate on Khalil and Rorrie.

I reached a bellhop as soon as I made it into the lobby. "Excuse me, young man."

"Yes, ma'am."

"Listen, I don't want to turn around but is there a black truck still sitting in front of the hotel with a man sitting in it?"

He looked over my shoulder. "Yes ma'am. Except the man is getting out of the truck."

"Thank you." I headed for the check-in as I corrected myself.

I'd give him two days.

10

KHALIL

I followed my therapist down the hallway toward her office. Due to her aversion to formality, from the first visit she'd insisted that I call her by her first name, Cameron. She led me in as always and I took a seat. She sat across from me, looking distinguished, yet carefully plain, dressed in a navy pin-striped blazer, white shirt, and matching skirt. Still she was attractive even while trying to take attention away from her looks. Her shoulder-length locks were dyed at the tips, framing her strong-featured face. Looking away from her eyes I scanned down and found myself next trying to avoid staring at her ample bustline. The blazers she wore to tone down her cleavage, and the glasses, were supposed to make her seem more like a doctor. I figured that she wanted to look the part and eliminate anything that might be disruptive to the doctor-patient relationship.

She needed to embrace that she was not only a licensed therapist. She was very good at what she did. The fact that she knew what she was doing made a nonissue of the fact that she came off as both sexy and confident.

At Cameron's hands I'd been able to shed a lot of the hatred and anger that dwelled within me. For as long as I could remember I blamed every bad thing that happened to me on two women: my mother and Frannie. After I was abandoned by both, there hadn't been anyone around for me to project that on. With Cameron's help, I'd been able to see that all the time I thought that I was dogging women out, hating them, I actually had been hating myself. Afraid to love, because I never felt worthy of receiving it. According to her, I had given myself the right to believe this because I had faced the terrible fortune of never feeling valued by anyone.

I also came to get help because I had recurring nightmares of being molested. I'd wake up panting for air many nights, thinking that I was being raped all over again. I wouldn't see myself as a little boy in those dreams though, which was weird. I was a grown man, yet I was still defenseless.

I'd been in therapy for two years off and on after the relationship with Kristen, a girl I'd dated just before I met Rorrie, came to an end. In a terrible incident, I'd punched the girl in the face. She didn't understand why in the middle of the night when she reached out to hold me, my reaction had been to throw a hard right jab that broke her nose.

I tried to explain and believed that she understood when I said she'd startled me. I was shocked when two days later I found out that her friends had convinced her to press charges against me. We parted ways and to avoid having any criminal record I was ordered to counseling. Shortly after, I found Cameron and the whole thing proved to be a blessing.

I'd never been able to make any real progress until I met her.

"So how are you, Khalil?" Cameron asked. She had a way of

making me feel as though I was in grade school even though she insisted I call her Cameron and she wasn't even ten years older than me.

"I'm fine, I guess." Cameron never asked what was troubling me. She'd wait for me to get comfortable with her. I don't know if it was the fact that I'd come to value the opportunity to talk with her or having another human being that I could spill my heart to. Being in her presence usually prompted me to open up, immediately. I fidgeted in my chair a little and then spit it out. "Cameron, I cheated on my fiancée."

She didn't respond. Instead she simply looked at me with inquisitive eyes, her hands flat on the desk. The office was dead silent except for the air blowing through the vent. I waited to make sure that she was blinking.

"I met her on a flight back from Miami. There was something about her the moment I saw her. I'm not sure why though, because I see beautiful women all the time. I had just spent a weekend in South Beach and the thought of cheating hadn't entered my mind so it was more than the fact that she was beautiful and sexy."

I paused and she offered an "Okay." I could have predicted what she asked next before the words came out of her mouth. "So how do you feel about it?"

"I'm not sure how I feel about it." Before I thought about what type of insight I could offer about my feelings, Honey's face popped into my head. Then I was surprised that instead of her chocolate skin, hazel eyes, her perfect grapefruit-size breasts, I thought of her voice and the things we talked about on the plane. I remembered that in the midst of whatever she was going through, she'd been able to make me laugh. She was witty and smart. But then just as quickly my mind drove me into the depths of what I viewed as my own depravity as I reminisced on how good it felt to be inside of her. There was no denying that she was incredible in bed.

"Well tell me what you believe you might be feeling about it? The first thing that pops into your mind," she said, now sitting back.

"I can't stop thinking about her. I feel bad because in spite of the guilt, I want to see her again. And it's more than sex. I feel like even though I don't know her, I want to. I almost *need* to. As if we have some type of weird spiritual connection."

"Have you been speaking with her?"

This is what was driving me crazy. It had been two weeks since I'd dropped her off at the hotel and I'd been by the hotel every day since then spending an hour or two parked out front hoping to see her coming or going. I didn't share this with Cameron. I knew it was crazy. "No, I don't have a number for her."

"If you did would you call?"

I nodded yes. "I know where she lives and I stopped by there to leave a note, but I could tell that she hadn't been past her house."

"How?"

"Fliers and junk mail jammed in the door. She hasn't been there."

"Did you leave your number or a note to let her know?"

"No."

"So what do you want to do in regards to your relationship?"

I sounded defensive when I said, "I do love Rorrie. I know I do, but I'm having a hard time concentrating on what we have. I don't know. Maybe it's just a thing I'm going through."

"A *thing*? Be more specific if you could."

"I mean ... maybe it was just me getting caught up in the excitement of someone or something new. I'm sure it'll pass, especially since I can't contact her anyway."

"Well you can. You said you know where she lives, right?"

"Yeah."

"So do you think you'll go back there again looking for her since you have no other way of contacting her?"

I wanted to tell Cameron that the day I'd dropped her at the hotel I'd sat in the truck for a moment before going into the lobby after Honey. I wound up practically begging her to give me her number. She'd told me basically that she thought I was confused and that by the time I had it all figured out everything would fall into place. At that moment it seemed that I didn't have a chance with her and even if I did, I didn't even know what I wanted a chance to do anyway.

I answered her question: "I don't think so." I paused and thought about how I was feeling. "I want to be able to let it go. I just don't know how. I don't want to hurt Rorrie, but I don't know if I can trust myself not to."

"Well there's nothing wrong with being confused. It shows that you're attempting to process some very conflicting emotions." She had a pencil in her fingers that she twirled a bit back and forth. "Let me ask you this, Khalil. What do you think will happen if you can't get over this? If you can't stop thinking about this woman or what you did with her. Will you proceed into a future with Rorrie?"

I shrugged my shoulders and bathed in the shame that her question brought me. We continued to talk about my dreams and my anger for the next forty minutes. I left my session feeling extremely heavy. Rorrie was due in this evening and I knew I'd be taking my bags of guilt to the airport with me when I picked her up.

$\mathbf{M}$y cell rang at a quarter past six. "What time you picking me up?"

It was my buddy David. He was getting married in the morning. Along with the other groomsmen, I was taking him out for his last night on the town as a single man. "Around nine thirty. I'm on the way to the airport to pick Rorrie up."

"Don't be late," he barked. We'd had the rehearsal dinner the night before, which worked well with all that I had to do.

"I wouldn't do that to you, partna. Hopefully *this* is the last time you do this." I laughed, referring to the fact that he was on his third crack at marriage and he was only twenty-nine.

"That's real funny, man. Just make sure your comedic ass brings plenty of ones, because I'm leaving my wallet at home."

I laughed, because I knew he was dead-serious.

$\mathbf{I}$ arrived at Reagan National Airport and pulled around as I searched for American Airlines. As I crept up toward the walkway just outside of the baggage claim I saw her. She was dressed in a pair of scrubs as she wheeled her one suitcase to the curb. I quickly stopped and climbed out to lift her bag, as she looked exhausted. She smiled and we embraced. For the first time I felt no electricity, only awkwardness.

"Hey you," she said. We climbed in the truck and the first thing she did was turn down my stereo. I turned it back up from the steering wheel. I loved that feature. Nas's *Street's Disciple* CD was pumping through the speakers. "Baby, could you please?" she asked in a tone laced with irritation.

"Headache?" I asked.

"Just don't feel like the noise. I've had a hell of a week."

I looked over at her as I turned the music down and a bout of fear swept through my body. She was staring straight ahead and didn't notice my careful gaze. I took in her profile, her hair and the trademark ponytail, the mole on her cheek, her bright white teeth, finally even her well-developed bustline. Just that quickly I'd judged her like a prize poodle in a canine competition and come up with a chilling verdict. For the first time I didn't see the beauty that had always hypnotized me.

The sight of her didn't move me at all; neither did her voice or her presence. My heart started to pound as I began to dread the thought of how I'd spend the next forty-eight hours sharing space with her while trying to come up with words to keep her from realizing that we had a problem.

A serious problem, because I needed to feel something for her as I always had, but I didn't. I glanced at her once again to confirm that there was nothing left about her that would bring me to my knees.

The condition of my heart had been just as it was since the day I'd left the lobby of that hotel, begging for a chance to get to know *her*. Even looking my fiancée dead in the face, I could see only one woman and it wasn't Rorrie.

11

HONEY

Miles Amory arrived on the East Coast early in the morning via his G4. Loaded with cash, he was a classy gentleman who didn't mind parting ways with large sums of money when it meant having a good time. I looked forward to spending the evening with him. He reminded me of a younger Harry Belafonte in poise and physical appearance. Miles had a high-octane lifestyle and already he'd concluded a ten A.M. meeting in New York and an early dinner at the Borgata in Atlantic City, where he usually spent the next hour or two gambling a couple hundred thousand dollars at the blackjack tables.

He'd wind up at his home on R Street in Georgetown, a nine-thousand-square-foot mansion that he slept in probably thirty nights a year. At fifty-two he was extremely well-kept. He was the only African-American on his entire street and I suspected one of the very few who lived in the heart of Georgetown. One look at how he lived and it was plain to see that he was important to a lot of people all over the world. He bragged about having five thousand employees and making money in five time zones. But to me, he was nothing more than a stream of revenue.

I'd met him at a fund-raiser that George Bush held for his reelection campaign a couple of years back at the Ritz-Carlton. Galas like those always brought out the deep pockets and were can't-miss events for those such as myself who were about the business of forming mutually beneficial friendships. Give me a shipping magnate, a technology CEO, or an oil baron over Allen Iverson and T.I. any day.

I pitied the groupies who didn't know where the money was. They studied ballplayers. I studied the person who signed their checks. I looked at the one exception that I'd made in dating an athlete, Priest, as a huge mistake. After all of the drama that I'd gotten caught up in, I was pissed at myself for ever breaking my own rules. Never again.

When Cheron knocked on the door of the hotel room I greeted her with a huge hug. "Hey, girl."

"Heeeyyyyyy," she screamed back. "Damn, you looking really hot, Hailey, and those shoes are banging." I grimaced when she called me by my government name and then she caught my glare and corrected herself. "My bad, I mean Honey."

Surprisingly, Cheron and I had become the best of friends over the years. There was no way anyone could have guessed that she wouldn't try to kill me on sight after Manny was killed over me, let alone that we could become more than fierce enemies. Life is unpredictable at best and when Manny had been killed, I'd realized that Cheron's ticket out of jail had disappeared with his last breath. For reasons I couldn't understand at that time I lost sleep thinking about her in a jail cell. A few days later I looked her up and when I found out where her mother lived, I went to visit her. She cried when I told her that I wanted to give her the money that she needed for a lawyer. It wiped out the stash of money that I'd collected from both Tank and Manny, but it kept her from doing any time.

She was smart and didn't look a gift horse in the mouth at the time, but the day we walked out of the district courthouse she asked me why I helped her. Before we climbed into our separate vehicles I admitted to her what I remembered. "Cheron, even though I always envied you, I respected you. Rorrie and I would sit outside and watch you as you left out the house dressed in the flyest gear." I'd laughed, remembering. "We couldn't wait to be grown so that we could be just like you. You were the closest thing we had to a hero. How could I let my hero go to jail if I could do something to stop it?"

Even now that she was nearly thirty-three and was the mother of a four-year-old daughter, Madison, she had managed to keep it together physically, usually looking the part of a model chick. We hit the gym together at least twice a week. Over the years I'd always been there for her when she needed my help, financial or otherwise, and in return she'd lend her wisdom.

Oddly, we never discussed Manny though. I'd formed my own code of honor and the disrespect that I'd shown her then would never happen again. I believe that she knew I'd learned from the past and that was obviously good enough for her to consider me a sister.

She set her small overnight bag on the table and I noticed that she'd changed her hair color. A few streaks, highlights, and a cut, and the chick was looking out-of-this-world. "I'm loving your hair, Cheron. When did you get it done?"

"Yesterday."

"The bomb."

"Thanks."

Then I pointed over to the bed. "Look through those and see which one you want to wear. We need to move because Miles will be here soon and we don't want to have him waiting."

"No problem," she said, approaching the bed where I had a few pieces laid out. Just as I suspected she went straight for the short white dress. "This is lovely," she said.

"Versace," I shot back. It was nice, but not nicer than the Salvatore Ferragamo number I was wearing. "You're a four, right?"

Cheron nodded. "Unless I'm bloated." Then she giggled.

"Well there you go." We wore the same dress- and shoe-size. "There are some matching kicks over there."

"You ain't nothing but the truth." Cheron stripped out of the khaki shorts and shirt she was wearing, in front of me. I quickly examined her panties and bra. They were nice enough.

"You're not going to be able to wear a bra with that dress, love. And grab a pair of those undies out of the bag." It was filled with nothing but La Perla. I looked at my watch. "Go on in there and freshen up. I'll be waiting down at the bar. Ten minutes max," I demanded.

"All right." She grabbed the items and moved toward the bathroom.

As I rode the elevator down I began to think of all the money I'd make tonight. I'd promised Cheron fifteen hundred to spend the night with Miles and myself. The second he greeted me, he'd hand me a cashier's check for twelve thousand dollars. And for that, he might not even want to have intercourse.

We cruised from the hotel just up M Street to Miles's favorite restaurant, Michel Richard Citronelle. I watched Cheron's body language, making sure that she didn't seem too impressed even though the food and the atmosphere lived up to the billing that it received worldwide. A mood wall that changed color every fifty-nine seconds, soft music, and the lure of a man made of money made it hard to resist actions that caused most women to appear foolish. This, however, was work for me and since Cheron was along for the ride and the commission, there were standards of decorum to be upheld.

The waiter treated Miles like an old friend and was at our beck and call. The world-famous chef even stopped by our table to ensure that everything was up to par and to make a wine suggestion to Miles.

The meal came quickly, allowing us to proceed with the evening. Custard-and-caviar-filled eggshells, a three-course meal, and two bottles later it was time to go.

Miles had long implored me to bring along another woman. I didn't have to tell him, he knew that I wasn't into women, and would never be, so any hopes of some girl-on-girl was out the window. He said he understood but still wanted me to bring a friend. So here we were.

We were headed down K Street when Miles's phone rang. He'd ignored every call before this one, so I was surprised when he took the call. "Yes, I'm in the city now."

I didn't listen closely until he asked the driver to turn around. Five minutes later we pulled up in front of a club. "Ladies, if you don't mind, I'd like to spend about thirty to forty minutes here. I have a client that I need to meet and it will only take a few moments."

I nodded, not wanting to appear fazed one way or the other since he was spending so much money. We climbed out of the

Maybach and walked into the door of the posh gentlemen's club.

We sat at a booth opposite one of the stages and within moments Miles had ten drinks delivered to our table. "Sip until you find what suits you," he said. He then walked to a table where three other men were seated. I caught their gazes. I knew the drill. He was telling the men that he had two pieces of ass that he was about to enjoy. Men were so predictable. He talked to them for five minutes and then came back to join us. The men spoke as they left the club together. Miles wanted to enjoy a few drinks before leaving and he had me climb out of the booth so that he could sit between us.

I drank sparingly, as was my policy, and kept my eyes on Cheron. She had a weakness for fine alcohol. I sat back and watched the girls get their hustle on—singles, fives, or twenties at a time. I thanked my stars that I wasn't one of them. They had to shake ass for a month or two in front of men who wanted to bang them, in order to make the kind of money that I did in one night.

A couple of them were really pretty and I thought about schooling them but logic prevailed. We are who we are and it took all kinds to make the world go round. They shook it on stages while I went all the way for a price. It was simply a matter of style.

"Cheron, go give her some money," Miles barked. He reached into his jacket pocket and pulled out a wad of money. "Here take it to her," he said, handing Cheron a twenty.

She looked at me and I winked and gave a slight nod. Whatever turned him on, *up to a point,* was my motto. Cheron looked out of place, as did I. We looked too classy to be handing out bills to dancers, even in a nice club like this one.

"That's right. Make her work for it," Miles yelled out. He was drunk, but that was cool. He'd been known to pass out from the liquor and rich food without so much as laying a finger on me. When that happened it was strictly his loss, as he paid for time, not sex, though the implication was always sex.

The white girl was gyrating slowly in front of Cheron. When she noticed the twenty she took her act to the next level, moving as if she were trying to entice Cheron.

Miles kept Cheron running back and forth, handing off twenty after twenty to every dancer who graced the stage. I reasoned that he must have been getting turned on, so I scooted closer to him and began to rub my hand on his thigh. I was shocked when he said, "I want her to do that."

"Excuse me?" I responded.

"No, I mean I want you both doing it at the same time."

I leaned in and whispered in his ear, "Here?"

"No, let's go back to my place."

He squared the tab and we prepared to leave.

Standing at the front of the club we were waiting for the car to pull up when I saw a group of men approaching the door. My heart almost sank when our eyes met.

It was Khalil.

"Honey?" Just then the car pulled up.

"Hey. I got to run, Khalil." The driver opened the door and I watched Cheron climb in as Miles stood there. I wanted to tell him that he'd been on my mind. Secretly though, I'd been afraid to go through with my plan to crush Rorrie, because I actually felt something with him that I couldn't yet comprehend. Instead I looked him in the eye and saw that there was so much that he wanted to say, yet all I gave him was, "I've got to run."

When we hit the corner and I glanced back again, he was still standing there.

My mind was blank as I put in my work that evening. Not that I enjoyed sex with my clients, but I usually was present. I never wanted to go numb to what I was doing for fear of losing my humanity. But as I sat naked on the chaise in Miles's bedroom my only thoughts were of Khalil.

I only responded when he asked.

It was strange but Cheron seemed to be enjoying herself. She had gotten caught up in the romance of the evening. The seven-hundred-dollar dinner, the ride in the Maybach, the endless string of Monopoly money that she tossed at the club, and now the three-million-dollar mansion had her believing that it was real. My session ended when I'd freaked out after the unthinkable happened. A broken condom. There had been a serious break in action as I made sure that he had not ejaculated anywhere near me.

I was completely through for the night but it was proven that one monkey didn't stop the show. Ten minutes later and Miles was bouncing up and down on Cheron as if his life depended on it. All the while he'd been making requests. "Rub my back, spank my ass," he screamed out. "Kiss her."

Cheron was drunk and surprisingly game. It was as far as I'd been willing to go. I knew that I could always hit a man when he was at his peak. "You know I don't do that, but if you really want to see it, it'll cost you."

"Okay, just kiss her. Kiss her while I nail her."

I smiled as I leaned in and gave her a long and sensuous kiss. It meant nothing to me and I felt nothing, but it paid my car note, twice. When I pulled away I noticed the look of un-adulterated pleasure on Cheron's face. In that instant, I knew that she'd been with women before. I moved away and let him finish up.

It was cool that I didn't have to remind him of the extra money when it was time for the driver to take us back to the hotel. On the downside, I left his home feeling way too strange. The entire ride back to the hotel I thought about Khalil as I stared out the window.

"What's wrong?" Cheron asked. "Did I do anything wrong?"

I shook my head no. "Not at all."

"Are you sure?"

I laughed. "Nah, girl. It looked like you enjoyed yourself though," I said, trying to change the subject from my blues.

"Hmmmph," she exclaimed. "The easiest money I ever made. Homeboy was all right. But . . . I wouldn't do it again."

"Really?"

She seemed a bit offended by my tone and immediately responded with: "Why you asks like that? No. *Really,* I wouldn't." She raised her voice a little.

"Why not?"

Her answer not only sobered me, it shot through me like a bullet. "Hailey, I have a daughter to think of. How could I face her if she ever found out? I wouldn't want this for her, so how could I expect different if it was something that I said was okay through my actions?"

"But you are saying it is okay. It's good enough for you to do . . ."

Cutting me off, she said, "I didn't do this for the money. I came along simply for the experience. Don't get me wrong. I'm a single mom and I can always use extra money, but I'm not hurting. I'm way past spending ridiculous sums of money on clothes and I'm not knocking you. It's your money. It's your choice. But for me, that's just not where I am. I simply wanted to hang out with you and one of these clients that I've heard so much about."

I was silent as we'd pulled up to the hotel. I felt every word she said but still it bothered me. After a few moments I said, "Can I talk to you about something?"

"Anything," she said. "I'm always going to be here for you, bitch. Just not tonight. I'm exhausted."

"Old Miles wore you out, huh?"

"You ain't never lied. His ass must have been on some Cialis or Viagra. Ol' boy got the coochie hurtin' a bit. Do you mind if I stay here and sleep it off?"

It was after two o'clock in the morning. "Go ahead, but I'm heading home, I have a Realtor coming the first thing in the morning, I'm putting my place on the market. We can catch up in the morning."

"Cool," she said as I packed up my belongings.

"You can bring the dress in the A.M. and I'll have the cash for you."

She was my girl, but chicks were famous for forgetting that they borrowed some gear.

I cruised twenty over the speed limit, stoplight to stoplight, pushing the engine of my M3 to the limit. I turned the music down as I turned onto my block and lucked up when I found a spot three houses down.

I took my shoes off and began to skirt my way down the sidewalk. It was humid and the ground felt sweaty under my feet but

I didn't care. My mind was on one thing, hitting the bed. Well two things, but I'd have to think about that in the morning.

I reached for my keys but was startled when I heard the voice behind me. "Honey, we need to talk."

Cornered, I had no choice but to face him.

12

KHALIL

I blew the entire mood of David's night on the town after I bumped into Honey. Seeing her looking so good and getting into the car of another man stunned me like a slap from Naomi Campbell. The guy was obviously wealthy but he looked old enough to be her father. Deep down inside I held out hope that it might have been, but I couldn't make sense of them being at a strip club. I wasn't in the club twenty minutes before I announced that I was leaving.

We had all met up at David's spot and then I'd left my car there, so I had no choice but to call Rorrie. She showed up asking twenty questions. "So what's wrong? What happened?"

I had thoughts of feigning sickness with the fellas but I didn't want David to worry about my making it to the wedding. I pulled him to the side and explained to him that I was having some problems with Rorrie and that I needed to get home. He wasn't happy but said he understood.

Now that Rorrie and I were driving to my car I realized that what I'd told him was true. "I'm not really in the mood to be around a bunch of drunk guys in a strip club."

"That's why I love you," she said. "Most men love that sort of thing, but you are only interested in a virtuous woman." She was smiling.

"That's me." I began thinking back to how I sexed Honey up a few hours after we met. Not much virtue in that, yet I couldn't figure out why for the life of me I'd begun to slip into this obsession over her. In all practicality, she could have been a whore.

My train of thought was broken when Rorrie spoke. "Khalil," she said. "I want to ask you something."

"Yeah, what's up?"

"Would you mind it if I didn't make it to the wedding tomorrow! I got a call from one of my old instructors and they are doing a clinic over at Greater Southeast Hospital tomorrow for children who suffer with HIV. It's like a free physical and treatment program. They are like five physicians short and I'd like to go over and volunteer. Of course I told him that I had a previous engagement and I'd have to ask my fiancé first."

"Oh, of course I don't mind. That sounds like a really great way to give back. To be honest, if there was any way that I could get out of going I would too." I half-laughed. I was relieved that she didn't ask me anything too heavy.

"You're not looking forward to David's big day?"

"It's not that. I'm just not big on weddings."

"What the heck is that supposed to mean?"

I thought about what I'd just said. "You know, big productions."

"Yeah okay. I guess that's why you haven't brought up ours in the past month or so. You think it's going to be too big a production?"

"Ummm, that's not it at all. I've just had a lot on my mind lately." We were nearly to my car. "Turn right here and then make the left at the stop sign. My truck is halfway up the block."

"Anything you want to talk about?"

"Just work and pressure that's it."

I looked over at her and I almost wanted to blurt out that I was confused about what I was going through.

We stopped at my truck and as I climbed out she asked, "You following me?"

"Yeah, but I want to stop and grab a bite to eat. You want something?"

"No. But you don't have to stop. I can cook for you."

"I got a taste for a sub. I'm going to slide over to Eddie's. I'll see you at the house."

She nodded and sped off. So did I, but in a different direction.

I sat on Honey's block for an hour before my phone began ringing off the hook with calls from Rorrie.

When I finally answered I said, "Hey, babe. Sorry, but I talked to David and the crew and they all begged me to bring them subs so I wound up turning right around and going back for them. Now I'm on the way back to the club. They really laid a guilt trip on me for leaving so I'm going to hang out with them for just a little while."

"Khalil, you could have fucking called me to let me know." I knew she was beyond pissed, because she seldom used the f-word. "I don't know what you're tripping off of lately."

"Sorry babe, but I'll be home in a bit."

"Whatever." Click.

I tossed my cell right back down in the seat and continued on my wait. I didn't give Rorrie's feelings a lot of thought as one hour turned into three. The entire time I sat in my truck listening to Maxwell singing "Matrimony: Maybe You," all the while being sucked into the fantasy world of his lyrics as I sang along. His words talked about finding someone who could turn out to be more than just a one-night stand. About finding the girl who could really be the one. My heart echoed the sentiments of the lyrics as I dreamed that perhaps Honey could be the wife that had been sent to me. Even though I barely knew her at this point, a part of me believed that just like Maxwell's words, she could teach me about me.

It didn't get any deeper than that. I had to find out if she was the one. Tuesday I had another appointment to see Cameron again and hopefully by then I'd be able to be honest with her about the things I was feeling. I'd at least know if Honey felt anything for me.

My phone finally rang again at two fifteen. Hearing it angered me. I was feeling too constricted to move. Either my conscience was getting to me or Rorrie sensed something and was trying to slip a noose on my neck. I glanced at the number to be sure it was Rorrie before I put it in the seat next to me and sat up. I finally decided that it was time to go home.

I started my engine and began to pull up the block when a car passed me and took my spot. Wishful thinking or not, I thought I saw Honey driving. I pulled out onto Connecticut Avenue just long enough to make an illegal U and pulled back up the block. When I saw her walking toward her house I felt myself growing light-headed, heart skipping a beat like a kid with his first crush. I saw a spot on the other side and pulled into it quickly. She didn't see me as I climbed out of the truck and crossed the street.

She was thirty yards or better ahead of me and I was about to call her name when I saw a figure step out from the bushes beside the door of her home. When the man grabbed Honey I heard her scream out. I couldn't move fast enough. I saw her jerk away and attempt to use pepper spray. She didn't react in time and he landed a blow to her face that dropped her to her knees. She would have hit the ground except for the fact that he held her.

He didn't see me coming as I lunged at him like Ray Lewis coming for a quarterback. He was huge, barely moving when I made contact. I did get him to the ground but it turned out to be a bad move as his weight allowed him to pin me down. From there we traded blows with me getting the worse of it. I was glad that he seemed to wind easily, almost gasping for air. I took the opportunity of his slowing down to go for his eyes with my thumbs. I jabbed him good in the left and this time he screamed out in agony. I easily rolled from under him and climbed to my feet. He struggled to stand, still holding his eye, and he wasn't paying attention as I swung my foot toward his balls with as much power as I could muster. When I made contact he groaned like a wounded animal.

Honey was now at my side as we watched him hit the ground. She moved toward him and began to empty the bottle of spray. Then she yelled out, "Khalil, come on, quick."

Thinking he was subdued I moved slowly but luckily she'd been more alert as he pulled a pistol from his waistband. My heart nearly burst open as he fired a single shot toward the security door a second after we'd cleared it.

From the second-floor window we watched as he headed for a vehicle that was parked up the street. Two minutes later sirens whirled out front as we sat nervously inside her apartment. It looked like she was in the middle of moving. There were boxes labeled and stacked neatly in the living room and more piled up in the kitchen.

"Now tell me again why you don't want to tell the police," I asked her as I sat nestled on her couch, holding against my cheek the frozen peas she'd given me. She was using the ice pack on hers.

"It's such a long story, Khalil. I don't even know where to begin. I will just say that I am really glad you happened to show up. I've been going through some changes with a guy I used to see. Obviously he isn't getting the message." She didn't seem as rattled as I would expect, almost like she dealt with things like this routinely. About a minute later she remembered to ask me, "So what are you doing here at two thirty in the morning anyway?"

Leaning my head gently back on her sofa I thought about the deeper meaning and what it may have looked like to her. I decided to open up to her as best I could. "I'm not really sure. I just needed to see you. I haven't stopped thinking about you since the day we met."

She smiled but looked reluctant in doing so. "Really?"

"You have no idea."

Her arms were folded. She'd dropped the ice pack on the coffee table after offering it to me. "Well it definitely felt a little awkward when I bumped into you earlier."

I couldn't resist the urge, so I asked her, "So do you normally frequent strip clubs?"

"No, it was actually the first time I'd been to one in years. I was just hanging out with an old friend and he wanted to go after we'd had dinner, so I went. Nothing serious."

"Did you enjoy yourself?"

"It was cool. It wasn't like I got my jollies off or anything. I'm definitely not gay, if that's what you're implying."

I laughed, relieved. "No, I didn't think anything of the sort."

"So," she breathed out. "How are things with your fiancée and you?"

I twitched nervously. "I'm not sure. Like I said, I can't seem to get this other woman off of my mind," I said in a playful tone. "I must be crazy. One day I spent with you and now I'm questioning everything." She sat there silent and I looked into her face. She still had a light coat of makeup on. Even sporting a slightly bruised cheek, she was beautiful. "Do you think I'm crazy?"

"Not at all, Khalil." She moved over next to me and kissed me on the cheek. "It's sweet really. I mean it. Also it's very flattering. I'm sure a handsome man like yourself can have his pick of women. For you to tell me that I've been on your mind, I won't even deny the fact that it means a lot." She stood up and said, "Listen I want to grab a few things. As you can see I'm in the process of moving but this incident is going to speed up that process. I'm gonna get out of here tonight."

I was still curious as to why she seemed unsurprised that she'd been attacked. "So where are you going to stay? You have family?"

"No, but I'll be fine. I'll get a room . . ."

Before she could finish I said, "I'm going to follow you and make sure you get there."

"You don't . . ."

I cut her off again. "I'm following you. You don't want the police involved. I'm following you."

———————

It was nearly four in the morning when she checked into the room at the Embassy Suites. Once she checked in I carried her bags up to her room for her. I knew it was late and I needed to get home but I wanted to stay. "I would ask you to stay but I don't think I should, Khalil." She was seated on the bed and had grabbed the remote. "I really appreciate everything you've done for me."

"I wanted to. You don't have to thank me." I walked toward her and once I was a foot away I leaned in to kiss her. She turned and gave me her cheek, sending my heart to the floor. "I thought you wanted me to stay."

"Not for that, though. Not for that." I didn't respond. Seeing my confusion she went on. "Khalil, I have a lot going on right now and so do you. I'll admit that I find you enticing." She stopped and laughed. "I really think you are mad sexy, but maybe we could just be friends for now."

"Friends, huh?"

She stood up and put her hands on her hips. "It's not like you can do much more than that. I mean what . . . we gonna get together, steal a few seconds here and there? You gonna sleep with me and then run home to her with my scent on your lips?"

She was now inside of my personal space, a few inches from my mouth. "I don't know, Honey. I just want to get to know . . ."

She hushed me by putting her finger to my lips. "Good night, Khalil. I have to get some rest. I'm going to have my things moved tomorrow. I'll be up early."

"So there's still no way that I can call you?"

She opened the door. "Good night."

"Good night," I said halfheartedly as I backed slowly out of her room, reeling from another round of her rejection. She winked, moved away from the door, and let it slam shut.

I reached my truck and started down Wisconsin Avenue toward the heart of the city, a million and one thoughts running through my mind as I drove. I flipped from WKYS to WPGC, trying to find some fast-paced beats to get my mind out of the weird state that I was in.

When my cell rang I was ready to throw it out the window. I was convinced that Rorrie had lost her grip. I picked it up ready to light into her. She didn't know that I was hurting over another woman but it didn't matter. She was there and I was going to take it out on her.

"Hello," I barked into the phone, making my disgust clear.

"If you want to get to know me, come back."

"What?" I looked down at the number. It wasn't Rorrie, as I could tell when I heard the voice. "Honey?"

"If you want to get to know me, come back to the hotel." I thought I was dreaming but then she said, "But don't expect me to have sex with you."

She didn't wait for a reply. Just like that she hung up.

13

HONEY

If I had been a gangster then Priest's days would have been numbered. He was fortunate in one way but as good as screwed in another. After he'd sent his enforcer to come and do me bodily harm I got angry. I did my best to hide it from Khalil, who'd been my saving angel. But from the second I realized that Priest had sent Big George back to my home, obviously to silence me, it was now a war. A war that I was sure he was too stupid to win. I'd never met an athlete smart enough to outwit a groupie, let alone a cunning diva like myself.

My belongings were in storage for the time being. I was going to go hotel-to-hotel until I got it all straightened out and once I did, money would never be an issue again. Priest had me fantasizing about what it would be like to retire from the life that I lived. I'd go somewhere, warm preferably, to open up a boutique filled with the types of clothes that I like. I'd be able to drive every day with the top down and a pair of Jackie-Os on my face.

I sat patiently in the rental car, waiting for the private investigator to arrive. On cue the silver Navigator pulled up. I hit my lights and he drove over to the corner of the lot where I was sitting. We were in the parking lot of Morton's, a steak house in Hackensack, New Jersey.

"How are you, Miss H?" he asked respectfully. He was a short man and I stared, almost rudely, as he climbed carefully out of the big truck. He might have been five foot three.

"I'm fine." I reached into my purse and pulled out an envelope. "Three thousand, it's all there. Mr. Amory spoke highly of you. Said you were the best. A real pro."

He handed me two envelopes. "You'll see for yourself. One of those is a set of copies. The third set, I mailed to the address you gave me. I hope that everything works out for you. I had to climb a telephone pole sixty yards up for some of those."

"Oh, I'm sure it will. You especially made sure of that. All I was looking for was a house, a wife, and a few other tidbits, but you, Mr. Cason, are a phenom."

He smiled and laughed out loud. My flattery had him tickled. "Well thank you much," he said. "I guess I'll be off. Call me if you need me."

"I sure will. As a matter of fact, I might need you really soon. Do you work out of town?"

"How far?"

"Not sure yet."

"How long?"

I shrugged my shoulders. "A day, maybe a week. No more."

"You call, I'll come," he said, grinning ear to ear. I was sensing that the black Danny DeVito had a crush. "I might go to hell and stake out Satan if the price is right."

I didn't laugh with him. Instead, once he left I sat in the car and looked into the envelope. I had two addresses for Priest and a few pictures of him with a woman other than his wife. Mr. Cason had taken photos of him carrying diapers and toys up to the door, kissing a pretty Puerto Rican girl and a baby. I was sure that this was going to be interesting to his wife, if the child turned out to be his, but what had me thinking about retirement were the next few photos. I smiled at the clarity of the images of him leaning back in a truck, getting head from none other than Big George. I couldn't believe the angle Mr. Cason'd shot the pics from.

What amazed me was that Mr. Cason had hit a goldmine himself, if only he'd wanted it. Instead he handed them over to me to do what I chose. He could have sold the pictures to any number of tabloids, but he gave them to me for the price we agreed upon. Either he was a real stand-up guy, or the name and face of the man he'd stalked for me hadn't rung any bells. I was inclined to believe that he simply operated out of integrity, since Priest had been an All-Star more than once.

Then again the pictures were worthless if you weren't going to sell them or you weren't planning to commit a felony with blackmail. I was.

When Priest walked out of the restaurant and to his car I waited for him to pull out into traffic and I followed him. The white man he'd eaten with was his agent. They were both riding high, I was sure. A newly signed contract, a fat signing bonus, and life was good for them.

He was heading for Englewood Cliffs, where he had a three-million-dollar mansion. I had the address written down and could have used the portable GPS to beat him there if I chose, but he was oblivious as he blasted the music out the windows of his Mercedes. I lagged behind when we reached the entrance to his development and carefully waited as he turned each corner before I pulled too closely. A few minutes later he arrived at his driveway and the gate opened.

Once he drove through the gate I waited for it to shut and then I pulled up right behind him and parked right in front of it. I looked up the long driveway; a half a football field away I saw his brake lights and then, a moment later, the reverse lights lit up. He began to wheel back toward the gate. I remained in the car until he reached the gate and stepped out. I opened the door and stepped out of the rental.

We were face to face now, separated by the white metal bars. "What are you doing at my fucking house? Are you crazy?"

It dawned on me that he had the nerve to call me crazy, yet he'd sent his henchman/lover to my door. "I think you know why I'm here, Priest. You're lucky I haven't gone to the police. What did you think you were doing having your goon show up at my house?"

He looked at me quizzically. I was sure he was wondering if I was setting him up. "I don't know what you're talking about."

"I think you do. As a matter of fact, you know he got his fat ass kicked that night by my man. And if he comes back . . ."

"Your man? Bitch, you're a fucking whore. A high-class one, but still a whore nonetheless. Any man who's claiming you has got to be some pussy-whipped idiot. C'mon now."

I don't know why but his words hit me like a ton of bricks. I don't even know why I had called Khalil my man, but I didn't appreciate Priest's sick tail having the nerve or the grounds to put him down.

He went on, "So what the fuck are you doing here?"

"It's okay with me Priest, that you've decided to take it there, but you should know you're way out of your league with me. I'm not going to talk you to death," I said as I stepped back to the car and reached for the envelope. I walked up to the gate and handed him the envelope. "It's really simple."

He opened the envelope and pulled the stack of photos out. It was like watching someone have their soul snatched from their body. I swear his eyes caved in and his bottom lip began to quiver. "Bitch, you've been following me? I'm going to kill you. You know who I am?"

I laughed at him. "You already tried that, remember? The fat faggot in the picture, you sent him to do a man's job."

He looked at me, his eyes full of hate. Just then his cell phone rang. He looked down at it then backed up toward his house. I waved him off and moved back a few feet but could still hear him clearly. "Hey, baby, I'm coming. I'm just talking to a Realtor. She's trying to convince me to sell . . . no I'm not. Gimme a minute I'll be there." He hung up. "Honey, listen. All I wanted was to talk to you." His tone had softened up and he'd changed his demeanor. "I only wanted to make sure that whole thing in Miami was going to stay quiet. I told my agent about it and he advised me to make an offer to you just to be sure . . ."

"To be sure that I was dead too?"

He shook his head. "No, no. Honey, you don't understand. There's a lot of money on the line. I have to keep my name clear of scandal. Like with that Kobe situation. You know how many millions of dollars other people lost when he lost his endorsements. It took him like three years just to get his image back to the point where he can use his persona to make money. I don't have that kind of time left and my agent has been riding me like crazy. All he asks is have you talked to the . . ."

"To the whore."

"I didn't say that. He's just been on edge like a motherfucker and that's gotten me on edge."

"So you sent your goon, or rather your boyfriend, to make sure that I'd keep quiet?"

"That's all. I just wanted to make sure you and I were cool. We went to your room and you weren't there."

"I came after you did and what you did was break into my room."

"Well you never even told us you were leaving. It looked strange. I thought you might have gone to the police."

"Yeah, right. You know Priest, your ass is sounding real guilty right now."

He shook his head "no." "I didn't do anything to that girl. I swear. The bitch just wouldn't put the brakes on with the drugs that night."

"What about her friend?"

"I don't know nothing about her friend."

"Yeah, well she was missing too and I've been following up on it and it seems like nobody has any answers as to her whereabouts." That was the reason why I had barely been home. I honestly didn't know what Priest was capable of. I was too smart to get caught slipping though.

"I swear I don't know anything about that, but I'll tell you this . . . the first trip to your house was merely because I wanted to drop some change on you to make sure everything with us was good. That's the only reason I sent the big man. I just don't need the controversy."

"That's exactly what I was thinking. But I'll *tell* you this." I reached into my pocket and pulled out a piece of paper. "It's gonna cost you more than some change, especially with these pictures."

His hands were on the bars as if he were an inmate. "So what do you want?"

"Two."

"Two hundred thousand? That's robbery," he shouted.

"Nah, my friend. Two million. I want two million dollars."

"Have you lost your mind? I don't have that kind of money. I can't afford to pay you that kind of money."

"From the looks of things, you can't afford not to." I looked at his house and the cars. "Suit yourself. I won't negotiate. I won't take one-point-nine-nine-nine and ninety-nine cents. Hell, I want a nice big house like this and someone to love me. Like you said. Who'd love a whore? It's time for me to give this life up and unfortunately for you, it's on you."

"There is no way I'm giving you two million dollars. I'll kill you and do twenty-five years first."

"Really? I doubt that. You just got a nine-million-dollar signing bonus. I suggest you dip into it unless you want these pictures all over the Internet and a story in the papers. Not to mention how much your wife is going to take when she finds out you have a little brown baby on the other side of town. I think two million is less than half."

He was silent. I handed him a card. "What's this for?" he asked.

"Wire the money to that account. I'll give you one week. Call me at that number and let me know when it's done. But don't call until it's done. If you do, the deal's off and I ruin you."

I walked away and climbed into the car. As I prepared to back out I yelled, "Once I get the money, you'll get the copies and the negatives. If anything should happen to me you can only imagine what the police and the newspapers will find waiting for them."

"Goddamned whore."

"Faggot."

As I pulled off and headed for the airport I wondered how long it would take him to pick his jaw up from the ground. Secrets are a motherfucker.

14

KHALIL

I made a few calls before I went to bed, or rather tried to catch up on some of the sleep that had eluded me as of late. The good-night call to Rorrie had been dry at best, as if the happiness was evaporating day by day. I felt like I was merely going through the motions with her. Usually my work was my sanctuary. I'd always found it so easy to escape everything, past and present, when I was behind the camera, but not this week. At this point, I was truly beginning to question my own sanity. I was well on my way to throwing my relationship with Rorrie away.

Right around the time Honey disappeared again I landed a job that was going to have me spend a week to ten days in Los Angeles, working on a project for Fox Searchlight. It was a nice reprieve from the heat of Rorrie's attitude as she'd now begun to tire of my "strange" behavior. I wasn't a complete fool though. Not for a minute did I question whether or not I deserved all of the strife that I was going through.

Ever since the night that Honey had invited me back to her

room there was no denying that I'd been acting like a complete ass toward Rorrie. After Honey hung the phone up I pulled over prepared to turn around, but then after looking at the clock I decided to drive home. I called the hotel and hung up when I recalled that all I had was her first name.

I was still in a relationship and though I'd come to terms with the fact that I was attracted to or lusting after Honey, I had to remain decent. True, I'd cheated on Rorrie the first time and for that I had no excuse. As deep as the desire was, I couldn't bring myself to do it again even after I'd pursued Honey. This, I would quickly regret.

The next day, when I went back to the hotel dressed in my tux, thirty minutes before I was due at the church, and knocked at her door, I got no answer. I'd gone back three times since then and hadn't had any luck. It took no time for my regret to turn to resentment. I was angry for denying myself what I wanted and began to resent Rorrie for simply being there, a reminder why I couldn't have the woman that I I'd become obsessed with.

When I left for California, I began to think that perhaps Honey had given up on me. It had been two weeks since I'd heard from her. Her face never left my mind even though I had no idea where she was. I was worried about her, but at the same time my intuition told me that she could take care of herself.

When my cell rang at five thirty in the morning, my first instinct was to start cursing. I knew it was someone calling from the East Coast. "Yeah," I moaned out.

"Oh God, I'm sorry. Khalil?"

"Yes."

"Are you sleeping still?"

"Yeaaah," I mumbled.

"This is Cameron. I was returning your call. Are you sick or something?" It was then that I realized that I needed to clear my throat.

I'd already told her I was knocked out, but from her inquiry as to my health, I was sure I sounded dead. She had no idea I was three hours behind her and was suffering from the early signs of sleep deprivation. And since it usually took my body a full week to adjust to the time difference, this had been only my second night getting a decent amount of rest. "I called your office yesterday evening to cancel my appointment, but I was also wondering if you could call me a prescription in. I'm in L.A. working . . . but I've been . . . It's been hard for me to relax."

"Having problems sleeping or the dreams again?"

"A little of both," I said, coming out of my sleep.

"You have a number or name of a pharmacy near you?"

"Uhhh, yeah. It's called Horton & Converse Pharmacy on Santa Monica. It's right around the corner from me."

"You got it. Did you reschedule with the receptionist?"

"Yes, for next week."

There was a little break in the silence as I waited for her to start with her normal probing but it didn't come.

"Okay, great. Khalil, call me if you need anything, or if you want to do your session over the phone."

"All right."

"Take care of yourself."

"I will."

I hung up and turned over burying my face in my pillow. A rush of emotions swelled through me and I almost wished that I could just keep it buried forever. I thought about all the problems that I'd carried through life with me. The *baggage,* as Cameron called it.

I wondered why my life had never been the way I'd thought it'd be, especially now that I was on my way to becoming a successful filmmaker and I had a beautiful, smart woman in love with me. Why was I feeling tortured while lying in this big bed alone, knowing that there was one girl who would want to be here, and another who I wanted to be with.

I thought about my father. I hadn't spoken to him in almost five years. The last time I saw him he was only a shadow of the man I'd loved and trusted as a boy. I think his letting me down had been the straw that broke his back. I also believed that the fact that I'd made something out of my life in spite of him was the ton of bricks that crushed him totally. He was expecting much less of me and I know it embarrassed him when we met up for the first time since I'd gone to foster care.

At twenty-one, I'd graduated from college and had landed a job paying me more money than he'd ever made in any two years. I'd only gone to see him because a job took me to Harlem, making the reunion convenient. That and the dozens of phone calls I'd received from his new girlfriend begging me to come. The irony was that it was a commercial that I'd shot, a PSA against drug abuse.

Walking into the same apartment that had been the source of so much pain for me didn't turn out to be as therapeutic as I'd hoped. Seeing my old room, where I'd been raped, nearly brought tears to my eyes as I stood there. My father had a new family living there with him. His girlfriend, who he'd met at a substance-abuse program, and her daughter along with her two babies now called the old place home.

My visit had been short and when my father walked me back

out to the street, he'd had the nerve to ask me for money. I didn't have any cash on me, but he rode in a cab with me to the ATM. I still don't know why I didn't refuse him. After I'd given him two hundred dollars, he immediately elected to walk home. As the cab prepared to pull out onto Lenox Avenue I told the driver to stop. Then I'd leaned to the window and called him back. "Hey," I'd said, clearing my throat.

"Yeah, son."

"If you don't hear from me again, please don't call and don't have your girlfriend call me either."

He opened his mouth to speak. "Khalil . . ."

I cut him off with an emphatic "Don't ever call."

I remember the look on his face as the cab drove off. He hasn't called since.

I spent an hour in the hotel's gym, running on the treadmill, trying to release some stress before the car service came to pick me up. We weren't working until two in the afternoon so I had a chance to grab a spinach salad before I slid into character. I was the hot young talent and I was lucky to get called in to work with this director.

Once I reached location I did my best to keep my mind focused solely on the project before me, shooting crowd scenes inside the Staples Center. I spent most of the day talking to the director, a quirky but brilliant guy who had the misfortune of being named Harry Ball. It wouldn't have been so bad but all day he answered his cell, "This is Harry Ball."

I actually laughed aloud a couple of times, imagining a set of hairy balls. Harry was cool though and when we finished shooting at ten P.M. he thanked me for a job well done. He whipped out the corporate card and we went upstairs to the Fox Sports Sky Box and grabbed stuffed burgers and a couple of rounds for the staff.

"Kid," Harry called out to me as we were heading to the lot where the crew's vans were parked. "How are you getting back to your hotel?"

"I had a car service scheduled but I think I missed the call while we were eating. I'm just going to catch a cab."

"Nonsense, I'll give you a ride. You're staying where?"

"The Hyatt in Century City."

"No problem," he said and waved me toward him.

We walked over to the bronze racing machine. He hit the chirp and we climbed in. "Nice ride," I said.

"Nice my pale white ass. This ride is what God Himself would drive if He were the driving sort. At least that's what the salesman told me when he sold it to me." He laughed. A quick elbow to my arm and he said, "No bullshit. I love to drive it and I'll take any excuse. Why else would you think I'd offer to drive you to Santa Monica?" He laughed again.

"So this a Ferrari, right?" I asked, not wanting to sound stupid as I scanned for an insignia.

"A Ferrari 612 Scaglietti. You won't see another on the road the whole time you're in L.A. You want to know how much this baby costs? Go ahead and ask me."

Harry had been pretty relaxed and a complete professional the entire day. But the moment he'd begun with the drinks it seemed as though that Harry had jumped out the window. This Harry was just as pretentious as the rest of the crowd I'd met on the set. "I don't think I even want to know."

"That's bull. Of course you want to know. Two hundred and

twenty thousand. But that's a whole other story. Listen, Khalil, you have been so quiet these last several days you've had me wondering if we were treating you okay."

"Oh, absolutely."

"You sure, because I've enjoyed working with you. I've heard some good things about you and believe me, contrary to popular belief, this business isn't about who you know, it's about who the hell knows you."

"No, Harry, everything was cool. I've just had a few things on my mind. Stuff going on back home."

"I understand. I really do. You definitely seemed a little tense when you got to work and you don't seem too much better off right now, but you know what? I have the perfect solution. Why don't you let me call my masseuse and have her meet you at your room? She's a magician."

"As much as I could use one, I'll pass this time."

"Nonsense," he yelled as we came to a stoplight. He then jumped out of the car. "As a matter of fact, you drive the rest of the way. I need to make a couple of calls." By the time I could tell him that I didn't know how to get back he was already at my door. "Just drive straight. We're taking Pico straight to the Avenue of the Stars, buddy."

He didn't take no for an answer and I was now pushing his death machine up West Pico like I owned it. The car was so powerful that I almost lost track of what he was doing. He'd taken the liberty of calling his masseuse and insisting that she drop what she was doing to come take care of me.

"She'll be a couple of hours but I have a place I want to take you to pass the time. She'll meet us there and then she'll give you a ride back to your hotel."

We wound up at Club Gotham. There was a nice crowd full of beautiful people and a line at the door. Harry pulled up at the front of the club and the valet ran over to his car. We bypassed the line and went right on in. I followed him up to a level called the Mezzanine, where a party within a party was in full swing. Blondes dancing, a few B-list actors playing pool, and an eclectic mix of folks seated at the glass bar.

Harry and I talked for a good while. It was strange. For some reason I found myself opening up to him, telling him about my dilemma with Honey and Rorrie. He was twenty years older than me, filthy rich, and firmly entrenched in white Hollywood, yet he seemed to be interested in what I was going through. Maybe he was looking for movie material. I couldn't guess.

"Khalil," he said as he sat next to me, puffing on a cigar. "Why would you trouble yourself with trying to make a decision? You're on the cusp of a super career. You'll be making a shitload of money in no time. Why not simply keep 'em both?"

I laughed and reiterated that I was already engaged and added, "I actually want a family. I didn't have one growing up and it'd be nice to have some people around you who you know are going to be there."

He slapped my shoulder playfully. "Khalil, that's insane. Family sometimes can be the worst thing in your life. I should know. I have two. My wife is back in the Midwest. I grew up in Chicago, married my high school sweetheart, we have two kids, and we've been together for twenty-four years. Married for seventeen."

"That's great," I said. You didn't hear things like that every day.

"Yeah, thanks. I also have a girlfriend that I've been with for ten years out here. She's twenty years younger than me, treats me great, and is a piece of ass like no other. I love her with every ounce of my soul. I'd die for her. As a matter of fact, she and I are trying to have a baby together." I was stunned. Not because of what he said, but how he said it, as if it were right. There was no time for me to judge him as he rolled on through with his message. "Moral is . . . why throw one away if you can afford 'em both?"

"I don't know, Harry, that could get a little confusing and dangerous."

"Bullshit. You'll never get far in this business with that attitude. You're making movies and you don't understand the one thing that makes it all possible." He paused and leaned in closer to me and poked my thigh with each syllable. "With money, any and every thing is possible."

He jumped up and said, "Darla." He greeted the tall, bronzed woman. "Meet Khalil. He's working with me. I'm taking care of it. Give him the deep tissue like you do me."

I stood up. She was as tall as I was. I looked her straight in the eyes. Not gorgeous by L.A. standards but strong from where I came from. She was thin in the waist and all silicon up top. I saw a little Korean in her face but then she also looked Native American. "Great," she said. We shook hands. "You ready to go?"

I didn't remember when I'd said that I was down, but in all actuality, now that I'd seen her, I couldn't imagine turning down a free massage. "Yeah, why not?"

She gave me a look as if she was a little insulted at my absence of complete excitement. "HB, I'll speak with you tomorrow."

He nodded and finished, "Sure thing. Khalil, enjoy yourself."

I was even more comfortable with the idea of the massage after the small talk we shared on the way to the hotel. Darla was a licensed masseur; she taught classes on holistic health at UC Santa

Barbara. She did well for herself, according to what she told me. She even managed to ask me a little about myself.

I offered to carry her table upstairs. She replied, "This is L.A., baby. Let the bellboys earn their keep. You're a star. They'll have it up in no time. You run on up. Take a quick shower while I wait for the table. I'll be up in five minutes."

"Room 712."

"I'll be right there. If you're in the shower leave the door slightly ajar."

"Okay."

As soon as I hit the elevator I looked at my cell. It was after midnight. I thought about calling Rorrie. I didn't want to wake her, since I figured that she'd be asleep, but I didn't look forward to having to deal with her attitude in the morning because I hadn't called either. I smashed the speed dial the second I stepped on the elevator. I was shocked when she answered on the first ring.

"Hey, you," she said. "I miss you."

"I miss you too."

"How much?"

"A lot. I miss you a lot."

She giggled. "That's good. But I'm sure I miss you more, as a matter of fact, I'm sure of it."

Oh shit. Here we go, I thought.

"So where are you?"

"I'm on my way in. I just called to say good night. I have an early day tomorrow, but I wanted to say good night to you."

"You tired?"

"Exhausted," I said as I stepped off the elevator.

"I wish I could help you get to sleep," she said seductively.

"Mmmmm, now there's a thought."

"Yeahhh," she moaned out as I pulled my room card out of my pocket. "Well guess what?"

I slipped the card in and out and the lock clicked as I said, "What?"

She was standing in front of me, ass-naked, cell phone in hand. "I'm here," she said with a grin.

I don't know if I mouthed the words *Oh shit*. I know I wanted to. I panicked. I'd just told her how tired I was. I needed a reason to go intercept Darla.

Rorrie was on me though. Hugs and kisses. "What are you doing here?" I smiled to keep from crying.

"I missed my man. I know things have been a little off for us, but I know it's just the jitters. But I just have to work harder to make sure you're okay."

"I appreciate that, sweetie. I do. Are you hungry? We should go out and eat."

"No, I want to eat you. That's it."

"Well let me run downstairs and cancel my order."

"No you can eat. You're gonna need your energy."

I was out of excuses that quick and it didn't matter because there was a knock at the door. I told her to drift out of sight due to the fact that she was almost naked. I planned to get rid of Darla through a combination of mouthed words, facial expressions, and hand signals. Before I could attempt any of it though, Rorrie and I both heard the words clearly: "Khalil, are you in there? The door is locked."

"Who the hell is that, Khalil?" Rorrie moved toward me. I put my hands up but this time she raised her voice. "Who the fuck is that?"

"Listen. I'm going to be honest with you . . ."

"Yeah, motherfucker, be honest."

Darla knocked again.

"Fuck this." Rorrie started reaching for her clothes. "It's about to be on up in here."

"Wait," I begged. "Let me do this. You'll know that I'm not lying. The whole thing is innocent."

I walked to the door and yelled through it for Darla to give me one minute. Then I walked over to Rorrie. I explained the whole night and how it had come to this woman coming to my room. "Now, I'm going to let her in and have her explain the story to you. There's no way she could tell you the same thing if it's not true. She has no idea what I just told you."

Rorrie kept her arms folded the entire time. Darla was great though. My story flew and she even showed her pocket license to Rorrie proving that she was a licensed masseuse.

It took about fifteen minutes to defuse the situation but once we did, Darla asked, "So are you still interested in getting your massage? It's paid for."

"No, but you can tell Harry that you did and that I enjoyed it."

"No, I wouldn't do that, but thanks anyway."

She was about to grab her table when Rorrie shocked the hell out of me. "Khalil, I want you to get it. You should get it. If she doesn't mind me in here."

Darla shrugged her shoulders. "It doesn't matter to me."

By the time I got out of the shower, the two women were talking like old friends. Rorrie had dimmed the lights, and the candles that she'd lit before I'd entered were the only light in the room. Darla instructed me to climb on the table and went to work.

Just as Harry had insisted, she was magic. My face was smashed into the hole on the pillow as she rubbed my shoulders. I was in heaven as she worked the physical tension right out of my body. My mind began to drift as her hands found knots that I didn't know I had. After twenty minutes I was somewhere between semiconscious and asleep when I began to think of Honey. I was longing for her touch as Darla's fingertips glided across my back.

When she had me roll over I was slightly oblivious to the fact that I was on the brick. I pretended to ignore it and thought that if Darla did then Rorrie might not even notice. I was wrong. From her angle on the bed Rorrie saw and scooted over to us.

She looked me in the eye and shook her head in disgust. I closed my eyes. I then heard her say to Darla: "I hope you don't mind."

In the next instant I felt her hand pulling the towel away. Darla never stopped working on my shoulders as Rorrie's hands began stroking my dick. "Wow," I heard Darla say as Rorrie leaned over and took me in her mouth. "I think I better leave you two lovebirds alone."

Rorrie didn't stop and in the next instant I felt Darla's fingertips on my nipples before she moved away from the table. We ignored her as Rorrie guided me onto the bed where she continued to pleasure me. Darla folded her table and crept out of the room while we went at it. It didn't take long before my breathing grew heavy and Rorrie began working my shaft, sending tingles up and down my body. My eyes closed, I thought of Honey, took a deep breath, and I came.

At four o'clock in the morning I was jarred from my sleep as I tried to escape my father's grip. He was holding me down while a faceless woman prepared to have sex with me against my will.

I woke up and saw Rorrie on top of me, riding me. She was on her way to an orgasm as she bounced her body up and down. I on the other hand felt the need to empty my bladder. She'd obviously taken advantage of a hard-on that had been caused by my need to use the bathroom.

I didn't stop her from getting what she needed. When she came she collapsed on top of me. Her chest heaving as she tried to catch her breath, she rolled over onto her side. I got up and used the bathroom. When I came back and slid into the bed she eased closer to me and said in a whisper, "Khalil, we need to talk."

15

HONEY

Priest was foolish and predictable. He came looking for me again and this time he actually had someone break into my apartment. I was nowhere near the place but I knew when the alarm company called that he'd been behind it. When his lover, or whoever he had do the job, made their way inside, all they found was the empty manila envelope in the middle of the floor. Inside was a single page from the centerfold spread of this month's *Playgirl* magazine. It made me laugh when I imagined the look on the culprit's face when he gazed at the picture of a white guy holding his cock. Honestly I figured he might get a kick out of it. I'd left a typed note inside as well.

It read:

> *This could have been your ass, if you know what I mean.*
> *You have until Friday. You can kill me later, but for now,*
> *fuck you. Pay me.*

I was sprawled out on a beach chair at Antigua's finest resort, working on my tan for the third day straight, when Theodore Rosemond came walking out to me. Theodore was the assistant to the manager, Mr. Wells, at the Antigua Barbuda International Bank. Before he could say a word I waved for the waiter to bring me a fresh drink. It was my third, or maybe my fourth, mai tai and I was feeling real warm and fuzzy. When the portly messenger stopped in front of me I smiled and he returned my grin.

"Good day, sir," I said, with my hands shielding my eyes from the sun.

"Good day to you also."

"So what do you have for me?"

He handed me an envelope. "Ms. Height, your wire has arrived. A receipt of your transmittal is inside."

"Thank you." I took the envelope. "Can you tell Mr. Wells that I'll call him in a few hours?"

He nodded. "Of course. Have a nice afternoon."

"Thanks." I could barely wait for him to leave. The second he turned his back and began to walk away I opened the envelope and checked the receipt. My heart began to thump as my eyes scanned the paper. Joy washed over me from head to toe as I read the bottom line, not once or twice but five times. Then a sixth. Two million dollars was actually sitting in my account courtesy of Priest Alexander. I didn't wait for my drink. I got up and walked coolly past the pool area and back toward the fitness area. I was so excited on the inside that I could have jumped on one of the treadmills and ran ten miles.

I continued on to the elevator and finally I reached the door to my suite. Once I made it inside I let out the triumph that I'd held back on my walk upstairs. I screamed at the top of my lungs, "Yeeessssss." I did a dance, ran in place, and jumped on the bed. "I'm fuckin' rich," I repeated over and over as I kicked the bed the same way Rick James had stomped on Eddie Murphy's couch.

A second later I was in the bathroom mirror staring at myself. "I'm reyaaattchh, beeeeyiiiiiitch." That was my imitation of Ashy Larry belting out Dave Chappelle's trademark line.

On closer review, I could see that I was sweating slightly, either from the excitement or from the kicking and stomping I'd been doing. I turned on the water in the tub and grabbed my Carol's Daughter bath gel, my iPod, and slipped into the oversized Jacuzzi tub. I'd forgotten one thing, so with water dripping from my naked body I climbed out of the tub and walked across the cold tile floor to the ice bucket that I'd kept filled with fresh ice for three days straight.

I popped the cork and carried the bottle of Dom Pérignon Rosé that I'd brought from the States with me, and one flute, back into the bathroom. This was a celebration that I'd prepared for. My body embraced the heat as I slid back into the warm water. Deep breaths and small sips were my order as my mind began to wrap itself around the idea that my net worth had just increased exponentially. I'd flirted with a six-figure bank account for years, but I'd always loved to shop. Any fly bitch will tell you that it's hard to hold on to fast money. I'd learned this the first time I saw a set of diamond studs that I just *had* to have, so I stopped trying. But this situation was different. I wanted my life to change even if I wasn't ready to admit to myself why.

I was going to invest in a modest home, start a legitimate business, get myself a 401(k), keep the rest in the bank, and live off the interest. I'd even come up with an idea on how to make even more money. It was all about leverage.

I'd need a hobby to fill some of the free time and maybe even some kids down the line. As for a man, there had only been one in my life who I'd thought of as much as I did Manny. Of course that had been Khalil. Manny was gone, but Khalil wasn't.

More sips of the champagne and I closed my eyes thinking of him. Cocoa complexion, high cheekbones, thick full lips, a perfect face. Shoulders like a construction worker's, defined but not bulky like the weight lifters who overdid it. He was blessed with an ass that would probably get him a lot of unwanted attention in jail. He had hips and thighs like an Olympic sprinter. I didn't even want to think about the boy's love muscle that must have been sculpted in heaven above. Enough to go plenty deep, but not so long that afterward it felt like I'd been punched in the stomach.

The strangest thing was that I wasn't really a sexual person and I had never been. It was such a misconception that any woman who had relations in order to get ahead was either promiscuous or a nymphomaniac. I was far from either. Sex for me had always been a means to an end and it had almost always been safe. Enjoyment hadn't been promised, nor looked for, on my part.

Khalil hadn't been the first man I'd slept with on a nonprofessional basis. There'd been a few others over the years. Just men I'd found attractive or intriguing. They'd pursued me with wine and food and occasionally with gifts. I'd given them the one thing that they all craved, great sexual pleasure. Still, I left them all wanting something that I couldn't give them, my heart. It had been easy to walk away from them since I hadn't allowed the connection to become any deeper than the day I'd met them.

I clearly had been missing the sensitivity chip. I preferred to believe I was simply focused.

This situation was different. I didn't want to admit it, but I was afraid. I was afraid that I could really care for Khalil and that could bring trouble that I wasn't ready to face. I didn't doubt for a hot second that I could snatch him from Rorrie, but I was afraid that I might not be able to keep him. When, or if, he learned who I was, would he want to be with me?

I'd studied men over the years, mostly out of boredom if for no other reason. Through the things they talked about with me during our interactions I learned that they all wanted the things that they were least willing to give. Every single one of them wanted to be loved, adored, worshipped, and appreciated. On top of this they wanted to feel big. It didn't matter if they made the women around them feel small. They wanted to be cared for while they cared only for themselves. But above all of this, they wanted to be accepted. Accepted for who they were. Rich, broke, fat, skinny, smart or dumb, they wanted a woman who would overlook their shortcomings, their situations, and their past.

I learned that us women asking for the same thing was nothing short of insane. For that reason alone, I was too petrified to love. Too scared to dream, until now.

I turned the jets on. As the tub began to vibrate, the motor forced the bolts of water out, causing a rumble that I felt from head to toe. Mary J.'s voice soothed me as I closed my eyes and dreamed of what it would be like to have a man love me right. I couldn't really imagine being able to trust a man to take care of me but I tried.

The beaches were beautiful in Antigua and I thought about staying there forever, though I knew I wouldn't. Perhaps Priest would be persistent enough to have the wire traced to the account. He'd never see me again and by this time tomorrow, I and the money would be gone from this island forever. I'd move it to another account and to another name and then to another. His money was gone for good and that excited me, it always had.

As the jets continued to send the water rumbling against my thighs I began to let my imagination run wild as my mind stared deep into a world of fantasy. I could see my home overlooking the ocean. There I was, sprawled out on a huge white couch, enjoying the breeze flowing from the ocean as a flame burned nearby, sending a mixture of hot and cold air to caress my body, which would be naked except for the thin piece of cotton that would serve as panties.

I'd be in heaven as my servant handed me small slices of melon dipped in honey, feeding me from his fingers. Tall, handsome, and ripped, dressed only in a swatch of fabric, he'd be black as the night and as beautiful as the Greek mythological hero Narcissus. I'd call him Khalil. Then there'd be another. A cross between a black and a Latino, who'd have skin that was so kissed by the sun that he'd be the color of bronze. I'd call him Manny. Golden brown skin, washboard stomach, white teeth, green eyes, and a pole like a black man.

They'd both smell of aloe, shea butter, and all things manly. Catching their scent in the wind would drive me crazy. Manny would have the soft and gentle touch, while the dark one, Khalil, would be rough.

They'd run their hands all over my body, caressing and then pinching until they'd touched every nerve. Khalil would reach for and yank my sheer panties from my body. He'd then drop to his knees, forcing my thighs apart. All the while Manny would be at my neck kissing me, while his warm breath danced against my skin. He'd move down to my breasts, cupping them, taking the nipples gently between his teeth.

Suddenly, I'd feel Khalil's tongue as it found my clit. He'd start a high-impact groove in and out as his fat lips held me hostage. I'd love every minute of it, the feeling of both men servicing me.

Manny would wait patiently for my permission to put it in my mouth while Khalil continued his violent licks against my center, pushing me closer to the edge. With one hand massaging my own breast, I'd begin to bring Manny toward my mouth. Before I could get him in, Khalil would pull his mouth from my pussy and place his huge shaft at my entrance and slam it home.

The surprised jolt of pleasure caught me off guard and I opened my eyes wide. I'd almost swallowed the water in the tub as I'd slid my body down so that my vagina was an inch away from the pulsing jets. My body was exploding and I could barely keep my head from going under water. I had no choice but to continue allowing the jets to send me over the edge. The orgasm was coming hard. "Ooooooooooohhhhhhh, shit," I screamed out as my body began to spasm. "Ehhhhhh, uhhhhh, ooooowwwwww."

As I came, the fantasy Khalil and Manny were long gone. Manny, who had always been the face of my desire, was nowhere to be found. As I bucked and slid against the bottom of that tub, I saw only Khalil.

In that moment, I knew that it was time to kill two birds with one stone.

A little before noon the next day my connecting flight landed in Puerto Rico. I was on my way back to the States. All morning I'd thought about my new life and what it would bring. As I made my way across the airport and through customs, I thought about what I'd say when I got him on the phone. Maybe I could have him come up to New York, where I had a meeting.

Everything was perfect until I saw that my flight into JFK was delayed by an hour. I grabbed a seat in front of the huge window and began to stare out onto the runway. I was the only one sitting there so I decided to plug my cell phone in the wall and steal a little juice. Before I plugged it in the urge swept over me and I flipped open the pink Razr. I scrolled down and pulled up his number.

I stared at it for a second before I pressed the green button to send. I let it ring three times and was about to hang it up when the voice on the other end answered, "Hello."

He sounded asleep but I went ahead and said, "Hello, stranger, did I wake you?"

"Excuse me," she said as suddenly I recognized that the voice didn't belong to Khalil, but to a woman.

"I'm sorry but I was trying to reach Khalil."

"Khalil is in the shower. Who is this?"

I needed to be a lady. I had no idea who it was on the other end of the line. It could have been anyone. But it wasn't anyone. I knew who it was so my response was what it was. "I asked for Khalil."

There it was.

"Okay, bitch. Who the hell do you think you are calling here at . . ." She must have taken the time to look at a clock. ". . . at six forty-five in the morning, asking for my man, not wanting to identify yourself, calling from a blocked number."

"Bitch, you need to calm down. It's almost eleven where I am."

"Who the fuck is this?" she yelled back into the phone. I paused for a second. There was silence. "I said who is this?"

I remembered Rorrie. The same girl I loved as a child. The same girl who I dreamed with as a kid. She was never that tough and I could hear in her voice that she was scared already. Shaken that someone was on her man's line, bold enough to disrespect her. It was time so I didn't let up. "Listen, I want to speak with Khalil. I have something important that I know he'll want to hear."

"Oh yeah, what's that?"

It was the oldest trick in the book but I didn't care. I wanted her man and I wanted her miserable. "He's going to be a father and guess what? It ain't with you, bitch."

"Whooooo the hell is this," her voice shrieked out.

"He'll know. Tell him, I'll call him later. Tell him to be alone so we can talk."

"When I find out who this is I'm gonna . . ."

"Rorrie, you ain't gonna do shit." I hung up the phone.

It was in effect. A smile fought its way across my face. I'd made my mind up. I was going to try this. A normal life, with a normal man, were both within my grasp. All I had to do was snatch them.

16

KHALIL

When the bathroom door swung open the draft caught me off guard. I didn't notice the look on Rorrie's face before I asked, "Did I wake you? I thought you were asleep."

Then I noticed my cell phone was in her hand as she began to approach me. In the time it took for her to take three steps I knew the tide of the day had turned dramatically bad and it was barely seven A.M. Slowly and deliberately she asked the question. "Who . . . is . . . she?"

Silence first while I processed her question and tone. "What . . . who . . ."

"Khalil, don't you lie to me. Who is the bitch? She just called your phone. She called me by my name and she said she's pregnant." I sat there with a stupid look on my face. "She said she's pregnant," she yelled. "Is that true, Khalil?"

I didn't know what else to say so I responded, "Pregnant? No. I don't know what's going on. This must be some . . ."

"Khalil, I will take this phone and hit you over the head with it."

The water was beating down on me as I looked her in the eyes. I looked at my phone and wondered what she could have learned. Had Honey called? It was crazy, because a part of me was hoping that she had and that maybe she'd done for me what I would have never been able to do myself. I didn't have an answer for her threat.

"Who is she?" she growled.

I looked her in the eyes and I think my silence gave away my guilt.

"Khalil, how could you do this to me?" Her voice was at its height as she yelled the words over and over.

"Listen, Rorrie, let me talk ..." I was cut off by my own reflexes. I ducked backward as my phone left her hand hurling toward my head like a fastball coming from a major league pitcher. The last thing I remembered was the phone shattering when it hit the wall just inches in front of me and my feet flying up into the air as I lost my balance.

"Sir, do you know where you are?"

My vision had blurred and I felt as if I were in a deep fog. This had been at least the fifth or sixth question, yet I couldn't remember answering any of them. "California?" I replied.

"Yes, but do you know what type of building you're in?"

I focused again and saw the pastel-colored walls and the machines. "This is the hospital."

"Yes. This is Century City Doctors. Do you know why you're here?"

I thought for a second. "Did I fall?"

"Yes, you did."

"Who are you?"

"I'm Doctor Culver."

I tried to remember how I got to the hospital. Then I remembered the beginning of the argument. "Is there a woman here with me?"

"Your girlfriend was here. As soon as we told her that you had only suffered a concussion, she elected to leave."

"She left?"

He nodded.

"What time is it?"

"It's a quarter after eight."

"In the morning, right?"

He laughed. "Yep."

He told me that they'd run a CT scan and found no injuries to my skull, or internal bleeding. He assured me I'd be fine, advised me to wait awhile before doing any strenuous activities and to see my doctor back East for a follow-up in a couple of weeks. I was free to go.

I caught a cab and realized quickly that I was just around the corner from my hotel. Once I got back to my room I expected to find Rorrie in there ready for round two. Instead there was no sign of her.

I looked in the bathroom and saw her toothbrush gone. I walked over to the bed and saw the pieces of my phone in a small pile. Next to it lay a note.

Khalil,

I am so angry and hurt right now. Literally I am too much of both to see or speak to you right now. I fear what I might do to you. You didn't have to say a word. I could tell

by the look on your face that you were guilty. I'm not sure
of what yet, but I'll see you when you get back to D.C. We
need to talk.
Fiancée?,
Rorrie

    P.S. Oh and by the way, if that bitch is pregnant, you
might not want to come back home.

I left the Nextel store with my bags in hand at eleven. When my SIM card worked in the new phone I was ecstatic. I immediately called my friend Duane. Duane was a lawyer by day, a wannabe actor by night. He was depending on me becoming the next John Singleton so that I could get him a real break into acting. I did pray that one day I'd surpass John Singleton, but not for the same reasons that Duane did.

He was excited to hear from me. "How's L.A.? You make any connections?"

If I didn't stop him I knew he'd get on a rant. "It's been great, but I need you to do me a tremendous favor."

"Yeah, sure."

In my mind that was the measure of a true friend. Someone who was ready to do whatever before they even knew what you'd be asking. "I need you to ride over to a place called Budget Lock & Key. It's on Florida Avenue. Ask for the owner and tell him you need to get an emergency lock change."

"Say what?"

"I need my locks changed on the house. But I need it done within the next couple of hours."

"That's pretty quick."

"Listen, Duane, can you do it or not? This is an emergency. I don't want to get anyone else involved and you and David are the only ones with keys."

"What's the rush?"

"I'm not trying to go into it right now, I have a plane to catch."

"All right, K-man. Keep your drawers on. So you want me to wait over there and get the keys."

"That'd be really helpful especially since I will need to get into my house."

"Does Budget accept credit cards?" he started.

"Go to the freakin' ATM and get some cash. Enough for a twenty-dollar tip. I'll pay you as soon as I meet you to get the keys."

"Man, you must be in some . . ."

"I'm out. You sure you got this?"

"I got you. I'm gonna leave out in about ten minutes."

I was staring out the window reading the ton of billboards advertising thirty new movies and television shows. All the while I was trying to meditate on my situation as the cab rolled slowly down the 405 headed toward LAX. I had jumped out there by changing the locks to the house. It was a bold move, but one that had been warranted. Once before Rorrie had gotten mad at me and gone through my closet, bagging up everything her money had paid for. The irony was that she didn't leave anything behind that I'd bought her.

This time I knew that she'd leave the house bare-boned naked, since she'd done most of the decorating, probably taking everything from the towels to the toaster. It's not like I was hardpressed and couldn't replace any of the material things but it was the principle. In all fairness, she wasn't going to turn around and pay me for all the months she'd lived there without contributing toward the bills. On top of that I didn't trust her in the emotional state that she was in. Rorrie getting in there and raiding a few items was the best-case scenario. What I truly feared was some *War of the Roses*–type drama, where she tore the house apart.

We turned off the 405 on to South Sepulveda and ran into a little traffic. I checked my watch, making sure I had enough time to catch my flight, when the traffic brought us to a complete standstill. My mind began to drift to thoughts of Honey. I recounted the conversation with Rorrie and wondered if it had been Honey on the phone. It couldn't have been anyone else. Then I wondered if Honey had in fact told Rorrie that she was pregnant. I gripped my phone tightly in my hand as I felt a twinge of anger and guilt. Anger because I was powerless to find out what was going on. She could call me; I couldn't call her.

Here I'd thrown my relationship down the drain over a woman who didn't care enough about me to leave me with a number. She could have been married, for all I knew. I was thinking to myself, *I must be crazy,* when my phone began to vibrate in my hand.

I looked down and didn't recognize the number. Nervous, thinking that it was Rorrie about to start in, I picked up anyway. "Hello."

"I hope I didn't get you into too much trouble." The second that I heard her voice all was forgotten.

"Honey?"

"Hey, Khalil," she said, sounding like an angel. There was not a hint of remorse for her having disappeared for two weeks.

"Where have you been? Where are you calling me from?"

"Slow down." She laughed out. "You got questions, huh?" she added. "It's all good. You sound like you've missed me."

I didn't want to sound too eager, but I couldn't help myself.

"Yeah, I have." I couldn't believe that I was spilling my guts. "I haven't stopped thinking about you."

"Is that so?" She paused. "When you didn't come back to the room that night I took it that you weren't interested."

"It wasn't that and I'm sure you knew that. It was just my circumstances." I thought about my dilemma as the traffic began to move. "So I'm assuming you called me this morning."

"Yeah, I hope I didn't get you into any trouble. She was very rude."

I laughed and shook my head. "Well according to her you told her that you were the other woman and that you were pregnant."

She chuckled into the phone. "That's nonsense."

I didn't really know what to believe. "Well I'm in the City of Angels right now, headed for the airport. I know that when I get home I'm gonna have a lot to deal with. She sent me to the hospital this morning after your conversation."

"What," she exclaimed.

"Well, she threw the phone at me, while I was in the shower. I slipped trying to duck and the rest is history. I woke up in the hospital and she was gone."

"She left you in the hospital? Man, that's rough."

"She did do that, but she actually left L.A. When I got back to the room she was gone."

"You sure she left?"

"Pretty much."

She was quiet for a second. I could tell she was either thinking or unsure of her next response. "Khalil."

"I'm here."

"I want to see you. There are some things I want to talk to you about."

"When?"

"Tonight. My flight just landed. I've been out of the States taking care of some business, but it's all finished now." She cleared her throat and then blurted out casually, "Khalil, I want to see you, but you need to go home and see what's up with your situation I'm assuming."

"Well, I'm not even sure she's going to be back in D.C. when I get there . . ."

"Say no more. If you want to see me, call me at this number when your flight lands. Did you drive to the airport?"

"No."

"I'll pick you up then."

"My flight lands at nine fifteen. At National."

"You call me. I'll be there waiting on you."

"I'll need to run home and change but I don't think it'll be a good idea for you to come past the house with me."

"No you won't. Just call me when you get there. I'll take care of every little thing."

"Honey, are you sure?" I asked.

"I'm more sure than ever, Khalil. You'll see. Have a safe flight," she said and then she hung up.

Something in her voice told me that my wanting was about to be satisfied. It was exciting but honestly a little scary. I didn't know what I was going to do about Rorrie. I even wondered if this was just a matter of cold feet, the whole thing with Honey.

My driver pulled up to the door of the airport. I gave him two twenties on a twenty-five-dollar fare. "Keep the change." I hopped out as he thanked me. There were a thousand thoughts racing through my head as I headed for the ticket counter to check my bags.

My day had been life-changing and it was barely noon. Just when I thought it couldn't get any crazier someone gently grabbed my arm. I turned and when I looked into her eyes I was stunned. When she opened her mouth and poured words out, my heart began to beat. It had been so long since I'd heard her voice.

"Khalil, look at you," she said. While I was trying to regain my composure she reached out and hugged me. "I've missed you so much."

The handle from my suitcase slid from my grip as her perfume invaded my nostrils. My hands found her back and I embraced her until the smile on her face was covered in tears. She looked exactly the same to me, though I wondered how she recognized me.

"I missed you too," I said. "More than you could ever know."

17

HONEY

Traffic was thick as I pulled out of the parking lot at Tyson's II in my spanking new Bentley coupe. I knew the car was a bit over the top, yet, thirty minutes after the money had cleared into my account, I'd been on the phone with a salesman, working out the details of my dream ride. I'd left the airport and driven straight to the dealer to pick the car up before heading to one of my favorite malls to burn up some more money.

Next on my list to prepare for Khalil was a stop at the ABC store, Best Buy, and the CVS, and I was nearly prepared.

Once I walked through the door past the Cheesecake Factory, tempted to stop, I made a beeline for Chanel, Nicole Miller, and BCBG Max Azria. Then I'd been able to find everything I needed for Khalil. From Hugo Boss to Saks, I'd bought him enough clothing to last for a three-day weekend even though I wasn't sure how much time we'd spend together. I'd sized him up the day I'd made love to him. One good look and I knew he was a forty-six long, a thirty-six waist, and a size ten-and-a-half shoe. I was sure he'd be impressed when he opened the bag full of goodies that I'd purchased for him.

As the sun began to set I made my way onto Route 66 and headed toward the airport. The thought that he might not call never entered my mind. I wondered where Rorrie was and was a little surprised that she'd given up so easily. It would make more sense to me to believe that she was off somewhere pouting, waiting for her man to come back apologizing and ready to explain. I had a news flash for her. It wasn't gonna happen. Not this time.

I looked at the clock on my dash and when it read twenty after nine I actually felt a twinge of nervousness. I pulled into the airport and prepared to wait and circle, but then my phone rang.

It was Khalil. "Honey, I'm headed for the exit as we speak. You here?"

"Of course," I replied as the butterflies began to flutter in my stomach for the first time.

"US Airways."

"Got it. Driving toward you as we speak."

"What are you driving?"

"The black coupe pulling up to the door. Is this you I see looking all sexy?" I laughed as I pulled up to the curb. He smiled and folded his phone shut. He moved toward me, looking like a real honey. Snug-fitting Kitson T-shirt and a pair of Rock & Republic jeans, and a pair of Nike Dunks. I was surprised to see him with nothing but a backpack on his shoulder and one small bag.

He opened the car door and climbed in. He gave me a somewhat nervous smile to which I responded with a quick hug and kiss. "Thanks," he said.

"Thank you," I shot back. "I see you travel light."

"Yeah, I've learned that art over the years." I nodded as we pulled off. "Is this your car?"

"Yeah, I just bought it. You like it?"

"I think I can appreciate something like this." He laughed. "You must be doing some hellified investing."

"I've done all right," I said as I tapped the gas. "So how long do I have you for?" Just asking a question that made me feel so vulnerable had me a bit off balance.

He was silent and seemed to sink into his seat. "I won't pretend that I don't feel bad about this, but Honey, I've done nothing but think about you since the day we met. And don't get me wrong, I do love Rorrie, but there's something between you and I that has convinced me that I don't love her enough to be with her." He seemed a little pained as he went on. "I mean what am I doing? I don't even know if this is real, if you want to be with me and here I am, without even considering her feelings."

I understood where he was coming from. I'd heard it so many times before from different men. The complaints and the confusion that had *led* them into bed with a woman who they had to pay to fuck. I didn't want to put Khalil into that category or better yet, allow him to put himself into that category, so I intended to set him straight. "Listen, Khalil. There is something between you and I, something very real. I can't explain it and I won't try. You're a grown man and you have to know that life isn't always easy or fair. So if you're gonna beat yourself up the entire time you're with me then I can drop you off. I want to take this time to get to know you, not watch you going through it. I'm not trying to be cold, but it is what it is."

When his face showed no emotion I suddenly grew scared that maybe I'd said too much. "So do you want me to take you home?"

He looked straight into my eyes and caused my soul to soar when he said, "No. I wanna be with you." I smiled and he asked, "So where are you taking me?"

"Does it matter?" I asked coyly.

"I guess it doesn't, but I just thought I'd ask."

I nodded my head and said, "To the moon. I'm taking you to the moon."

Khalil had drifted off by the time we reached Front Royal, Virginia. I kept the volume down as I listened to my favorite CD, *The Emancipation of Mimi,* letting Mariah talk to me since Khalil had run out of fuel. I didn't blame him, knowing how a cross-country flight could wipe you out. He looked like an angel as he slept and every few moments I found myself looking over at him, thinking to myself, *This is how my life ends and my fairy tale begins.* He'd found me and I'd chosen him.

When I pulled off the interstate I punched in the navigation system the address to the cabin I'd rented. We drove for thirty more minutes into the Shenandoah Mountains as the winding roads took me up and down. I couldn't wait until the morning to see the view that we'd have. Finally after it seemed we'd driven skyward at a thirty-degree angle for an eternity, I saw the street that led to our cabin. I cruised down the long driveway and pulled up in front of the house.

It was just as I remembered it. I'd been here before but not with someone I wanted to. I remembered sitting on the deck imagining what it would be like to be able to share this with someone I loved and thinking that I'd never know. I parked at the front door and went to the digital lockbox, pressing the code to get the keys. The company that I'd rented the place from was top-notch. I'd been able to tell them everything from what type of thread count I wanted on the sheets to what brand of bacon I wanted stocked in the fridge. Ready to head in I leaned over and nudged Khalil. He was sleeping soundly. I nudged him again, this time grabbing his shoulder and saying, "Khalil, wake up."

Like a wild animal getting the jump on me, he came out of his sleep and swung as if he was fighting for his life. The pain of him striking my arm had me fearing my forearm was broken. The second I saw the fear in his eyes as he realized what he'd done, I knew that sometime, somewhere, something bad had happened to him.

18

KHALIL

My body was all out of whack from the time change, plus the fresh air seemingly had me in coma-like sleep. Still, I woke to the strong smell of bacon and fried potatoes coming from the kitchen below. It was ten thirty when I sat up in the bed to stretch and yawn. I realized that Honey hadn't slept next to me and I wondered if she was upset about my swinging at her arm. I had wanted to tell her that I was having a nightmare, though I knew it might seem weird that anyone would have nightmares while sleeping in an automobile.

The ceiling fan was whirling above me and I collapsed back down as I contemplated making my way toward the bathroom. "You're up," she said, poking her head up the steps. "I made you breakfast."

Inhaling deeply, I commented, "Smells really good."

"I'll bring your plate up here."

"No, I'll come down. I have to use the bathroom anyway. I need to grab my bag from the trunk though to get my toothbrush."

"I already have that taken care of. Everything you need is downstairs in the bathroom."

I nodded. The bed I was on was in the loft and as comfortable as it slept, I wondered why she hadn't shared it with me. I got up and made my way down the steps in nothing but a pair of black Calvin Klein boxer briefs. I looked across the cabin at Honey. She was in a silk robe that covered her cotton tank top. From the way her ass was jiggling so freely I didn't think she had on any bottoms. The cabin was laid out. A combination of wood floors that matched the walls and a stone floor in the kitchen, where there were Viking appliances. There was a huge Navajo rug covering the floor between the couch and the plasma television.

I walked into the bathroom, which was the size of a small bedroom. The floors and the shower walls were done in a decorative ceramic tile. There was a black towel on the counter with every possible toiletry that I could imagine. Also she had lined up an electric toothbrush, a Cellmen travel set, and a bottle of Clive Christian cologne. I didn't mean to let it slip but I think I mouthed the words *This bitch must be rich*. I meant no disrespect but I couldn't believe that she was going out like she did. I'd shopped in Saks for years, but I'd never thought about purchasing four-hundred-dollar facial scrubs or five-hundred-dollar bottles of cologne.

As I emptied my bladder I started to wonder if she'd robbed a bank. I stepped out after washing my hands and she was headed toward me with a plate. "Let's go out on the deck."

"Cool."

We sat down and as she placed my food in front of me I noticed the view. We were well up in the mountains. I couldn't believe that I'd slept through the ride on the way here. We held

hands as I blessed the food and she waited for me to take a forkful before she ate.

All smiles, she couldn't wait to ask, "How is it?" I was sure she
knew.

"Mmmmmmm, damn girl. Delicious."

"Like Momma used to make?"

"Not quite . . . not my momma."

"Excuse me," she said, rolling her eyes playfully.

"No, no. I'm saying that my moms never cooked for me. At
least not that I can remember."

"Oh I'm sorry. Did you lose her at an early age?"

"I guess you could say that. She wasn't around and I don't really know the story behind it. I assume it was drugs, but I'm not
sure. She was gone for as long as I can remember."

"Khalil, I'm sorry."

"No, it's cool. I'm a grown man now. And being a grown
man, I can appreciate this meal that you made." I took another
forkful. "These are delicious." We were both quiet as we chewed
and stared off the deck down the mountain. "You know what's
crazy?" I asked.

"What's that?"

"Yesterday at the airport, after I spoke with you I saw someone
from my past."

"Someone you used to date?"

"No. Not at all. The woman I saw was like a mother to me
early in my life. She was my father's girlfriend for a long while."

"You hadn't spoken to her in a while?"

"More than thirteen years."

"Wow. She lives in California now?"

"No, Philadelphia."

"I bet it was nice to see her after all this time."

I thought back to that day when Frannie took me back to the group home. The day she promised to help me before disappearing forever. Then I said, "Yeah, I guess in a way it was nice to see her."

"Did you exchange numbers?"

"Yeah. She wants to come to town and visit and catch up."

"That'll be nice."

"Yeah, maybe."

The conversation switched gears and still it came easy for us as we sat on the deck and finished our food. "C'mon, we'll clean up later." She led me by the hand to a huge hammock on the other side of the deck, which wrapped around half of the house. "Get in slowly and lie still until I get completely in, or we'll both wind up on the ground," she warned me.

I followed orders and she climbed in on top of me. She put her head on my chest and closed her eyes. "Can I ask you something?" I whispered.

"You can ask me anything, but there might be some things that I'm not ready to tell you. Is that going to be okay?"

I thought about that for just a second. "As long as it goes both ways."

"Deal," she said. "Now go ahead and shoot."

"First . . ."

"Hold on. Hold on. You said *a* question; you're trying to turn this into twenty questions."

"Maybe so. Twenty questions. That sounds good. You ready?"

"As I'll ever be. Are you?"

"It's my game."

"We'll see."

"First," I said. "Why didn't you sleep in the bed with me last night?"

"No real reason. You were tired and I wanted you to get a good night's rest. Plus I was down here with some ice on my arm," she said in a lighthearted tone, letting me know she wasn't angry.

"I'm sorry about that."

"It's okay. I must have scared you pretty bad."

"Yeah, I hadn't been sleeping well the whole week and for some reason I slept in the car like a baby."

She nodded. "Understandable. Now my turn," she replied. "Why are you here with me? Is it because you wanna fuck me or something else?"

I took a deep breath. "First, I'll admit. I am definitely sexually attracted to you but there is more to it than that. I've never had such a strong desire for someone so fast. All my life I've kept walls up, not wanting to love anyone, mostly because I never really believed that they would be there for me. When I met you and we talked it was crazy. I was almost sad when the plane landed. I knew then that I needed to know you and I haven't stopped needing you since."

"Why?" she said softly.

"That's not fair. It's my turn to ask a question."

"Why?" she repeated.

"Honey, I didn't grow up with a lot. In fact, I grew up with very little. I actually spent five years in foster care. I learned that we don't get everything that we want, but sometimes we do.

"At seventeen, what makes a kid who hasn't had any examples of success qualified to make a decision that will affect the rest of his life? I remember one day I was down in the Village and saw some NYU students shooting a film for their coursework and I stopped to watch. They were all so into it. They looked fulfilled. I sat around until they finished then I asked a few questions and one of them gave me a magazine that had information on film schools.

"I didn't see a school that I wanted to go to, but I did decide I wanted to find out where black people went to learn the same thing. When I heard about Howard's film school, I knew that I wanted to go there."

I could tell that although she was listening intently, she didn't really understand the point I was trying to make. I decided to simplify. "The point is, when I came across Howard, I knew that was where I wanted to go. I just knew. I had no references or experiences to go by. I just knew. That's the same way I feel about you. I just feel connected to you and I know that we're supposed to be together. I don't know for how long, but I know that I'm supposed to be here. With you."

She was silent for a few seconds and then she lifted her head up and I felt her lips on my face. "Are you sure?"

My lips found their way to hers. They met and with a slight shift of weight she was on top of me kissing me. The hammock began to rock slightly as the flames of passion began to ignite between us. My hands began to caress her back and her ass. Instantly I was rock-hard and wanted nothing more than to be inside of her.

It was as if she read my mind. Without foreplay she reached down for my manhood and found it ready. Just as I had suspected she wasn't wearing any panties and when she climbed on top of me I reached for her and found that she was moist. She leaned in for a deeper kiss, sticking her tongue in my mouth. With the other hand, she pulled my underwear to the side. I felt her sliding down on me as she guided me inside of her.

As I entered her I felt as though I was sliding into heaven. She was like no other woman. Up to this moment I had wondered if my mind had been playing tricks on me the entire time. Perhaps her sex had caught me off guard and really wasn't that good. Maybe I had just gotten used to sex with Rorrie and the second I felt someone different I made more out of it than I should have. All those theories flew away as she moved up and down on me. My eyes were closed as she sent me drifting away.

I heard the words but I didn't know where they'd come from, my mouth or hers. "*I love you.*"

Maybe I was imagining that I'd said it or that she had. What we were doing was beautiful. Grinding our bodies together, getting it in. She brought her upper body down on me and began to grind as she wiggled her pelvis up and down in order to stroke me faster. I wanted to make it last but I lost control.

"I'm going to come, Honey," I whispered. "I'm . . . gonna . . ."

She didn't stop. She kept on riding me, giving me pleasure until my body began to buck. I tried to hold on but then she suddenly sat up and yelled out, "Ohmigod, Khalil." She trembled and shook as jolts of pleasure took her over as we came together.

I felt no remorse or nervousness as I emptied my seed into her. The thought immediately entered my mind: *What if I get her pregnant?*

The answer came to me behind the question as I smiled welcoming the possibility. In all actuality I had little reason to believe that I would, after sleeping with Rorrie, unprotected most of the time, for two years without even a scare.

We spent the rest of the afternoon making love and watching movies. There was a Jacuzzi out on the deck that we spent what seemed like two hours in, drinking wine and eating fresh fruit. Once the sun began to slide behind the mountains off in the distance we decided to take a walk.

We trekked forty minutes up the hill toward the top of the mountain to a clearing that looked like a camping spot. "Wouldn't this be romantic to sleep right here and watch the stars?" I asked.

"Would you do that?" she shot back.

"If I had a shotgun and a tent." I laughed. "Make that an Uzi and a tent made out of bricks."

She laughed. "Yeah, you know black folks don't do crazy shit like that."

We sat there and talked for a while but decided to get a move on before it got dark. We held hands the entire walk back to the cabin. "Khalil," she said. "What do you think is going to happen when we get back?"

"You mean as far as you and I?"

"As far as everything. What if she wants you back? I mean assuming you want me and you're not confused."

"I'm not confused."

"So what happens if she doesn't want to let go?"

"She will, if she hasn't already."

"So if she does let go, what are we doing? I mean do you think we're moving too fast?"

"I think we're moving fast. I do, but at the same time the speed feels just right."

I looked over and saw her smile. Then she looked at me and asked, "What if I was pregnant?"

I was quiet. "You told Rorrie that you were pregnant didn't you?"

She stared me right in the eye and said, "Absolutely . . ." She paused then burst into laughter. "The bitch shouldn't have gotten smart."

A part of me was angry but then at the same time, I chuckled slightly on the inside. "That wasn't right." I had a flashback. "You know it's your fault that I wound up in the hospital."

She reached up and rubbed my head. "I'm soooo sorry. What can I do to make it up to you?" she asked seductively.

We stopped and started to kiss right there on the path. Our hands began to roam all over each other. When she pulled away I said, "Don't start what you can't finish, Ma."

"Bring it on. Last one to the cabin is a rotten egg," she shouted as she took off. I ran after her but surprisingly, she was fast as hell.

When we made it back to the house she ushered me into the shower. I felt like a million dollars after I climbed out. She laid me on the bed, where she began to lotion my body from head to toe.

After we ate dinner we found ourselves in bed, snuggled up, spooning as we relaxed in complete silence. "I have a lot to do when I get back," she said. "I'm homeless right now." She laughed.

I laughed back. "You're kidding right? I mean you are driving around in a condo."

"No, I'm not kidding. I'm between places. I sold my place and I wasn't sure where I wanted to buy, or if I even want to stay in D.C."

I began to panic. "Where else would you go?"

"Khalil, it's a great big world out there. Who knows."

"So if you move away, how soon?"

"I didn't say I was leaving. Calm down."

But she didn't say she wasn't. The fear came back. The fear of losing that which I cared for. Once that came, the words came right out of my mouth without a second thought. "You can stay with me. You can move in with me. I want you to."

I had no idea how I'd work this out but when she leaned in and kissed me with three soft pecks and said, "I want to," I knew I had to figure it out.

19

HONEY

The hotel room looked like a dressing room. Shoe boxes stacked high, Gucci, Dolce & Gabbana, Jimmy Choo. Purses, dresses, jeans, lingerie, and new suits lining the closet. I had passed most of my newfound free time burning up the malls like Mazza Gallery in Upper Northwest. I'd even made quick one-day trips down to Atlanta's Phipps Plaza and to Chicago's Michigan Avenue to grab a few things.

Khalil had asked for a couple of days to get Rorrie's things out of the house before he moved me in. I'd been impressed when he'd come home and begun packing her stuff the night we arrived from our trip to the mountains. I had to admit that it was going to be awkward for me. I also knew that it would have to be somewhat wrenching for him, with one woman here this week, a new one the next.

But I didn't feel bad. There was a lesson in it for her. Love is like a boxing match. The referee says at the beginning of the fight: "Protect yourself at all times." The logic is simple. Both people are throwing punches. Even if you think your opponent is beaten, you have to keep your guard up. Here Rorrie had let her guard down to the point that she was defenseless. Somewhere along the line she'd stopped paying attention to her man. Maybe it was because she was so busy studying to become a doctor. Now she'd lost him. One thing was certain. Rorrie would be crushed once she finally found out that she'd lost him to me.

I did feel a little bad having Khalil believe that I intended to live in his house. I was planning to put a contract on a new home within the month but it was necessary that he throw Rorrie out. I had to know that he'd do that and he did. In fact, he surprised me with his icy demeanor. I overheard him telling her mother that he was going to leave her things on the back porch of their home while she was at work. Rorrie, it turned out, had gone back to Richmond once she'd left him in L.A. She had thrown herself back into her work while she tried to make sense of the situation.

If she tried to contact Khalil, she couldn't. The day I began to bring my things over he changed the numbers to his cell and the house. He did everything he could think of to make me more comfortable. He asked me what colors I wanted the place painted, and even cleaned out the garage and put an electric opener on it for me to park the car in.

My second night there I sat on the couch relaxing, waiting for him to come home from a job. Khalil only worked on location five or six months out of the year. The rest of the time he did some freelance work filming performances at the concert venues such as the Warner Theatre, the 9:30 Club, and Constitution Hall. It was two thirty in the morning and I couldn't sleep. Staring up at the ceiling I began to wonder what I was doing. I had cooked and cleaned. The house smelled so good that it could have passed for a Bath & Body Works store. Had I really gone domestic? Would I be able to keep it up? Was it really possible to turn a hooker into a housewife?

I heard Priest's voice in my head the day I'd referred to Khalil as my man: *"Your man? Bitch, you're a fucking whore. A high-class one, but still a whore nonetheless. Any man who's claiming you has got to be some pussy-whipped idiot. C'mon now."*

I thought about what he said and I wondered if he was right about me. I tried to fight it but tears welled up in my eyes as I hugged the pillow. I had allowed him to not only judge me, but to label me as well. This was something that I never did. Who was he? He was a fag and a cheat.

I'd done what I had to. The world had taken everything from me that I needed most. My father, my mother, Manny, and even Rorrie. I had nothing to push me but me. Was I wrong because I chose not to be poor or work a job I hated, probably in the food court or retail, for a few bucks an hour, while I watched women who didn't look half as good as me live the good life and shop?

I didn't have a college fund. I didn't have shit. The only thing I had was my looks and this special package between my legs. And even though I'd questioned it for years, there was no denying that *it* was special. I'd watched man after man go crazy in it, and jump through whatever hoops I required in order for them to get it again. Looking around the house and the life I'd stolen from my childhood friend, I began to wonder if my ability to sex men up was a gift or a curse. Here I'd landed a man, one who, for the first time, simply made me feel good, and I felt like an impostor. What started as nothing more than revenge had now become the future I desired, yet I was worried that it could all be snatched away.

I picked the phone up and dialed Cheron, looking to get some support. I was shocked when she answered. "Girl, what are you doing up?"

"I just got in. I went to see that group I was telling you about, Fertile Ground. They did a show at a club in Baltimore called Sonar."

"Was it nice?"

"Really nice, but my date was whack. The entire night he talked about his job and his motorcycle. Plus you know we can't stand niggas who wear cheap shoes."

We both laughed. "Bad, huh?"

"Bad ain't the word. I coulda sworn that Hush Puppies weren't in season or in style the last time I checked. I mean what type of guy wears suede shoes with shorts anyway? And this fool actually thought I was going to go home with him. I started to tell him that I'd take a bullet with no batteries over a night with his ass." I laughed again but when I trailed off she said, "So what's up with you?"

"I don't even know. I'm sitting up here in this house, kinda wondering if I belong here. Wondering if I belong with him."

"Are you crazy? Why wouldn't you?"

The words were burned in my brain. *"Bitch, you're a fucking whore. A high-class one, but still a whore nonetheless. Any man who's claiming you has got to be some pussy-whipped idiot. C'mon now."*

"It's my past . . . I just keep thinking that if he ever found out . . ."

"Hold on," she said. "Let me pull my shirt off." A second later she continued with, "Listen, sweetie, you know I'm not about sugarcoating things so I'ma tell you straight up. What you do, or did, for a living wasn't right or you would be proud of it. But dammit, we've all done things that we aren't proud of. You are no different from anyone else who's used crime to come up. The Rockefellers, the Kennedys, hell even the Bushes kept it gangster for the oil. The difference is that you didn't hurt anyone to get yours."

"But you still didn't answer what if he finds out?"

"Cross that bridge only if you come to it. Listen, you could always tell him yourself and that way no one could have anything on you."

"Yeah, right. Tell him that I sold pussy?"

"You know what's funny?" she said with a serious tone. "Most women have slept with more guys for free than you have for money."

She didn't really know that for sure. I'd only told her about ten guys. In truth there'd been far more than that over the years. Still I replied, "You're right."

"So why don't you just get over this nonsense and be happy you found someone. You have left that life alone, right?"

"Absolutely. I am retired."

"Well then. Just concentrate on being that homemaker and *his* whore and I assure you, he'll ask very few questions. Men are just dumb like that."

Cheron was nuts. She went on for ten minutes telling me that I was worthy and deserving. She claimed that men wanted good sex and a woman who they were attracted to. As long as a woman knew what she was doing and treated her man to as much loving as he could handle, a man wouldn't care if she landed on this planet from Mars. I thought about how many men had used the line "Let me take you away from this." They'd all promised marriage, kids, and a home. Here, Khalil had done all I'd asked and more that I didn't to make me feel at home.

In between being crude, she made some good points. I appreciated her efforts to make me feel better. It had worked a little. "Thanks so much for talking to me."

"Girl, whatever. When are you going to come pick Madison up? She keep asking about you."

"Next weekend. There's a festival down on the Mall I'd like to take her to."

"Sounds good."

I remembered another important thing. "I had one last date on my books and I was wondering if you wanted to take it before I called to cancel it?"

"Hmmmm," she said. "Is he a gentleman like that Miles?"

"If you liked Miles you'll love this guy. He's a hotshot lawyer. Really laid back, loaded with money, and even though he lives in town he's very discreet."

"That means he has a wife."

I laughed at her sharpness. "Exactly."

"How much?"

"Ten, fifteen grand. He may get a little kinky for that kind of money and I'll just put it out there about the wife. He said she likes to watch."

"You have got to be kidding."

"No, I'm not. They'll try and videotape if you let them, but for that you can charge double."

"Are you saying you been with them and let them tape you?"

"No, I didn't, but if you want to make the money, the option's yours." The truth of the matter was that I'd never worked with this guy before, but if I'd told Cheron that she would have balked at the opportunity to earn the money. What I knew I'd learned from him through our e-mail correspondence.

"Wow," she said. "So you're really leaving it alone. This man of yours must be either rich or he must have a dick made of pure gold."

I giggled. "Girl, you sick." Then I added, "He ain't rich."

We laughed together. "Well I'll tell you what, I'll do this appointment, because hell, ten Gs is ten Gs, but please don't tempt me anymore. You are not going to turn me out as if your name is Heidi Fleiss."

"Deal."

I gave her the date and the time. It was three weeks off. We hung up and I sat up and wiped away a couple of tear stains that had formed on my cheeks. By sending Cheron on that appointment I was completely done with that world. I was walking away from money that sometimes seemed too easy to make, yet I was overjoyed. All I could think of was the future with Khalil.

I couldn't tell, because I'd never been here before, but I was beginning to think that I might be in love. I dozed off on the couch, wrapped in a blanket, thinking of him.

"Hey, baby," he said, nudging me awake. I looked up and saw Khalil's body standing above me. "Sweetie, let me help you up so we can go upstairs."

I was so out of it he bent down, picked me up, and carried me. Feeling the heat from his body I wanted to make love to him but I was in too deep a fog. As usual I was stirred by the fact that he smelled so good, but I still couldn't snap out of my haze. In fact, I barely remembered us going up the stairs or us sliding into bed.

I do remember the banging that stirred us awake at six thirty in the morning. "What in the world?" I heard Khalil say as he sat up in the bed like a shell-shocked veteran hearing a loud boom.

The second set of bangs came harder. He stood up. I did the same thing as I watched him head out of the bedroom door. He didn't look for a weapon, which told me that he wasn't really scared of anyone who might be on the other side. Me being a woman, I was prepared for what I believed was the inevitable. I'd been doing sit-ups, crunches, push-ups, and Tae Bo for the last month, getting ready for this.

I grabbed a pair of tights and slipped on a pair of Air Force 1s. I already was in a wife beater. As I headed down the steps, I heard her voice. I put my hair into a ponytail and began to stretch my arms behind my head.

I walked through the living room and stood ready to step out-side when Khalil looked back at me. He pushed the door closed so that Rorrie couldn't see inside and then he shook his head no. He pointed back to me and said firmly, "Go back upstairs."

I folded my arms as if to let him know that he was going to have to handle this and that I was ready to do whatever if he didn't. His face turned into a scowl and he repeated: "Go back upstairs, now."

I stood my ground but still stepped back and took a seat on the wooden chair that sat in the hallway. I was going to listen at the least. "Rorrie, I've taken all of your things to your mother's. You don't have any reason to be here."

"How can you say this to me? After everything we've been through. How can you throw it all away for some other bitch? I'm a goddamned doctor. I know I'm beautiful. What does she have that I don't?"

"It's not about that. But you can't just come over here like this."

"Well I've been calling you, but you changed the numbers, just like you changed these locks."

"Rorrie, things had been bad for a while with us. It's not like you didn't have any warning."

"How can you say that? I never thought you'd cheat on me." She began to cry. "I hate you."

He was silent.

She kicked the storm door and yelled again. "I know that bitch is in there."

"Rorrie, don't make me call the police."

"Go ahead and call the police you faggot. As a matter of fact, you'd better call the fire department too, 'cause I'm going to burn this motherfucker to the ground while you sleep."

I would have been cool but the threat sent a jolt of anger through me. I knew that she had it in her to be incredibly jealous, but to hear her make threats like that was shocking. Khalil may not have known what she was capable of doing in desperation, but I did. She was still mouthing off, "Khalil, you sorry son of a bitch. Your movie isn't gonna be shit. You'll be nothing without me. What's so great about this bitch? Tell me . . . tell me . . ." she was yelling now.

Suddenly I heard my mother's voice. *Hailey,* she said. *Go ahead and whip her ass. Beat her like she stole something.*

With that, I stormed the door and attempted to get past Khalil but he was much faster and stronger than I would have guessed. With only one arm, he grabbed my waist, spun me around, and with his free hand slammed the door shut.

"I don't want this," he said. He had me in his grip. "I don't want the fighting. We can move. We can leave here today." Rorrie began banging. "I'm calling the police," he said. "I don't want my woman fighting like this."

"No Khalil. Let me go."

His next words froze me. "What if you're pregnant?"

I stood still when he said that. The banging had stopped. Everything was quiet again. I thought about his words. They were full of concern and it was the strangest thing. I hadn't had anyone speak words of concern for me in so long that it actually stunned me. I hadn't had anyone worry about me in years. The look on his face assured me that the season of me drifting through life alone was truly over. I wasn't alone anymore. In that moment I knew that our spirits were connected. I didn't need to get Rorrie back. I didn't need revenge. Life itself had taken care of everything. She was out there broken. She'd taken everything from me first and now I was doing it to her. I didn't need to lift a finger against her. She was reaping what she'd sown.

We were eye to eye. No hint of sadness or remorse for having to turn Rorrie away. He belonged to me. I finally responded to his question. "Why would you ask that?"

He shook his head. "I don't know. It just popped into my head. But if you are, I don't want you fighting. So please go up . . ." he didn't get the words out when the sound of breaking glass scared us both. We looked down and saw a brick on the floor.

He moved toward the door and yelled out to her. A second later she pulled off and her tires squealed as she reached the corner. I knew that Khalil didn't want me fighting. He'd said it. I also knew that he was concerned about me and the possibility that I could be pregnant, which blew my mind.

As I stared down at the brick the only thing I could focus on was the fact that I knew where Rorrie's mother lived and then I tried to imagine the look on her face when she saw the same brick on the floor in her mother's living room.

20

KHALIL

Imagine my surprise when I walked through my therapist's door and saw her swaying slowly to the music that she played through the speakers on her computer. She was standing up and listening to Janet Jackson while she sipped from a bottle of fruit O water and dancing in a manner that was actually enticing.

Her secretary had sent me in even though I'd arrived ten minutes early. Cameron obviously hadn't buzzed for me. She usually wore a blazer but today she was clad in a snug-fitting, Baby Phat, polo-style shirt and a jean skirt that shocked me by revealing an outstanding shape.

I knocked on the door to get her attention. She turned around and from the look of embarrassment on her face it was apparent that if she were white she would have turned as red as a can of Coca-Cola. "That must be some bottle of water." I laughed to break the ice.

She looked at her watch and then laughed it off. "You're early. Was Jackie at the desk?"

"Yeah, she sent me in."

She nodded then grabbed her sweater from her chair. "Excuse me for one second." Cameron headed out of the office, surely to go chew her secretary out.

When she walked back in three minutes later she was wearing her sweater and she seemed fine. I'd already taken a seat and she was ready to get down to business.

"So how have you been Khalil?"

"I've actually been good."

"The dreams? No recurrences?"

"No not really. I mean no." She nodded suspiciously or my mind was working too hard. Changing the subject I blurted out, "I saw the woman who abandoned me as a child. I saw her at the airport in L.A."

"You mean your mother?"

"No, Frannie. She was my father's girlfriend."

She scribbled down something. "So she wasn't your mother, but you chose to use the word *abandoned*. Why do you think that is?"

"Well, she was like a mother to me. The only mother I knew for the early years of my life."

"I remember the story. I have to ask you a question though. Now that you are an adult, do you think it was her responsibility to take care of you?"

"Not legally, no I don't, but morally, yes. Yes I do. In the same position, it's what I would do. She knew what she was leaving me behind to face."

"You mean the drugs or the sexual abuse?"

"All of it. She left me behind. She knew what I was facing. She knew my father was on drugs, though it did get worse, or rather, out of control when she left. She still had to know that there was no way I'd be okay after she left."

"So do you blame her or your father for what happened to you? For the life you lived."

"You mean the life I didn't live."

She shrugged. "Or do you blame yourself?"

My eyebrows rose. "Why would I blame myself?"

"You'd be surprised. Victims do it all the time."

"But I was only a kid. What could I have done?"

"That's the question. Maybe you think you could have done something. Fought her off. Told someone. Gone to the authorities about the drugs or the abuse."

"Cameron, no kid does . . ."

"You'd be surprised. Each case is different though. We're talking about you."

"I blame my father. He wasn't a real man. A real man takes care of his child. I blame my mother. She was weak and evil and selfish. And I blame Frannie, because she wasn't like my parents. She could have helped. She could have saved me." I felt the tears beginning to come. I was embarrassed that she was taking me there.

Her face showed compassion now. "Khalil, if you need . . ."

I interrupted her as a thought flooded my mind. "I could have done something but . . ." The same compassionate stare. She was waiting for this. ". . . I could have stopped it, but I think I liked it. I liked what she did to me. I hadn't had anything good in my life for a long time. No one else paid me any attention good or bad. Tenille was the only one," I said as I began to cry the tears of shame. I covered my face and let it all out.

"It's okay, Khalil. It's okay." A moment later and I heard her shut the door. She then kneeled at my side and handed me a Kleenex. "Let it out. It's okay to feel all that you feel. Those feelings are yours. Own them and then we'll work on letting them go."

I continued to cry for at least a minute as I thought about everything that I'd been through. My chest moved in and out as if I'd just run a four-minute mile. "I loved Frannie. I did and she left me."

"It probably really hurt her to do that. She probably didn't think there was anything she could do, Khalil. Did you get her number when you saw her at the airport?"

"Yes."

"You need to call her and talk to her. Just be honest with her. Just be honest."

I tried to calm myself. I was in so much pain. Cameron handed me more Kleenex. She reached up to wipe my face and I felt her hands on my cheeks. I looked up from my palms and she was right there in my face. And I couldn't have written a worse ending to the session, but she leaned in and kissed me on the mouth. I never realized that I felt anything for her emotionally that would have made me respond. But physically, she'd always enticed me. Many times I'd fantasized about bending her over this desk. I kissed her back and we stood up, lips locked.

A second later and my right hand was up her shirt caressing one of her globes and hers was at my crotch. It was like a lightning bolt when I heard her use the words, "Fuck me, Khalil."

The words were different but they triggered the memory of Honey's request. *"Take me upstairs and make love to me . . . Now."*

I pulled away and said, "Stop."

She was stunned. The look on her face told me so. "Please, Khalil. I know it's wrong, but I want you. Just this one time."

My head could have fallen off my shoulders and rolled out of the office. I couldn't believe that my therapist had lost control like that. I wanted to ask her who *she* was. Instead I told the truth. "I'm in love. I can't do this."

"You can." Her voice was seductive. "It'll never happen again. I..."

I cut her off. "I have to go." I turned and walked out of her office and didn't look back.

21

HONEY

Call me petty but I felt a sense of exhilaration as the glass crashed. I'd launched the same exact brick through Rorrie's mother's window that she'd sent through Khalil's. As a matter of fact, I'd wished that I had another so I could have thrown two. When I heard the alarm going off inside of the house something told me to take off running. I must have looked like a lunatic for certain as I scurried toward my vehicle looking like I'd just stolen something.

I was half hoping that Rorrie would come out of the house and get some but instead I had to take satisfaction in sending the message that she could be touched. It was ten after two in the afternoon and I was running late. I'd dropped Khalil off at his appointment and set off to run a few errands. The dry cleaning and grocery store, he knew about, the brick I'd hidden in my Chloé bag, I had decided was classified. No need to worry him.

I zipped up Alabama Avenue, headed for Pennsylvania, and turned left. I blew down the hill, glanced over at Pope Funeral Home, where my mother's funeral was held, and blew a kiss. I crossed the Anacostia River and was in Capitol Hill in no time flat. When I pulled up in front of the building where I'd dropped Khalil off I didn't see him so I put on the hazards and double-parked. I climbed out and prepared to grab us a couple of lattes from the Starbucks next door.

I didn't make it to the curb when he came walking out of the building. He didn't see the woman behind him, because when she reached for his arm he was startled. He yanked away and said, "Let it go."

When he turned around and saw me he looked a little shocked but went right with, "Come on, let's go."

I tossed him the keys and I moved toward the passenger door. The woman who'd followed him outside stood there watching us. I looked back at her and gave her a real good look, since she'd been staring at me so hard. I was thinking, *Take a picture, bitch. It'll last longer.*

We pulled off and I asked, "What was all that about?"

"Nothing."

"So, that was your therapist?"

"Yeah."

We drove in silence for the next few minutes. I knew enough about men to know when they want to be left alone. He had that look. I sang along to the radio. We were listening to Michel Wright's show on WPGC. After a quick voiceover, an oldie came on, Case's "Faded Pictures."

I sang each word, *"As she turned through the pages, the tears rolled down her face, I could see her reminiscing why her life had to be this way."*

"I didn't know you could sing."

"I can a little."

"Nah. You sound good. Really good."

"Thanks, you're too kind."

We pulled up to the house and I told him that I had a few groceries in the back. He climbed out the car and said, "I'll take it around and park in the garage and bring the rest of the stuff in the back."

"Cool." I climbed out with two bags in my hand and he pulled off. I made it to the first step and I heard the voice again.

"Bitch, you're fucking my man." I looked a few cars down and there she was, finally. Rorrie in the flesh. As she approached, she said, "We need to talk ... and ..." She stopped mid-sentence when I turned and looked her in the face.

It was then that I saw she realized who she was talking to. If I could have taken that picture it would have won a prize. All of the emotions that must have been running through her mind at the time appeared on her face at once. The part that was hating the other woman, the shock that she absorbed when she realized that it was me, the deep shame for what she'd done to me, and finally, the fear that she was about to take a beat-down for killing my mother.

She tried to speak but initially only air came out of her lungs. "H ... Hai ... Hailey, is that you ... you?"

I paused and looked her in the eye. "Yeah, it's Hailey. Do I know you?"

"It's me Rorrie. We grew up together," she said.

I couldn't believe that she bought that I didn't recognize her. She hadn't changed a bit: always book-smart, she was always gullible. In all fairness I had to admit that she was still cute though not as cute as me. Same shape, same everything. How could I not have recognized her? "Oh yeah. Rorrie." I played it cool. I was going to wait on her to jump out there. It was obvious she hadn't seen the brick through her window yet.

"What are you doing here?" she asked.

"I live here. With my boyfriend."

"Khalil? Khalil is *your* boyfriend?"

"Yes. We just started dating."

"Khalil is my fiancé," she squeaked out. "Are you the woman I spoke to on the phone a couple of weeks back? Did you say you were pregnant?"

I smiled, finally ready to stick the dagger in her and watch her crumble. "Rorrie, I know all about your now-canceled joke of an engagement. I was also here this morning when you threw a brick in the window. You'll find that same brick in your mother's living room when you get home. If that's where you're staying?"

"My mother lives in Temple Hills now. She's been there for six years. What are you talking about?"

Oh shit, I've bricked an innocent person's home. Oh well, I thought. "Never mind me. So how can I help you?"

"How can you help me? You are sleeping with my man. He and I are getting married."

"You mean you *were* getting married."

"No, this is just a thing he's going through. I'm going to need you to back off." She was beginning to sound frantic. "How did you meet him anyway?"

"Does that matter?"

"I just want to know." She shook her head in disbelief. "I don't understand any of this."

"If you must know, we met out of town. I've been living out of state until recently. Khalil and I, we met on a flight and joined the Mile High Club."

She looked like she was turning green. "I can't believe this."

"Believe it, skank. And you'd better be glad that I might be

pregnant or else I'd be forced to beat that ass simply on principle."

"Pregnant?" It was too much for her to cope with. First, I
watched as her face contorted as if she were going through labor
pains. Then, like I'd set off a bomb, she began to shriek at the top
of her lungs and without warning she began to charge me. She
lowered her body as she got close to me, reached out, and tried
to tackle me.

I responded by sidestepping and dishing out several punches
to her face, watching her fall to the ground. She was a wild
woman but not wild enough for all the pent-up rage that I'd carried for years. *Who comes to a fight with her hair out?* I thought.
To keep Rorrie from getting her bearings as she tried to make it
to her feet, I reached for the top of her head. I had a fistful of her
locks in seconds and I wasn't letting go. I was like a heavyweight
wrestler exacting punishment on an opponent; everywhere my
hand moved, her head followed. I began to pound her face with
my free hand, ignoring her cries of pain.

It was insane. I wanted to destroy her but something told me
to go easy on her. I wasn't interested in catching a charge but I
needed to send her a message.

"Let me go," she yelled.

"This is what . . . you . . . wanted," I panted as I whaled on her.
My Tae Bo paid off. I wasn't throwing girly punches. I hit her so
hard I think I could have knocked a man down with a few of the
blows.

She swung wildly, trying to free herself, and one of her fingers
poked me in the eye. I let her go and I was surprised that she still
had so much fight in her. She was on me while I recoiled from
the pain. I tried to back away but lost my footing and suddenly

she was on top of me. Instead of punching me she wrapped both her hands around my throat and tried to choke me. She was actually trying to kill me.

Out of the corner of my eye I saw the front door open, and Khalil appeared. "Heyyyyy, stop," he yelled out as he made his way down. Though I knew I'd gotten the best of her to this point, there was no way I was going to let him pull her off of me. Before he could reach us I swung my knee up into her back and she screamed as I tried to crush a rib. When this didn't instantly break her grip, I pulled my legs up and out, the benefit of my bedroom skills. Before she knew it my calf muscles were at her neck. I had no problem yanking her off of me. As Khalil jumped in between us I told him to step back.

"This is bigger than you, Khalil. Just chill and fall back for a minute."

"What? I'm not going to sit up here and watch you two fight."

Rorrie then chimed in, "How could you do this to me, Khalil? How could you do this with her? I told you about her."

"What are you talking about?" he asked.

"I told you about my friend Hailey. The whole incident about her mother being killed."

"This is Honey."

They both looked at me. "My real name is Hailey, but no one has called me that since my mother was killed. I didn't let anyone call me that. Hailey died when my mother died."

"That's bullshit. Ask her where the name Honey came from."

I jumped at Rorrie, ready to swing again. Khalil grabbed me and stopped me from round two.

"So you recognized Rorrie when you saw her picture?" he asked. "When you asked about her, you knew who she was?"

I nodded my head. "I recognized her. Yeah, I did."

"You conniving little . . ." Before she could finish her sentence I swung lightning fast with accuracy and slapped her so hard saliva flew from her mouth.

She tried to charge me but this time I had my feet planted and I swung both fists in her face, creating a clothesline effect. Her legs kept coming but her head stopped. She fell to her back.

"Stop it," Khalil commanded. "Honey, go inside."

I stood still. "I'm not going anywhere. She needs to leave before she gets hurt—" We both looked down at Rorrie and I finished with "—Worse."

He nodded. I watched him lean over and help her up. "Rorrie, you have to go. You can't keep coming around her starting trouble." My arms were folded. I'd won the battle and the war all in one day.

The tears began to fall. It was the part of the story where the sad, slow song would have started if it was a movie about her life. "If that's how you want it. Then I hope you two are happy." She turned and began to walk away. I knew she didn't mean one syllable of what she'd said. Almost to her car, she turned and said, "Khalil, don't forget that I told you why her mom was killed because she was sleeping with anyone who had a pocket full of money."

I charged her and she, realizing she'd had enough of me, jumped into her car. As she pulled off we made eye contact and I knew that, in spite of the box of whoop-ass I'd opened up on her, there was a chance I'd see her again. I just wanted to make sure that if I did it would be on my terms.

22

KHALIL

A week had passed since I'd found out that Honey had known all along that Rorrie was my fiancée. I was still trying to reconcile her reasoning for not letting me know: *"If I had told you then you might not have known that I wanted you for you and not as some prize in a scheme for revenge. Remember, you came after me."*

She had a point. I'd pursued her with all my might, but a part of me couldn't stop thinking that the initial fuck was exactly that, revenge. It bothered me as I tried to pull it together. I didn't want to end things with her. I hadn't felt so alive ever.

Still, tired of my distant mood, Honey boiled over and we had our first argument. I had been sitting on the couch, trying to watch some clips of my work, when she started up. She came out of the blue with, "Khalil, I don't have to stay here. I can leave if you want me to."

"Maybe it's you who wants to leave. You've definitely shown that you have a talent for disappearing."

"Maybe I should disappear. You're not talking to me. I don't know what's going through your mind. Ever since Rorrie's crazy ass showed up you have been acting like you're having second thoughts."

"What do you mean by not talking? We've talked."

She shook her head. "I mean *really* talked. You've kept things very surface with me and I'm tired of it. If you are having second thoughts about us I'll understand. Just let me know," she said so coolly that it had me doubting that she cared about me at all. "I'm going to head out and give you some time to think about *things.*"

I was about to comment when she walked away and headed upstairs. I sat there for a few moments. I began to wonder why I'd been distant. Maybe I was mad that I'd allowed Honey to hurt Rorrie or that I'd even helped. Maybe I was insecure about what was going on with us. Was she going to wake up one day and feel as if her mission was completed and then abandon me like my mother and Frannie had?

I got up and moved toward the steps. I heard the shower running when I walked into the bedroom. There was steam coming out of the door to the bathroom as she'd left it open. I walked to the door and peeped in to see she had her back to the door and a washrag in her hands, holding it to her face.

I could see her shape through the steam and the glass and instantly I became turned on. It had been a few days since we'd made love. I didn't know how she'd respond but I pulled my shirt off and dropped my shorts and underwear down to my ankles. I stepped out of them and moved to the door. When I pulled the shower door open she looked shocked. Then as I moved closer I saw that she'd been crying.

"Baby, what's wrong?" I said.

She shook her head and the tears continued to fall. "I . . . I . . . don't." She paused and looked down into her cloth.

"Talk to me," I said, moving closer to her.

"I don't want to lose you," she murmured out. "Khalil, I'm so happy with you. I don't want you to be mad at me."

I realized that I had been angry with her, but in that moment I released it. Her vulnerability allowed me to. I moved closer and kissed her. "I'm not mad at you. I don't want you to leave. I don't ever want you to leave."

She lifted her head up and kissed me back and the sparks ignited. She never stopped with the tears but I was sure they became tears of joy and pleasure as I lifted her left leg to my waist and entered her.

I started slowly but our passion erupted and before I knew it we were fighting to possess more of each other. Her hands on my ass, pulling me in deeper while mine were locked on her to hold her in place as I pierced her target. We got lost in the moment as we banged bodies together with the warm water beating down on us.

I heard the words again; this time I knew that they'd come from her mouth because she said my name, "Khalil, I . . . love . . . you."

For once in my life I felt free. I knew the difference between what I was feeling now and what I'd felt with Rorrie, who I'd always loved with my mind. This was heart and soul, a spiritual connection.

I let her leg down and she asked me what was wrong. "Let's go get in the bed."

"Did you come?"

"No."

She looked surprised but not as surprised as she looked fifteen minutes later as I worked out on top of her. Her eyes were rolling up inside of her head. "No one . . . omigod," she cried out. I grunted and kept moving as I inched closer to ecstasy. "Khalil, I haven't ever been . . . fuhh . . . fuhh . . ." She didn't get the words out before she let out a high-pitched scream as she thrashed her head back and forth.

Her throes of passion excited me to the point where I came hard and collapsed on top of her. I took a moment to catch my breath and then asked, "Honey, am I too heavy?" She didn't respond.

I lifted off of her and was shocked to see that she was out cold. I tapped her face, thinking that she was playing games. A cold rag and a few shakes later and we both realized that she'd passed out.

"That was incredible," she whispered as she came to with a smile on her face. "I didn't know it could be like that," she said three times back-to-back. She went on about the mind-blowing sex, the shock that I lasted so long, and all of the things that she felt as she had a gut-wrenching orgasm.

We turned on the radio and listened to Justine Love and Todd B as they played slow jams that fit the moment we were in. "The Way" by Jill Scott and then "Emotional Rollercoaster" by Vivian Green played as we stared at the ceiling. My chest poking out like King Kong's, I dozed off with her in my arms.

Honey had urged me to make the phone call to Frannie. After I'd talked with her about her promise to be at my side, I felt the strength to do it. Now two days later, there was a twinge of nervousness as I approached the home that was located in the part of Philly where Germantown connected with Mount Airy. Her street was well kept and quiet.

I knocked on the screen door. The door inside was standing open, allowing the slight breeze to enter. Frannie came to the door in a pink dress and greeted me with a huge smile.

I introduced Honey as my girlfriend and she gave her a big hug. "This is so wonderful," she said. "I can't believe you're here. I've missed you so much over the years."

I caught Honey's gaze when Frannie'd said the words. She was checking on me for a reaction. I'd confided in her about all of my feelings and my anger, some of which I'd never shared with anyone other than Cameron.

We weren't in the house a good five minutes when she said, "I want you to take a seat. I've whipped up a little something for you to eat. Don't even think about saying that you aren't hungry," she commanded like a general.

I didn't deny the fact that I'd been hungry all day, but too anxious to eat as we cruised up 95. The house was old and had a door to the kitchen. When it swung open I could smell the aroma of home cooking that had my saliva nearly dripping from my tongue.

Over light conversation we ate collards, fried chicken, macaroni and cheese, cornbread, and then as if we could get any more stuffed she brought a freshly baked apple pie out of the kitchen and a tub of Häagen-Dazs out for dessert. Throughout the whole dinner memories of Frannie cooking for me and feeding me as a child flooded my mind.

"You okay, baby?" Honey asked a few times.

"Yeah, I'm good. The food is great," I'd said. It was great having my woman there to act as a buffer to the discomfort that was choking the air out of me.

"As a matter of fact, I'll take another slice of pie, y'know to go with this second scoop of ice cream." Honey smiled.

"Where are you putting it all, chile?" Frannie asked and laughed as Honey ate like she hadn't had a decent meal in a while herself.

"Miss Frannie—" Frannie had insisted she call her by her first name. "—I love a good meal like this so you won't catch me acting shy when I get a chance to partake of some good ol'-fashioned soul food. My mom was a good cook and if she hadn't died while I was young, I probably would be a size six or an eight." She laughed then added, "Or maybe a ten or a twelve."

They both laughed. "I like this young lady, Khalil. She's a keeper. You do what you have to do to keep her around."

I wasn't sure where it came from but I felt compelled to let it out. "Sometimes it's beyond a man's control though, right?" The conversation and the laughs came to a halt that quick. "I wanted you to stay, but you left. Remember?"

Then I got up from the table. "I can't do this. I don't forgive you." I reached into my pocket and pulled out a hundred-dollar bill and placed in on the table. "Thanks for the hospitality but this was a bad idea. I'm sorry Frannie, but we're leaving now."

Honey's eyes showed horror. I felt bad that she had to see me act this way as I headed for the door but I was hurting too bad. "Khalil, no," she said.

"Was it something I said, Khalil? Please don't go like this," Frannie pleaded.

"I just can't do this. I needed you then. I don't need you now. I needed your food when I ate in that lousy cafeteria on Thanksgiving and Christmas, not now. It was stupid of me to come. I'm sorry."

I watched briefly as Honey stood up and began to follow me. I could hear her thanking Frannie for the meal. Then as we stepped out of the door and down the steps I heard the woman who'd at one time been my mother crying. "Khalil. I know you don't need me." Her tears were evident now. "But I do need you. I . . . need . . . you."

I hit the alarm switch as I climbed into the Bentley. I didn't look back as we pulled off. As we turned onto Windrim Avenue I wondered if she felt even a fraction of the pain I'd endured when she had done the exact same thing to me years before.

23

HONEY

Khalil had definitely fallen into some state of depression after we'd gone to see Frannie. I felt bad for urging him on. It had been too much for him though he didn't come right out and say it. I had noticed that he'd been having a hard time sleeping, tossing and turning. Four nights in a row I listened to him grunting and moaning, sweating and fighting.

When I looked over at the clock, it was five A.M. I couldn't take it anymore. "Baby, wake up." I rubbed his head and tried to stir him as lightly as possible without startling him. "You're having a bad dream, Khalil."

He opened his eyes and I was relieved when he didn't take a swing at me. "Huh?"

"Wake up. What are you dreaming about? Do you remember?" He was out of it still.

"What?" he said softly.

"Are you okay?"

"She was doing it again. Frannie was doing it again. She was touching me on my . . ."

He sat up and looked as though he'd just seen a ghost.

"What did you say?"

As if he'd just discovered electricity he looked amazed. "Frannie . . ."

"Frannie what?"

He looked me in the face. "Frannie did it to me too," he said as tears began to pour down his face. "She did it to me first." It was like my heart exploded inside of my chest. My brain hurt and I had to force myself to breathe as I realized what he was going through at that moment. I'd insisted he reach out to her and now this was on me.

As far as I was concerned from this point on, it was me and my man against the world. In our short time together I'd learned that we had both been victimized by life. Neither of us had a chance to experience true love. My mother had always been so busy keeping a roof over our heads that at times it felt like I almost raised myself. Once she was murdered, my aunt did nothing more than put up with me for a couple of years and that was it.

Khalil for his part had been abandoned and abused in his young life and spent his crucial teen years in foster care. It was a miracle that he'd turned out how he had. Not only was he a viable member of society, he was successful. Following your dreams took courage, even more than I had. I never even dared to develop my own. I think what I wanted most was to be loved and have a family. To have a man that I could call my own, that I could dream with.

Khalil didn't let what he'd finally admitted to himself stop him from showing me how much he cared for me and I wanted to show him my appreciation.

As we drove out toward Annapolis he had no idea of the surprise that I had in store for him. We crossed over the Severn River and got off of Route 50. Once we turned into the exclusive neighborhood he began to ask questions. "Who are we visiting?"

"Just hold tight."

I kept driving down the street and when we'd almost reached the end of the block I pulled up to a gate where a portly white woman was parked in a Mercedes wagon. I rolled down my window and she waved as she walked over to the car. "I'm sorry about the mix-up, Ms. Height. Here is the control for the gate and the garage. Congratulations to the both of you."

"Thank you." She waved at Khalil and climbed back into her car.

"What's going on? What is she talking about?"

I hit the remote and the gate opened. I pulled the car in and past the garage up to the front door. "Welcome home, Khalil." I motioned for him to get out of the car.

His mouth dropped open, as it should have. He was standing in front of a one-point-five-million-dollar home. "Are you kidding? I know . . ." He couldn't even get the words out. "How can you afford this?"

"I'll tell you all about it tonight. For now let's just take a look."

He continued shaking his head in disbelief as he walked through the front door into the foyer. The house was wide-open and you could see past the winding staircase into the family room. He didn't know which way to go first so he said, "Gimme the tour." He continued to mumble that he couldn't believe it.

The huge kitchen, Egyptian-stone floors, and the dark cherry cabinets were breathtaking to me and I'd seen the place at least ten times. There was a great room off of the kitchen, with one-story glass windows giving a breathtaking view of the Severn River and the dock that was at the bottom of the hill.

It took us ten minutes to see the entire house. There were six bedrooms, a huge recreation room, a theater room, and a parlor. We headed outside and when he saw the gunite pool that was equipped with a built-in spa he broke into a huge smile.

"This is beautiful. I don't know how you can afford this."

"You mean *we*." I pulled out a piece of paper and handed it to him. It was the deed. I'd added his name to the deed, though not the note. "You own half of this."

"How?"

"I purchased it. Went to settlement a few days ago. Wanted to surprise you with *our* new home. One that we can fill up with babies," I said, smiling.

We stood there suspended in time for a few quiet seconds while I did nothing but capture the excitement that was flowing from not only his eyes but from his heart as well. I could feel his thoughts. In that moment I felt safe and valued. The house and the money would have been great for either of us alone, but together we had everything that we could have wanted and needed. With him, I knew that was more than I should have ever asked for.

I wasn't really all that sure what I believed in as far as a higher power, at least not the way I'd suffered so much, but in that second I honestly felt as though I knew what people meant when they used the term *heaven-sent,* because that's what I thought of Khalil.

He moved closer to me and asked why I was crying. I hadn't realized that while I wasn't bawling like a baby, my eyes had filled with water. I was overwhelmed. The thought of living in a house like this with the man of my dreams had never really entered my mind.

"I don't know," I responded. "I'm just so happy that I've made you happy. It's all I want to do."

Summer was definitely coming to an end. As I strolled out of the hotel lobby on Lexington Avenue in Manhattan I felt the sun fighting to keep the heat on the back of those who dared step out into it. I had no choice. One more bit of business called me.

I'd chosen a navy-colored suit, slight white pinstripes in it, and it wasn't helping me at all in my efforts to stay cool, calm, and collected. It was a bold move that I was making and I was feeling hot, worried, and nervous. I hadn't even told Khalil where I was headed to; in fact, I'd given him a half-lie as I told him that I was merely checking in on an investment. I did feel bad about it.

I'd collected lump sums of cash, thousands of dollars at a time, from men all my life. Now I could actually say millions when counting Priest, but this was different. I was meeting with some white-collar folks now who had the ability to send me to jail possibly, if they weren't afraid of what I was bringing to them.

In the week leading up to my purchasing the house I found out two pieces of information that piqued my interest and prompted my actions. The first was that Priest had just signed on with Mark-One International, one of the top agencies in the world. They represented nearly every top name in the sports-and-entertainment-game, which hadn't been snatched by either William Morris or IMG. This of course meant that he was valuable to them for one reason only. He was going to make them a ton of money.

The second piece came to me via Mr. Cason, the same detective I'd used to get Priest's photos to start with. I'd had him lay off a couple of weeks until Priest felt comfortable that he wasn't being followed anymore, then I had Mr. Cason get back on him. Call it intuition but I knew there'd be more for me to learn. But instead of more undercover behavior, I got the word from Mr. Cason that Priest managed to keep his nose clean. I figured that with the publicity he was getting from his new deal he was probably lying low. That's when the idea came to me to have Mr. Cason check on Janice Sears's family. Janice, who had been introduced as Jan, was the girl who'd been found dead from an overdose in Miami after spending the night with Priest.

What I learned from my hired friend struck me as insane. The second girl, who'd accompanied Jan the night she died, had also made headlines. The day after Jan's death she was locked up in a Dade County jail after being caught in a stolen car, headed to the airport, with a kilo of cocaine, unknown quantities of ecstasy, and bunch of stolen credit cards.

She never made bail, because three nights later she was found dead inside her cell, an *apparent* suicide by hanging. The first thing that crossed my mind was that Priest couldn't have been connected enough to have the girl killed in a Miami jail cell. It had to have been a coincidence. This was until Mr. Cason stumbled across the fact that before Priest played college basketball for St. John's University he'd transferred from the University of Miami. What was more interesting was that the girl he dated for the two years he was there had a brother who had become a resident of the Florida penitentiary system after his violent and lucrative drug organization had been invaded by the police and DEA, who eventually brought him down. Though the brother was still in jail, his third appeal was being paid for by none other than Priest Alexander, shedding light on a connection between Priest and someone who'd have the power to conduct a hit inside of the prison system.

After I learned all of this, it would have made sense for me to be fearful but I wasn't. Instead I made the call to Brad Persons, Priest's agent, and here I was in a cab headed to Brad Persons's office on Sixth Avenue. The cab dropped me off and I headed into the building. After signing in I hopped the elevator to the thirty-eighth floor.

"Ms. Height, Mr. Persons will see you now," the headset-equipped receptionist stated. No one came to greet me, she only pointed and said, "To the end of the hall and make a left. You walk straight into his office."

"Thank you," I said confidently and headed off.

The Mark-One headquarters were huge and the hallways were wide, filled with a bunch of offices on each side. I did walk straight to where she directed and it looked more like a wing. Parquet floors, huge glass windows, oversized mahogany furniture. The office was amazing. "Please come right in." I heard the voice and then looked at the man in the doorway to see a tall, slender, fit, silver-haired gentleman. He was also wearing a headset. He reminded me of TV journalist Anderson Cooper.

"Can I offer you anything? Coffee, tea, bottled water?"

"No thanks. I'm fine."

"Okay great. Let's get right down to business."

"Okay let's. The first thing I'd like to do is walk with you into your restroom and watch you undress, then after I've checked your clothes we can go take a cab ride or a walk to somewhere where I'll be comfortable talking."

We sat there staring at one another for twenty seconds before he asked me if I was serious. I explained to him exactly how serious I was. "It's your wallet Mr. Persons, but I don't have much time."

He smiled and nodded once he realized that I wasn't some crackpot with dreams of pie in the sky. He pulled the tiny recorder from the inside pocket of his jacket and then motioned for me to follow him into the bathroom. As he stood there in nothing but his boxer shorts I realized that he now accepted that I was a force to be reckoned with. I patted his clothing and went through his pockets inside of his bathroom, which itself was larger than some people's offices.

Ten minutes later we hopped out of a cab and walked into McCormick & Schmick's. We grabbed a table and he insisted that I order something. Again it was time to get down to business. I handed him the photos. "I know you have a lot riding on Priest. This would be a problem, though I'm sure he wouldn't be the first or last homosexual who sold sneakers for Nike or Adidas, whoever you have the contract with, but I'm aware this isn't the kind of thing they smile upon. I also know you have Sprite and McDonald's interested, among others. All of these companies are selling an image, one that is way different from the person you are now representing."

"So what exactly are you suggesting?" he said. I knew he was looking for terminology, something he could use to tie me into a blackmail charge.

"Mr. Persons, I did not take these photos, but I won't deny that I know who did. All I'm saying is that I would like to assist you in protecting your investment and your right to be rewarded for your investment. In addition to the photos, I have some very disturbing knowledge about your client that might bring embarrassment and possible criminal charges that would make a lot of people very uncomfortable."

"Knowledge such as?" he said, for the first time sounding smug.

"Well let's just say this. If I told you, he'd have to kill you," I said, smiling as I sipped my French martini. He didn't smile back. "Your client has been involved in some things in the past few months that I have knowledge of. As long as you don't learn of them you can represent him in good conscience and make all the money in the world."

"Is that so?"

"Absolutely and of course I don't want to be involved in any of this. I want to just fade out and let things fix themselves so that everyone is happy."

"So what do I need to do to ensure that you can keep all of this quiet?"

"I'll need four million and for you to have a talk with your client."

He looked as if he wanted to spit his drink out. "Four million dollars?"

"All things considered I think that's cheap. This type of assistance will enable you to make that ten times over at least."

"I'm not sure if I can get you that much for the assistance that you are offering. In fact, we may have to consider letting Mr. Alexander go in light of these circumstances."

"Please, and walk away from a client in a contract year, when you've already secured a sneaker deal and the kind of fast-food deal that will put his face on a billboard in Times Square as big as the one of Diddy. Let me be frank with you, Mr. Persons. I don't much care for Priest. If there was ever a less deserving person . . . I mean truly, he doesn't deserve the admiration showered on him. I think he's a clown, but kids love him and so do most of the people who buy jerseys, sneakers, and tickets. I wouldn't be upset if you tell me to go screw myself and don't offer a dime for my assistance. I'll gladly give these photos to the press for a fraction of what I'm requesting from you." I took a sip of the water with lemon, rinsed my mouth, and swallowed. I pulled out a card and put it on the table. "When I leave New York tomorrow afternoon, this business will be settled one way or the other. Thanks for your time and for lunch. The crab cakes were scrumptious. Call me early if you want to stop the ball from rolling." I stood up and headed for the door.

Before I could hail a cab he was on the curb next to me. "I can give you two-point-five. When we get back to the office I can cut you a check, but that's as high as I can go and still have it make sense for me to do business with Priest."

I looked down at the curb to hide my smile. Once I'd suppressed it and was able to keep a straight face I looked up. "I think I can live with that."

"One thing, Ms. Height." His face had turned to stone. "Some of the people who invested in this company to begin with are a little . . . how should I phrase this? Some of them have a propensity to behave in a less than savory manner when a situation calls for it. You taking his money and reneging on the deal would be one of those situations, meaning that you have now gone as deep as the well will go, which means I shouldn't see a copy or any other version of these photos come across my desk at your hand or anyone else's. Digging any further, now or in the future, could create a dangerous situation. One where you would wind up on the short end of a very tough stick. You do understand what I'm saying of course."

"I do."

What he was saying was that he'd have me killed, or locked up at best, if I ever showed my face looking for more money. This of course I knew ahead of time, but what could I say. I needed the money. I'd blown through most of what I'd gotten from Priest in the past couple of months.

"Let's go," he said when the cab pulled up. As we drove back down to his office he made a couple of calls and didn't seem angry at all. I'm sure I wasn't the first to play this game with him. Inside I was beaming. I'd have settled for one million.

I returned home to an empty house. Khalil had sent me a text message letting me know that he was going over to his house to pack up the rest of his belongings. He had found a renter on Craigslist and agreed to have the house ready for them in two days.

I walked out the back door and took in the view. I was amazed at what I saw. Boats out in the middle of the Severn River, a clear September night sky, all the perks of the small mansion that I now owned free and clear. I took a seat on one of the stone benches near the Jacuzzi and began to reflect on all that I'd done and endured to get here. I wondered if it had all been worth it. I was happy now, finally. Money had always given me joy, as had being able to afford nice things. I loved the security of a fat account, the glitter of diamonds, and the smell of a new Louis Vuitton handbag. I didn't understand people who didn't believe that money could buy happiness. That was a lie. What it couldn't buy was peace or salvation, but happiness it bought by the truckload.

I stood up and headed back into the house to get a bottle of water. I thought I heard Khalil's truck pulling up, so I looked out the window. That's when I saw a car parked out in front of the gate. I headed to the front door and decided to go investigate. No sooner than I reached the driveway did I hear tires spitting gravel and spinning out as the car began to disappear at warp speed up my street and out of sight.

Completely weirded out, I dialed Khalil's phone but got no answer. He said he'd be painting so I wasn't surprised that he didn't pick up but I was a little scared. I shook my head trying to convince myself that it was nothing more than the price of the business I'd conducted. I'd be watching my back for the next few years probably, but so was every hustler, politician, and entertainer in America. Getting a little freaked out every now and again was a small price to pay to live well, I reasoned as I walked into the wine cellar. Forty-five minutes and three glasses of Merlot later I'd calmed completely. So much so that I'd drifted off on the couch with nothing but dreams of my future with Khalil dancing around in my head.

24

KHALIL

When she walked through the door and saw the house completely empty except for the last two boxes and a bag of trash that were sitting by the window I saw the look on her face. It was the first time that she had to face the finality of what was going on.

"How did this happen, Khalil?" I was sitting on a stepladder, my body positioned like the statue *The Thinker* while I tried to come up with an answer that might make some sense. "How did we get here? Two months ago we were going to be married. Now you've given up the house that we were going to raise a family in to be with her."

I knew she needed this, to vent. I had no idea what would be safe to say. "Rorrie, I don't really know how it happened."

"Did you ever love me?"

"Of course I did."

"What did I do wrong? Did I dream too big? Was it my career, the time I had to spend away?"

I shook my head no. "I did love you."

"So you don't anymore?" Giving me no time to answer she asked, "Do you love her?"

It slipped off of my lips like a song: "Yes."

The tears burst from her like a sudden volcanic eruption. She fell to her knees and began to whimper like a baby. Over her cries her words were almost completely inaudible. "Why?"

I moved to her. "I'm sorry." I put my hand on her back.

"I . . . loved you. I did all of this for you. I wanted to be a success for you."

"No, you did that because it's your calling to be a doctor."

"What is it about her? What can she do for you? She doesn't have anything."

I felt her pain as the images of the house we lived in now flashed through my mind as well as the Bentley. It would have crushed her to know that. "It's not about that."

"Well what's it about? Is it about the pussy? Are you leaving me because of how she fucks? Because I can tell you all about that, about how she got a man killed over her and how her mother died because she was selling her pussy."

I shook my head in disgust. "I know you're hurt but . . ."

"But nothing. Hailey is a whore. You've left me for a whore."

Growing angry, I said, "I agreed to see you so that we could talk, not to hear you go on about her."

"We are talking. We're talking about you leaving me, the girl who loved you when your raggedy ass was striving to hold a camera at a fucking Bison game for free. When you were waking up trembling like a bitch at night, I was right there chasing those demons away. You were a week away from St. Elizabeth's, Khalil. Do you remember that? Does she know that I nearly had to get your ass committed?"

"Rorrie, leave. Fuck this. I tried to talk to you. I wanted you to feel better, but you came to be nasty."

"What did you expect?" She stood up. "A motherfucker I'm engaged to starts creeping while I'm working my residency, trying to build my career for our future and you expect me to come in here and talk all nice. You're leaving me for Hailey, Honey . . . whatever you call her. She's always been a selfish bitch, a liar, and a whore. I hope you get exactly what you deserve." With that she stood up and kicked over one of the boxes, sending the contents out onto the floor.

We both watched as the can of paint that was inside poured out onto the floors. I looked at her with eyes that showed my patience had vacated. "What you gonna do?"

"Just leave, Rorrie."

"Fuck you. I'll burn this motherfucker to the ground."

"Leave."

She stood in my face and her scowl conveyed that her love for me had now disappeared. "Fuck you."

I looked at the paint and imagined another day's work, trying to clean the floor. My anger got the best of me and I grabbed her by her neck. "Get out of here."

"Before what?" she gargled out.

"Rorrie, don't push me."

She approached me and took a swing at me, slapping me. I laughed to keep from exploding. She tried it a second time and I grabbed her hand. With her free hand she reached for my crotch. "What's this? You want to say good-bye to me. A proper good-bye?"

I jerked away feeling violated and oddly attracted to her. We'd always had adequate sex but maybe what we'd always missed was the natural sexual connection. Rorrie had always been willing to try anything, but usually it felt forced or too much like she was trying to be more sexual than she really was. Right now though, she was different. No love, just anger and pain. I couldn't figure it out then but perhaps all that I knew about love and attraction was that together or separate, they brought anger and pain.

"Leave, all right?"

"Fuck you," she said again. "I'll leave, after you fuck me one last time."

"You'll leave now." I grabbed her and pushed her toward the door. She began to struggle.

I had her in the foyer and reached for the door when she blurted out, "I'm pregnant."

"You're lying." I stopped in my tracks.

She grabbed her purse and pulled out a package. "These are prenatal vitamins."

"Rorrie, you work in a hospital. This means nothing."

"You think I'd go through all of this to deceive you."

"I do."

She stepped back and as we locked eyes she lifted the black dress that looked more like a shirt up over her breasts. The first thing I noticed was that her belly-button ring was gone. I was shocked when I actually noticed a bulge. Then she rubbed her belly. "I have a small hump, but it's coming and look at these." The dress was now up on her neck. She wasn't wearing a bra and her nipples did look a little puffy as they stood at attention. She had a pair of white cotton-and-lace panties on. She leaned back on the wall. "I know you don't want me though. I know you'll want me to have an abortion. Two kids at one time . . ."

"She's . . ." I cut myself short. She hadn't paid me any attention. Instead her hand had slipped down inside of her underwear.

"Just let me feel you this last time and I'll leave you alone. You won't have to worry about anything."

I stood there as she began to masturbate in front of me. I didn't realize that I had begun to watch her intently. In my mind I was merely looking for a clear sign that she was lying about being with child, but my eyes were locked on her fingers as she began to moan.

As quickly as she'd kicked the paint over I found myself behind Rorrie, thrusting into her as I bent her over the steps. "That's it Daddy, fuck me hard."

I couldn't deny that as good as Honey's pussy was I was still enjoying the familiar wetness and feel of Rorrie's womanhood. As I pounded her I thought about our first date, a play at the Warner Theatre and how we ended up tearing each other apart in her apartment that night. I thought about the plans we'd made to be together. "Yes, yes, yeahhhhhh," she screamed.

I pounded harder, knocking her head into the steps. I continued to ravage her as if I were a man possessed. "Ohhh, shit," she yelled. I lost all track of time and space intent on doing one thing, tattooing her ass as if she'd stolen from me.

I grabbed her by her hair and yanked her head back as I bulldozed into her hard enough to knock a building down. Her knees buckled and she cried out, "Uhhhhhhhhh, I'mmmm coming."

I fucked her hard through her orgasm until I felt her go dry and I continued to pound her like a piece of meat. "It's starting to hurt, Khalil," she said softly. This only caused me to increase the ferocity of my assault.

A few minutes later she realized that her plan had backfired as she began to cry. "My hair, you're hurting me."

I continued. Nothing but heat and friction. My loins banging against her ass. "Stop."

Finally I let go of her hair and gripped only her hips as I reached my peak. With no care or affection, I pulled out of her. "Ouch," she yelped. I stepped back and yanked my underwear up.

"What the hell is wrong with you?" she said as she took a seat on the steps looking as if she'd been beaten-down. She was holding herself. "Shit, my pussy hurts."

We stared at each other again.

"Are you sure you're pregnant?"

"Positive."

I had a smirk on my face. "So, I guess you'll be leaving me the hell alone for good."

"What are you talking about? I know you don't want a baby with me."

"Rorrie, shut the hell up," I yelled, sounding like I'd gone mad. She recoiled. "I told you a lot about me over the years and some real shit that happened to me. But there are some things that I didn't tell you."

I had her full attention.

"Like what?"

"Like, there's a pretty good chance that I'm fucking sterile. The disease that I caught from Tenille in middle school might've ruined me. All this time we've been together there has to be a reason why I've never gotten you pregnant. I know this is just a lie you're telling to keep me. Have some dignity."

I didn't believe in ghosts but you'd have thought that from

the look on her face, she'd seen one. "Now, Rorrie, just leave and never try to contact me again."

"Please, Khalil. Let me explain."

"Nothing to explain. It looks like you shouldn't be calling anyone a whore."

"Please."

This time my strength scared her as I yanked her from the steps and pushed her out of the door. "What about her? She said she was pregnant."

One final push and the door slammed in her face in more ways than one.

25

HONEY

I was learning a little bit about relationships. Having a man wasn't as easy as I imagined it would be, but still worth it. Khalil would have to deal with my moods the same way I dealt with his and so far he had. So when he seemed distant the day after moving the last couple of boxes out of his house I didn't worry about it too much.

He sat around the house and decided to watch college football instead of riding out to the mall with me. A little pissed, I decided to keep the disappointment to myself. I reasoned that he was dealing with some type of feelings behind the move.

"I may not be here when you get back," he said as I gathered my belongings to head out the door. "I spilled a can of paint on the floor last night and I need to go get it cleaned up. The tenants are coming to get the keys tomorrow."

"Okay. I'll see you when you get back. I hope you're in a better mood." He didn't say a word but I noticed that he was nursing a glass of Hennessy.

I headed for Annapolis Mall and decided to ignore his funky

attitude. I was going to kill him with kindness. As superficial as it may have been, I believed that a new watch and a bag full of gifts would cure anyone's crankiness. I stopped off at Pier One first and then headed over to the mall. I was thrilled to find a spot near the door outside of Nordstrom.

I waved to one of the managers, who knew my face, which was a sure sign that I shopped too much. I couldn't resist scanning through the latest pairs of True Religion and Seven jeans. I ended up buying a couple pairs of each.

As I made my way out into the mall my cell rang. The ringtone belonged to Cheron. "Hey, girl you ready for tonight?" I asked. Tonight was the night that Cheron was going to meet the client who I hadn't canceled with. In fact, he'd wired the money to me two weeks prior.

"That's what I was calling you for. I'm not going to be able to make it."

"What do you mean? Why would you want to cancel?"

"I don't want to cancel but my period came on. I'm cramping and I have a migraine that is kicking so bad that I've already thrown up twice. There's no way I can make it."

"And why the hell are you calling me with this now? You're supposed to meet this man in a few hours."

"You can't call someone else?"

"Like who?"

"I don't know. I'm sorry. Believe me, I would have dragged myself out if it was just the cramps, but when my period came flowing like crazy a couple hours ago, I knew it was a wrap." She paused for a second.

"Well he had the money sent over via wire last week, cash. It was twelve grand."

"Shit," she screamed out through the line. "Well why can't you just do it since it's your last time anyway."

"Because the last time was my last time. I'm in a relationship."

"Wow."

"What's all that?" I asked.

"I mean this sudden blast of morality is mind-boggling. You've fucked married men for years and now you don't want to cheat on your boyfriend because it's wrong." She laughed.

I didn't like her tone. "Cheron, fuck you and now I see what I get for trying to help you out."

"Screw this guy. He's paid you already and you're about to cut that phone off anyway, right?"

"I don't get down like that. I've never cheated anyone out of their money. Fair exchange is no robbery and I sleep well behind that. Plus this guy is pretty well-connected; I wouldn't want to make an enemy over twelve grand."

"For twelve grand, I'd make O.J. my enemy."

"Let me call him and see what I can do," I said, hanging the phone up in her ear. Then I realized that I'd left my other cell phone in the car.

I walked into the Bose store to price a new Wave system to surprise Khalil. It was expensive but it didn't make any difference. The same thing applied when I grabbed him a pair of LeBrons, of Evisu jeans, and of Gucci shades. I was determined to cheer him up. In all, he'd be sporting a fifteen-hundred-dollar smile. He could act funky if he wanted to. He would find himself ducking from the stereo instead of listening to it.

Climbing back into the car I went into the compartment in the trunk and grabbed the other cell to call the client. With Khalil gone I'd have time to return the money and show up at the house to help him get the floor cleaned up. "Hello, Brian. This is Honey."

"Hey, I can't wait to see you. Are you available to come earlier than we discussed?"

"Well there's been a little problem and I'm going to need to return the money to you."

"Excuse me?"

"Something has come up at the last minute and I won't be able to entertain you tonight."

"You call and tell me this at the last minute. I have to tell you I really don't appreciate this."

"Like I said, I'll return the money to you personally, I can have it to you within the next couple of hours. You can call another service . . ."

"If I wanted another service, I'd have gotten one from the jump. You were highly recommended. Miles called you the best and I settle for no less than that. What if I wait until tomorrow or later in the evening?"

"Well actually, I'm stepping away from the business. Moving on to some other things."

"So you are saying that I won't be able to indulge in your company at any time in the future either," he huffed out.

"I'm sorry, but like I said, I'll bring the money to you right away. Just tell me where you are."

"My wife is going to be so disappointed. She has been so stressed lately and she was really open to trying something new. She's been distant lately and I needed this spark. What would you say if I doubled that money, for the same three hours?"

"I'd say thanks but no thanks."

He was silent, thinking. "I'm at the Bethesda Marriott Suites right by NIH. Room 1114. I want every penny of the money here in an hour." He was angry and suddenly the nice-guy routine was out the window. All men reacted the same way when they didn't get what they wanted. All except Khalil.

I blasted my sister Mary's CD as I sped home to get the money for him. I cursed Cheron the entire way but realized there was nothing that she could have done. Mother Nature was the queen bitch.

I climbed the stairs and found the suitcase where I'd kept the envelope stashed. I yanked it out and counted it up. Forty fifties and one hundred hundred-dollar bills. He'd know that his money meant nothing to me as I hadn't touched it. I thought about changing my clothes out of habit, but I wanted to get it over with as soon as possible.

Back out the door I reasoned that my having to return this money personally was akin to my actually closing the door on this phase of my life myself. I needed to do it and as I sped toward the Capital Beltway my mind played pictures of the life I'd lived. I couldn't really put my finger on the lesson that I'd learned from the things I'd done. The only thing that bothered me was that now I had a secret, a past that my man would be ashamed of.

I wondered if that in fact was a lesson or just one of life's laws. We all do things we're ashamed of, some of us for a living.

"Nice car ma'am," the bellman said as he helped me out.

"I won't be but a moment. Can I leave it here?"

"Unfortunately, no. They give out two-hundred-dollar tickets out here in the blink of an eye. Are you checking in?"

"Just running upstairs to drop something off for a friend."

"Well, you leave the keys and as long as no one comes by I'll leave it here. Worst case I'll have the valet take it for you."

"Thanks," I said, catching his eyes going up and down my body. I gave him a ten-dollar bill and hit the revolving door.

I reached Brian's door and knocked hard and deliberately. "Just a moment," he called out from the other side.

The door swung open and he stood there, surprisingly tall and handsome. He looked a little too earthy though to be a lawyer, with the short dreds and five-o'clock shadow. He reminded me of an older Eric Benet. "Hello. Again, I just want to apologize for the inconvenience. Here's the money. I can wait here while you count it."

"Please, Honey, step inside for just a moment. I also want to apologize for the tone I took with you. Things happen and I had no right to get indignant with you."

I nodded and stepped in. He went on, "It's just that I've been trying to get my wife to go along with this for a while and now that she finally agreed to it, you canceled on me." He walked to the wet bar and emptied the envelope. "Can I offer you a drink?"

"No thanks. I just wanted to return the money and be on my way."

He was counting. When he finished he pulled a second envelope from his pocket and asked, "Are you sure you won't take this? It's another twelve thousand."

"I'm leaving." I turned to walk out the door.

"How about just to watch she and I? You keep the twelve I gave you originally. All you have to do is watch me make love to my wife. That's it."

He was desperate. For some reason I stopped and listened to him. I didn't need the money, but I loved it. The part of me that lived to separate fools from their money had been stirred. "All you have to do is watch us. One time. Twenty, thirty minutes tops."

I paused for a minute and he sensed my indecision. "She just got in the shower. I'm going to join her. You could just wait until you hear us and then come into the room and take a seat. Like I said, if you don't want to join in you don't have to. But if you do, you can take all of that," he pointed at the stack on the counter.

His words, smooth and convincing, had me out there. In that second I recalled why I did this. It was for the power. It had never been about the sex. And while it had been how I made money, the only way I had been able to do it for all these years was because of the rush I got. "I'll take the twelve I brought here. When you two are finished, I'm leaving."

"Fair enough." He stood, dimmed the lights in the room where I was, and I watched him walk into the other room, which was illuminated only by candles, and shut the door.

I waited for a moment and my heart began to beat from my indecisiveness. *I should leave,* I thought. *Set the money down and leave.*

I grabbed one of the bottles from the counter and twisted the top. I chugged down the liquor without reading the label on the tiny bottle. I took a second and then I sat down in the chair. "This is the last time," I whispered to myself.

Time must have moved quickly because I heard movement in the room in no time flat. I got up and walked to the door. The room was dimly lit by only a single candle on the nightstand. It was enough light for me to see that Brian was on top of his wife, kissing her passionately. I leaned back against the wall and watched while trying to go unnoticed until it was over. He began to work his way down her body with his mouth, giving her small doses of pleasure the entire way.

A minute passed and he was now tongue-deep in her pussy,

causing her to moan like a woman possessed. Brian was sexy, but I had no desire to touch him. I knew then that I was completely into Khalil. I might as well have been watching two robots.

There were oooohhs and aaaahhs galore. They were excited at the idea of being watched. I had made a mistake in staying. I was over this. I had to admit though that when he began sawing in and out of her, I felt the twinges of moisture begin to form in between my legs.

They changed positions and she was now on top of him with her back to me. He was staring around her trying to make eye contact with me. I stared at him, giving him what he wanted for the twelve grand he was spending. He then motioned for me to come closer to the bed where his woman was riding him.

I obliged him. Now a foot away from the bed, he asked me to caress his wife's breasts. I shook my head no. He then continued to push up and into her. I did run my fingers through her hair. She had shoulder-length locks that were surprisingly soft. She seemed to rise and fall higher onto her husband once I'd began running my fingers through her hair. Suddenly Brian yelled out, "Grab her breasts, make her come. Take all the money."

Without thinking, I reached forward and cupped her breast, flicking my finger over her nipples before pinching them. The second I touched her she seemed to go over the edge.

"Oh gawd, yesss, babeeee. I'm about to ... uhhhhhhggggg-hhhhh." She erupted into a series of grunts and jerks as she had her orgasm.

He began to moan, "I'm coming too. Yesssss, oh shit."

I stepped back as I watched her collapse onto her husband. I stood up off of the bed and he called my name. "Honey."

"Yes."

"Are you sure you can't stay with us?"

"No . . . I can't . . ." as I was speaking he flipped the light on. His wife and I made eye contact and I wanted to die.

It took her a second to figure it out, but I knew instantly that his wife was Khalil's therapist.

I turned and raced for the door. I was so upset that I left the rest of the money on the counter—a first.

26

KHALIL

I was walking out the door of Solbiato in Georgetown, after grabbing a couple pairs of Prada shoes and a couple of shirts, when my lawyer called me from Los Angeles. The first words out of her mouth were, "Are you ready for this?"

My heart soared when I heard that. I could tell from her tone that there was nothing coming but good news. Aretha Towns was one of the most powerful black women in Hollywood and I was lucky to have her representing me. I loved her from the first day we sat down, and her enthusiasm was the reason why. She believed in my ability to become a great filmmaker at the start. Now here she was on the other end of the line, so excited for me that she couldn't even get the words out.

"I'm ready," I responded, having only a guess at what she wanted to share.

"An offer from Fox Searchlight came in today. They want to buy your movie and offer you a three-picture deal. I have a contract that they sent here for you." I was speechless. I stopped in my tracks just as I reached my vehicle. "Khalil, you there?"

"Yeah, I'm here. Just not believing what I'm hearing. When?"

"Well, I told you about the screening, but I didn't mention that I'd pulled some strings to get a few more execs to view it, with the intent of creating a buzz. It just so happened that the people I pulled in turned out to be interested. Now, here you are with a dream deal in your lap."

"I don't know what to say. Thank you." I went on uttering a few more statements expressing my disbelief at my good fortune.

"You deserve it. You did a great job with your first shot and I'm sure you'll make the most of this opportunity. I'll look it over and have it out to you overnight."

"Hold up. I have a new address. Let me get it for you." It felt strange saying that. "So what are the terms as far as dollars and cents?"

"A million and a half for your movie, and the development deal is worth anywhere from six to ten. With the right movies and right budgeting you could walk away with at least a couple million in your pocket easily."

As I pulled onto P Street I digested her words. I couldn't believe it. I'd made it. Nothing could stop me from this point. We talked as I cruised toward the house. Aretha outlined every detail to a T. "A lot of money and work are headed your way. Get ready for the bi-lifestyle." She laughed.

"Say what?"

"Bi-coastal." She giggled. "You're gonna need a place out here in L.A. What did you think I meant?"

"Hell, I didn't think I heard you right." I laughed.

As I pulled onto 395 my line beeped from a call. *Private Caller* appeared on my screen. Against my better judgment I ended my call with Aretha, told her I'd be on the lookout for the contract, and clicked over.

"Khalil?"

"Who's this?"

"It's Cameron."

"Hello."

"Hello to you. I haven't heard from you and I just wanted to reach out to you . . ." she paused and then she added, "I wanted to apologize to you for what happened."

"Well it's done and I don't hold anything against you."

"That's good."

Then we both went silent as if there were things to be said but neither of us knew what to say. After the silence continued for nearly half a minute she blurted out, "There's something I need to tell you . . ."

Sensing that she was about to confess her feelings I cut her off. "Listen, Cameron, I'm a man and I've realized that even though there are some things in my background that might cause me to blur the lines when it comes to boundaries, I can't make excuses for myself or my actions. The situation that occurred, I should have handled it better. I'm in a relationship and I am happy for the first time. I don't blame you, because I know that for you to come on to me like that, you would have had to be in a very vulnerable state."

"Khalil," she tried to stop me but I continued on.

"Don't be embarrassed. I was actually flattered because I've always found you attractive and I still do, but . . ." Time stood still as I delivered the end of my sentence. ". . . I'm in love."

I heard sniffling coming through the phone then she said, "I have to go. I'll have my secretary call you . . . about an appointment."

"Yeah, I was going to call this week because . . ." I got the feeling that we had gotten disconnected as the other line grew dead-silent. I looked at the screen and saw *Call Ended*. I wondered for a moment if she'd hung up on me.

It didn't matter. I was so excited about my deal that I felt instantly yanked from the funk that I'd been in all week. Ever since I'd screwed Rorrie I felt horrible for multiple reasons. Most serious of all was the guilt that had been sitting on my shoulders. I could barely face Honey and was fearful that the bad dreams would kick in again. Trying to handle it alone made me want to see Cameron for a one-on-one, but I feared an uncomfortable situation.

I called Honey and got her on the first ring. "Hey sweetie, what you up to?" I asked.

"Nothing, just surfing the Net, trying to find some info on vendors for my boutique." She sounded really laid back, almost monotone. She'd been acting strange for the past few days. I didn't know if she was acting on some intuition or if she was feeding off of my energy, which I knew had not been right since my encounter with Rorrie.

"Sounds good, but I want you to get dressed and be ready for dinner when I get there. I have some news for you and we're going out to celebrate."

"Oh really, tell me now."

"No, it's gonna wait. I want to tell you in person. I have one more stop to make and then I'll be there to spend the evening and all night holding my queen."

"Well you finally sound like my Khalil again, so it must be some great news. What do I need to wear?"

"You know you're always beautiful, so it doesn't matter."

"I'll be waiting on you," she said and then she paused. Before she hung up to get prepared she said, "Khalil."

"Yes."

"I've missed you."

I knew exactly what she'd meant. We'd gotten off track for just a minute, but we both were mature enough to know that things like that happened sometimes. I said what I felt and responded, "I've missed you more."

It took me an hour to get in and out of the urologist's office in Bowie. He'd run some tests and given me a quick checkup. I won't deny having been freaked out after the conversation with Rorrie the other night. I had a flashback of her yelling *I haven't been with anyone else.* I was anxious to get the results of the fertility test. On one hand my sanity was on the line. If it turned out that I was sterile and that Honey was pregnant by someone else I don't know what I would have done. On the other hand, if I was able to procreate, then I could possibly have two women with child.

At a little after seven P.M., I pulled off of Route 50 and into my community. It was always strange driving down the street that I now lived on. A mix of emotions ran through my mind. Sometimes I felt as though I didn't belong, I was here only because of Honey's bank account. I knew in my mind that if I'd married Rorrie, it might take us years to get here. Between her student loans and my career being at its starting point, who knew how long it would take for us to live like this. Now in the blink of an eye my life and my plans had changed.

As I hit the gate and pulled into the stone driveway I glanced up at the sky wondering what had caused God to rain down such blessing on me. I said a quick prayer, asking for forgiveness for what I'd done to Rorrie and headed for the front door.

Hitting the steps, I had the strange feeling that I was being watched and when I turned around I caught the tail end of an automobile moving up the street. Could have been nothing, I reasoned and headed inside.

"Honey, where are you?" I yelled at the top of my lungs.

The house was growing dim as the sun was preparing to set. There wasn't a single light on and no sign of Honey. I moved toward the steps and then up toward the bedroom. Still not a trace. I reached the bed and saw a note,

> *Khalil, I'm so happy for you and I don't even know what your news is yet. I do hope that you weren't set on going out as I had already planned a little something special for you before you even called. I suggest you slip into these and head out the back door and there I'll be.*

I looked down at the bed and saw a silk bathrobe and matching loungewear. I smiled as I played along. I got naked and changed into the silky clothing.

I headed down and out toward the backyard. She wasn't in plain sight until I looked just down the hill and saw a blanket on the grass, surrounded by tiki torches. She was clad only in her lingerie. "Nice of you to join me," she said as I approached. "Have a seat."

I obeyed and took position right next to her. She got up and headed over to the gas grill and lifted it, bringing over a covered tray full of food that smelled so good my mouth began to water.

She set the tray down and then pulled the bottle out the ice bucket and handed me a glass. "A toast to . . ." I didn't respond and she repeated herself as she poured: "A toast to . . ."

I laughed when I realized that she was ready for me to share my news with her. "A toast to dreams coming true. A toast to me being offered a fantastic deal for my movie as well as three more and enough money to make me feel like I deserve a woman like you."

She laughed and smiled. "Wow, that must be a lot of money," she said jokingly. "No seriously, I am so proud of you baby. More than that, I am happy for you."

I noticed that she didn't sip from her glass. "You're not drinking with me."

We were eye to eye and when she spoke I was thrilled and frightened at the same time. I didn't know what to think or make of it when she said the words "I can't. I can't drink with you. You see, I have some news for you as well. I'm pregnant."

27

HONEY

I had been hoping with all of my heart that his therapist hadn't recognized me, but deep down inside I knew that she did. It was a bold move but I was prepared to do whatever I needed to in order to protect what was mine. I loved Khalil and I was carrying his child now and nothing or no one was going to cause us any trouble.

I couldn't stop laughing to myself at the look on his face when I told him. He looked as if he was going to pass out and when he couldn't catch his breath we both realized that he'd enjoyed too much excitement for one day. It's not every day your one-chance-in-a-million dream comes true and then you come home to find out you're having a baby all within a few hours' time.

A soak in the huge tub and a glass of cognac had calmed him. I'd bathed him and then had him sit on the edge of the tub as I'd given him the blow job of a lifetime. By the time I finished with him he was so relaxed he could barely move. I prayed that I would feel the same level of relaxation once I handled the business that I had at hand.

———

I walked into Cameron's office before she had taken her first patient. She was behind the counter, talking to her receptionist, when she looked up and saw me standing there. Her eyes squinted a bit as if she was trying to adjust her sight. "I'll just need a minute," I said.

She waved me in. "Hold Mrs. Lords if she arrives before I'm finished," she barked to her receptionist.

We walked into her office and she didn't elect to sit down. I took a seat without her offering one and crossed my legs. "I need to know where you and I stand."

"You need to know if I'm going to mention to Khalil that you're a call girl."

"Formerly. I was a call girl formerly."

"Well you were on duty a few nights ago."

"I'm sure you know that I canceled the appointment and I told your husband the reason why."

"My husband?"

"Oh, that wasn't your husband?" A smile came across my face. I believed now that we both had something to hide.

"My husband and I are separated. He was just someone that I've been dating."

"And you were comfortable enough to get down like that?"

"Are *you* judging *me*?"

"Not at all. It's just a little strange."

"Well isn't this whole thing?"

"Well he mentioned to me that you were his wife, on the phone."

"You and I know that people say things that aren't true all the time. Now don't we?"

"I just need to know if you're planning to mention this, because if you are then I'd like to tell him first."

"Hmmmm," she said, nodding her head. "So he only deserves to know if someone else is threatening to tell him. That's the only way that you believe he's good enough for the truth?"

"It's not about that. You're a woman and don't sit up here all high-sidity, acting as if you don't have any secrets. Not after seeing you so willing to ménage with someone outside your marriage. And, baby, I'm sure that wasn't your first trip to the freaky side."

"Hold up . . ."

"You hold up. I'm pregnant by Khalil and I need to know if I need to have this talk with him, because I don't want to raise a child without a father."

I wasn't sure where she got the nerve but what came out of her mouth was: "Are you sure it's his child?"

I jumped up and pulled my hand back to slap her right across the mouth but when she flinched from fear, I caught myself. "I'm sorry." I took a step back. "I'm sure it's his child. I haven't been with anyone other than him since the first time he and I slept together and I've always had safe sex."

I looked at her and saw the look on her face and it dawned on me right then. "You have feelings for Khalil?" She didn't respond. "Have you ever been involved with him?"

"No." Her words were soft, she sounded defeated.

I moved toward her. "Please don't lie. If you're lying then I can't trust you."

"I don't owe you anything. You don't have to trust me . . ." Maybe it was the hormones, or perhaps just anger, but I swung for her face. She jumped back out of the way and I missed. "I'm calling the police," she screamed.

"No, please don't," I begged. "I don't know what's wrong with me . . ." I began to cry. "I just love him so much. I'm so sorry. I'm so . . . sorry," I whimpered as I covered my face with my hands. "I just love Khalil."

"He loves you too," she said. I looked up at her. Her face looked calmer. She handed me a Kleenex. "Let me ask you this. Are you sure you're going to stop doing this?"

"I already have. I swear."

"This might sound strange coming from me, but have you been checked out for . . ."

"Absolutely. Every three months, and I am completely clear and disease-free."

"It's just that I care for him and I want him to be happy and . . ." she paused. "Khalil's been through a lot."

"I know and I'm going to change all of that. Not only do I love him, I can take care of him in a lot of different ways."

"Financially?" she said. "Khalil has a lot more needs than that."

"Please don't sit up here and tell me about my man."

She sat down and reached into a drawer on her desk. "I won't tell you about him." She pulled out a folder and thumbed through the pages like a bank teller flipping through money. Then she stopped at one page and nodded her head. "I do however think you have a problem."

"And what might that be?" Our stares were now locked.

"In a session some time back, Khalil confided a bit of information that right now tells me that this whole thing is about to get very interesting."

"And what might that be?"

She closed the folder and put it away with a smirk on her face. "Khalil once told me that there was a chance he was sterile."

"Well . . ." I rubbed my belly and added, "We know now that he's definitely not sterile."

"Well I guess that remains to be seen," she said smugly. I was beginning to think that she was the one who needed counseling. She'd gone from professional to compassionate to hostile and wound up at condescending. I believed that in light of her feelings for my man, she didn't know how to feel.

I resisted the urge to call her out of her name and stood up. "I'm leaving, but I just want to know what to expect."

"Khalil has made it clear to me that he won't be coming back. So as far as I go, expect nothing," she said as I walked toward the door. Then, if my ears weren't playing tricks on me, I believed she mumbled, "Expect everything."

When I glanced back she wasn't even looking up. I shook it off and headed out.

The Realtor who'd found my new house in Maryland had put me in touch with her sister-in-law in New York, who, along with her husband, owned commercial real estate all over the country. I was hoping that she'd have something perfect for me in Atlanta or Miami that I could use for my boutique. When she called back a few days after our initial conversation, it was easy for her to get me excited when she told me that she'd been able to find a great location for my store; the only catch was that it was in New York City. As if she cared, I posed the question to her. I actually asked her how I was going to have a baby, open a boutique in SoHo, and keep my man happy.

Her response was: "Sweetie, I couldn't tell you that. All I can tell you is that this location has made two previous tenants a mint selling shoes and clothing. There'd be very little build-out for you as the place looks fabulous."

I'd wanted to tell her then that I'd take it, but what I did promise to do was drive up in the morning to take a look at it.

I was meeting Khalil for dinner to talk about the whole thing before he left for the West Coast for a few days of meetings with his distributor. We agreed to have a meal at Clyde's in Chinatown. I beat him there and when he walked in, my heart melted as usual because of his beauty. He moved toward me with pride in each step.

"You're looking really dapper," I said. He was wearing a Façonnable shirt that I'd bought for him, a tan blazer, and a pair of perfect-fitting jeans that had him looking like he'd jumped out the pages of *GQ*.

"Thanks, baby. You're not looking too shabby yourself," he shot back as he leaned in for a kiss.

We both seemed to play with our food while I discussed my news. Khalil's face didn't show approval so I asked him, "What's wrong?"

"Nothing. Just thinking about the things you said."

"I don't have to . . . I mean . . . we won't have to live in New York. I just think that I could make a lot of money there."

"I know we haven't discussed this yet but how does this work if you have a baby?"

"What do you mean *if* I have a baby? Do you not want to have a baby?"

He was silent for a minute and stared down at the table. "Honey, I need to tell you something."

"Go ahead."

"When I was molested, the woman who did it to me gave me a disease. I was young and didn't know to seek treatment. By the time I did the doctor told me that there was a chance that I'd be unable to have children. That I could be sterile."

I'd heard this from Cameron, but hearing it from my man seated across from me at the table with tears in his eyes almost caused me to break down. My heart was tearing in two as I leaned in and took his hand. "Listen, Khalil. I don't care what the doctor told you then. If I can carry this child then you *will* be a father." He pulled his hand away and I gathered quickly that he was doubting my words. In that I knew that he needed to hear what I had to say. "Khalil, look at me." His teary eyes were now locked on mine. "I haven't been with anyone else since we made love the first time. This is your child."

As I spoke the words I thought about Miles Amory, my last client, and the broken condom. Then just as quickly I dismissed it, thinking that life couldn't be that cruel. "Khalil, whatever your doctor told you back then was wrong. Your boys can swim," I said and felt relief when he cracked a smile.

He took my hand again and said, "I'm happy." Though his face showed the weight of the world, he seemed to be convinced that I was telling the truth.

We finished our dinner as I outlined a plan as to how it would work. We were going to be a power couple, like Russell and Kimora, Jigga and Beyoncé, Bill and Hillary, no less. By the time we paid the check and were heading out he was saying things like "As long as you know the baby has to come first."

It warmed my heart as I felt it all coming together. He'd parked in the garage and I'd used the valet. "I'll drive you to your car," I insisted.

"Cool," he said.

Khalil handed the ticket to the attendant and he headed off to get the car. As usual we caught the oohs and aahs of bystanders as the car pulled up. The black paint shining like a piece of art. It was a showstopper. I handed the attendant a tip and started for the car when I heard a voice come from behind me. "So this is what you're wasting my money on?"

I looked back and saw none other than Priest Alexander and two of his cronies standing behind me. I tried to ignore him and headed for the door but he began to follow me. It was then that Khalil realized that he was talking to me. "C'mon sweetie, let's go."

"Don't rush off on my account, I'm sure your man knows all about your scheme." He was close enough for me to smell liquor on his breath. I looked out the corner of my eye and saw Khalil headed around the car toward us. "Awww man, what you gonna do? You wanna fight me over this money-hungry whore?"

With that Khalil charged him and was about to swing when two of the valet attendants jumped between them. "Please, sir. Not in front of the restaurant." Seemingly out of nowhere the whir of sirens shot out from the corner and a D.C. squad car approached.

Priest stepped back from my side of the car and as he moved back toward the sidewalk he said a quick "Nigga, you lucky."

"Let's go," I said one more time. Without a doubt I'd have some explaining to do and as my blood boiled inside of my veins I shot death eyes in the drunken fool's direction, which screamed out to him that I'd be returning the favor. We both climbed in and as I was about to pull off I got the chance to eyeball him one last time. The look on my face let Priest know that he'd just made a mistake.

A serious mistake.

28

KHALIL

I resisted the urge to call her on the cell while she drove behind me. We were headed back to the house and I needed a face-to-face with her. Needed to see her expressions as she explained to me. The entire drive my mind finally allowed the curiosity that I should have attended to a while back to bubble over to the point where I was now ready to drill her with questions. If she was such an adept investor, why didn't she ever talk about her work? The only thing she talked about was the boutique that she'd yet to open. Where did the money come from? And what of the accusations thrown by Rorrie, though I knew that they could have been rooted in jealousy or anger? Rorrie's words that night echoed in my mind: *"Ask her where the name Honey came from."*

Now she'd nearly been accosted by Priest Alexander. As fine as Honey was I didn't find it hard to believe that she might know or have dated some famous men, but why the animosity? She had some explaining to do and the second we pulled up and made it into the house it was on.

"So Honey, break it down for me. What's the deal with you?"

I was already seated on the couch when she came through the front door. She walked past me into the kitchen and came back with a bottle of Deer Park. She exhaled as if she was preparing to go through it and then she sat on the floor in front of me, Indian-style, and leaned her back against the ottoman. "Khalil, there are some things about me, about my past that you don't know."

"I've gathered that."

"I'll be completely honest with you. I'm not proud of them, but I don't regret doing them either. I may not have always made the best decisions, but I was faced with some very rough circumstances. My mother was murdered." Her voice was steady, no sign of cracking or nervousness. "And to be honest with you I don't want to talk about them."

"Honey, I deserve to know what I've gotten into . . ."

She patted her heart. "You've gotten into me. You've gotten into my heart," she said emphatically. "My past is exactly that, my past."

I looked down at the floor. This wasn't how I visualized the conversation going. I was about to get up and walk away but she began to speak again. "I want you to know that when we first met, I was attracted to you and it wasn't about anything that you could give me. It was about your spirit. I hadn't felt that way about a man in so long, but still, I had no intention of sleeping with you."

"Until you saw the picture of Rorrie?"

She nodded. "You're right. When I saw her face so many emotions ran through my mind. So much pain, anger, and hatred. The second I saw her I wanted to hurt her. You were there. You wanted me too and so it was easy . . . but then."

I waited for her to continue. "Then what?"

"Then I fell in love with you. I couldn't get you off of my

mind. It was easier for me at first to convince myself that it was just about revenge, but I got caught up."

"So why did you disappear?"

"Because I had things to take care of. I wanted to be with you, but I had issues with Priest to take care of."

"Did you date him?"

"Sort of. We hung out from time to time, but the last time we did something bad happened."

"Did you sleep with him?"

Hesitantly, she nodded her head yes. "But that wasn't what I was talking about."

"Are you in love with him?"

"Hell no. Not at all."

"Is he in love with you?"

"Khalil, you were there just now. There's no love lost between us."

"So what happened?"

"I don't think I should tell you details, but I will say this. I think that Priest hurt someone, or was the cause of a couple of people being hurt. He knows that I know and for that reason, he paid me to keep quiet."

I was stunned. "So that's why he asked you about the car? He gave you enough to buy a Bentley?"

She nodded again. "Yes, he did."

"You blackmailed him?"

"Yes. I did."

We talked for a few more minutes as she outlined the details of what had happened in Miami. I couldn't believe my ears. It was like something out of a Lifetime movie. Sex, scandals, and cover-ups.

"How can you feel safe after doing that, Honey?"

"He has more to lose by harming me. I had told him that as long as nothing happened to me, he'd be good with *all* of his secrets."

I sat there now wondering about the woman who I'd fallen in love with. If she was willing to blackmail a famous athlete for some major money and keep his possible crimes a secret, what wasn't she willing to do?

"Honey I have something to confess to you as well."

She stood up and came to sit next to me. "What is it?"

"I saw Rorrie."

"And?"

"She told me that she was pregnant. If I'm the father it would have had to have happened in L.A. the night before you called."

"Wow." She leaned back and sank into the cushions.

"I didn't believe her. In fact, I cursed her out and basically dismissed her. Now, that you're pregnant, I believe you. But if I fathered your child then I could have fathered hers as well."

We sat in silence for three or four minutes. Finally she asked me, "Do you love me, Khalil?"

"Yes, I do."

"No matter what? As long as I do right by you will you always love me?"

"Yes."

"Then I don't care about that. Don't stress over it," she said so calmly that it made me uneasy. Then she said, "I want you to go upstairs and get undressed, put on some Maxwell or Gerald LeVert. I want to make love. I need to grab a couple things from the kitchen."

Uneasy or not, I wasn't a fool. I got up and headed upstairs.

—————

It was four A.M. when we finally went to sleep. I looked over at Honey sleeping as hard as a coma patient. She'd earned her rest in high fashion, making love to me like a woman who knew that in three months her belly would be swollen and that her *sexy* as she knew it would be transformed to *pregnant chic* for several months.

I'd been on my back in amazement as she bounced up and down on me, flipped positions like a gymnast, and worked my body as if it belonged to her. In the past five hours she'd taken me on a physical journey that transcended any lovemaking experience that I'd ever known. Honey had begged me to spank her until she claimed it hurt so good. She'd broken body oils out of the drawer, which made my skin tingle before she massaged me. The grand finale had to be her pouring honey all over my manhood and licking it off before having me return the favor to her, showing no care toward our nine-hundred-thread-count sheets. The feeling of licking honey off of Honey was indescribably erotic.

Now I sat there staring at this woman, watching her chest rise and fall with each breath. I was completely content and somewhat relieved that we'd talked and she'd told me everything. I had to admit that the entire drive home from Clyde's I'd contemplated hearing the worst.

When I drifted off beside her, my heart was full. I realized that as much as I'd gone through in my life, now things were evening out for me. I deserved her. I deserved to be happy and by the time I'd had my first dream I had a plan.

At eight A.M. I rolled over and scrolled through my phone. I noticed that I'd missed a couple of calls and messages. They must have come while I was in the restaurant or during the drama out front with the guy Priest.

I checked my messages and when I heard my urologist's message I was filled with joy. *"Mr. Graves. I'm sorry that I missed you but I know that you wanted to have the results as soon as I got them. It turns out that your sperm count was very healthy and you are in no way, shape, or form . . . sterile. Please call the office on Monday to confirm that you've received this message or if you have any questions."*

I left the house at nine A.M. in the Bentley, headed for Wisconsin Avenue. I pulled into the parking lot and walked into Tiffany & Company like a man on a mission.

"Hello, may we help you with something today?"

"Yes, I'd like to purchase an engagement ring." The words rolled off of my lips as if I'd planned this for years.

"Congratulations," the thin brunette said. "Right this way. Do you know what you'd like?"

Actually I did. I chose the ring I would have selected for Rorrie if I could have afforded it back when we got engaged. I picked out a three-carat, emerald-cut diamond in a platinum setting. I braced myself when she pulled it out of the case. "Oh, this is a great price. It's only forty-eight thousand dollars, and for a ring of this quality, you can't beat it."

I wanted to slap her for saying that but it didn't matter. "That's the one."

She was all smiles. "So you'll take it?"

"Yes."

"Do you know her ring size?"

"No, but I have this." I reached into my pocket and handed her one of Honey's rings. "She wears it on her right hand, ring finger."

Ten minutes later I had a fifty-thousand-dollar balance on my Black Card and a proposal to take care of.

Cruising home, I made a couple calls down to the harbor and set up a day that hopefully neither of us would forget. I stopped off at Target and the Gap and picked up a few things that Honey would need in case we didn't come home that evening. I didn't want to have her pack a bag. Once we dressed and left the house, she wouldn't have a clue where we were headed.

"**W**here have you been?" Honey was walking around in her bathrobe when I returned to the house.

"I had a run to make. I need you to shower and put on something comfortable. I'm kidnapping you for the day," I said as I leaned in and kissed her.

She smiled and said, "Mmmm, sounds interesting. Should I be worried?"

"I think so."

We drove to the marina and pulled into the gravel parking lot. I had Honey wait while I talked to the owner of South River Boat Rentals. I signed the paperwork and waivers and headed down the dock while he gave me the crash course on the operation of the boat.

"What are we doing here?" she asked once I came back to the truck. "Don't tell me you're buying a boat."

I laughed. "Just test-driving one. You aren't scared are you?"

"I'm not scared of much, big guy. You should know that."

"I'll keep that in mind. Let's go." I went into the trunk and grabbed the bags.

As we climbed aboard the boat she asked me, "So you know how to drive a boat? You never mentioned that. You are full of surprises."

I laughed thinking that she didn't know the half of it.

I guided the thirty-seven-foot boat out onto the South River as if I were the Skipper himself. Once we made it into the channel I had her come and steer the boat and taught her the basic controls of the boat just in case anything happened to me. She caught the hang of it pretty quickly and I let her continue at the helm while I went through the bag to make sure she didn't find the ring once I allowed her to sift through the bag. I took the ring out and put it in my pocket. I'd rented the boat for twenty-four hours though I planned to have us back before it got completely dark.

We traveled south from the marina about six nautical miles before we reached the waters just off the banks of Quiet Waters Park and dropped the anchor. We switched into our swimsuits and jumped into the water, which were both calmer and warmer than I hoped.

Honey was a good swimmer and we had a good time until I heard her screaming. I swam toward her and had just enough time to ask her if she was okay before I screamed out, "Oh shit." We were swimming in the middle of a school of jellyfish. "Come on."

A few minutes later and we were laughing about it. The sting went away after about thirty minutes. Too far from the shore to be visible and without another boat in sight, we both showered and headed out onto the deck without a stitch of clothing on.

"You tired?" Honey asked.

"A little, you know you did put it on me last night. Why, do you want to go down and take a nap?"

"No, I want to take one right here on the deck. Is that okay with you?" she asked as she put a towel down.

"Fine with me," I said as I lay down with her. The sun was still beaming but the breeze coming across the water made it feel perfect. We dozed off as Mariah Carey played on the portable speakers that I'd hooked my iPod up to.

When I woke up it was nearly an hour later and I was hungry but too nervous to eat so when I saw the wine rack in the cabin I popped open a bottle of wine instead. Honey was still sleeping as I drank nearly half a bottle of white zinfandel.

"What're you thinking about?" I heard her ask as I sat a few feet away staring out at the water.

"I didn't know you were up."

"I can't believe I was sleeping like that," she said as she stretched her arms and stood up. "So what were you thinking about?" she asked again.

"You."

"Good things I hope," she said, wrapping her arms around me.

"All good things." I felt her smiling into my neck as we gazed out at the water. Neither of us spoke for a few minutes.

"What made you decide you wanted to be Captain Stubing today?"

"Oh you're taking it way back to the *Love Boat*." I laughed. "Well at least you didn't call me Isaac."

"No but I appreciate it. It's beautiful out here especially now that the sun looks like it's about to set."

"Yeah, it is beautiful," I responded as I stared at the tangerine ball of fire as it was beginning to slide into the horizon.

I opened a bottle of water for her while she ran in to grab the terry-cloth sundress and slipped it on. When she came back from the cabin I took her in my arms and kissed her passionately and then, staring into her eyes, I began to speak. "Honey, I want you to know how much I love you."

She smiled. "I love you too."

"I feel that from you. It's like nothing I've ever felt. Having you in my life has done something to me. I hate to bring her up, but even though I was in a serious relationship with Rorrie, I was never able to get to this level. It's like I carried around all this pain until you came. I carried around so much hatred, but you've saved me from that. Even with each success, I felt like I was always trying to achieve in order to spite the demons that haunted me, never to enjoy it. It's different now. I feel alive."

"I don't know what to say," she said in a whisper as a tear formed in her eye.

"Baby you make me whole. I've walked around all of these years not knowing what it feels like to have someone understand me, and love me. I don't ever want to lose you."

"You won't, baby. I'm here for you. I always will be. As long as you let me."

I reached into my pocket. "Honey."

"Yes, baby."

I took one knee in front of her and pulled the black box from my pocket. She covered her mouth. "Will you . . ."

Before I could even open the box or get the words out she was in tears as she answered, "Yes. I thought you'd never ask."

When I flipped the box open she screamed out a playful "Hell-o."

"Can I slip this on your finger?"

"On one condition," she said.

"What's that?"

"Don't make me wait too long to marry me."

"We can be on a flight to anywhere in the world by midweek."

She nodded yes. "Then please, Khalil, slip it on."

29

HONEY

Cheron rode with me to Richmond and waited in the car with me for two and a half hours after we arrived. She said she didn't want me to get into another altercation with Rorrie, not while I was pregnant. I had been on cloud nine since Khalil had proposed to me a week earlier. It didn't really faze me when he broke the news to me about Rorrie telling him that she was pregnant. It happened before he and I were together and to be honest, I wasn't convinced that she actually was. I didn't want to bring it up to my man, but I, of all people, knew that women ran some serious games when the fear of losing their man came into play.

Cold, hard proof was what I came for. I had gotten her address off of the Internet and her schedule from the hospital that she was doing her residency at. She must have been doing overtime, because it was eight o'clock and she was supposed to get off at five. I didn't mind waiting, since I had Cheron in the car with me; we actually joked and laughed our way through the wait. Because of my newfound cravings, we had a cooler full of Yoo-Hoo and Sprite and a bag of snickerdoodles that I had been devouring, when I saw a car pull up. My heart began to beat faster when I saw the door open. A second later Rorrie climbed out.

Without a care in the world she made her way toward the apartment and Cheron and I exited the silver Taurus rental slowly. By the time she reached her door and pulled her keys out she hadn't even noticed we were behind her. When she finally looked over her shoulder I thought that she was about to use the bathroom on herself.

"What do you want?" she yelled.

"Calm down," I said. "I just want to talk. I don't want to fight. I can't fight . . . I'm pregnant."

She looked timid as she tried to place Cheron's face. "Talk about what?"

"Khalil told me that you said you were pregnant."

"I am."

"Are you planning to keep it?"

"I'm not sure. Why is it your business?"

I held out my ring finger. I might as well have thrown a brick in her face. "He and I are getting married next week. I just want to know for sure that you're pregnant and that it's his."

"Where do you get off? Of course it's his. He and I have been together for . . ."

"Were together," I cut her off. "You *were* together. Look, I'm gonna need you to use this," I said as I pulled the EPT box out of my purse.

She covered her face and exhaled. "What's that going to prove?"

"If you have to ask, then maybe you're not really pregnant."

She turned her keys and tried to enter her apartment quickly but Cheron blew past me and grabbed the door. "Are you trying to pull some shit?"

"You cannot force your way into my place."

"Rorrie, we can handle this like adults or we can get ignorant up in here. You might not recognize her face, but this is Cheron, Manny's ex-girlfriend. The Manny you got killed because of your little plot to steal Tank from me. I'm sure she would love the chance to tear you apart, but I've been trying to keep her calm the whole three hours that we've been waiting for you to get off work. Now if you want me to back out of it and let things pop off however they do, I can do that." I paused and watched Cheron give Rorrie a stare-down that Mike Tyson would have been proud of. Clearly Rorrie was shaken. "Just take the test and we're out of here."

"Okay, I'm not pregnant," Rorrie cried out. "I'm not. I told him that to try to keep him."

"Screw that. She needs to take the test. We gotta be sure," Cheron said.

I extended my hand and the test. "It'll take a few minutes."

She looked at me and then at Cheron, who seemed like she was fuming. I followed her to the bathroom, where she peed on the stick. Four minutes later and I had a negative result in my hand. Rorrie collapsed on the couch and erupted into tears as we headed out the door. I looked back and took what I was sure would be my last look at her, only to see her staring at me.

"Hailey," she whispered. My eyes and hers were locked together as if we were peering into each other's soul. "I'm sorry."

There were so many things that she had to be sorry about but I knew that those words were for my mother. I turned and headed out the door, finally confident that the book was closed on her in both mine and Khalil's life, forever.

We rode in silence, listening to Beyoncé's *B'day* for the first hour. Finally Cheron broke the silence. "So how do you feel?"

"I feel great."

"That's good. I'm happy for you."

Twenty minutes passed before I realized that Cheron had something more she wanted to discuss. "Hailey, I don't know how to say this . . ."

"Just spit it out."

"Okay, I will." She paused and turned the volume down a notch. "You're doing really well. New house and driving a car that cost a fortune. A husband and a baby . . ." She took a deep breath. "I think that if the shoe was on the other foot and it was me who had run into all of this good fortune, I would have looked out for you."

I was a little shocked at what she'd said. "Say what?"

"I would have broken you off. It's obvious that you're rich and I still live in my little apartment in Southeast. I'm just saying. You know things aren't easy."

"Cheron, you have a lot of nerve. I've always looked out for you and I always will. But what do you expect me to do? Buy you a house, a car? I've always given you money. Hell, I paid for Madison's tuition last year. What do you expect?"

Her feelings were hurt but she didn't come off like a victim. Instead she told me: "I'd like some money. I'd like a couple hundred thousand dollars. If it hadn't been for you, Manny and I would have been together and he would've had me living like a queen, but I didn't get that chance."

I shook my head. "Cheron, Manny had a wife and a baby on

the way. He was fucking me on the side and who knows who else. On top of that, he probably would have been locked up by now."

"You don't know that . . ."

"This is ridiculous. But you know what, I'm glad I see where you're coming from. You should know that I have your daughter in my will. I love you both and I'll always look out. She'll never go without, but I'm the one who was on her fucking back for all these years not you. You made your choices and I made mine. You think this shit was easy. You don't know the half of it. I'm ashamed and I'm just beginning to forgive myself for what I did to me, for what happened to my mother. My life has been torture for years. Yeah, I've had money and material things but absolutely no peace and surely no real happiness. Until now. Until Khalil.

"And yeah, I do have plenty of money. But if you think I'm going to give it away you're crazy. What you can do is run this boutique that I'm about to open. I've had you in mind ever since the opportunity came for me to open it in Manhattan. I was planning to set you up in a nice place and have you . . ."

"I'm not moving to New York," she said, cutting me off.

"You really should . . ."

"Hailey, forget I said anything. Forget it. You do you."

Her voice was cold and chilling. I decided to drop it and we rode in silence the rest of the way home.

30

KHALIL

I needed to do it alone. If I was going to move on and bury my demons once and for all, this was the first stop and hopefully the last. I didn't call before I came back here on Honey's advice. No need to give a warning or time to prepare an excuse; I simply walked up to the door.

"Khalil," she said, shocked to see me.

"Can I come in? I'd like to talk to you."

Frannie took the lock off of the screen and said, "Of course." She opened the door and when our eyes met she seemed a little misty. "I'm so glad you came back. I haven't stopped thinking about you since you left."

She led me into the living room where I took a seat and then she immediately began trying to offer me food and drink. I accepted a Sprite. I'd been craving them lately. She came back with the soda, a cup of ice, and an envelope. "Here's the money you left here. I was going to keep it until I saw you again."

"What made you think you'd see me again?"

"I prayed on it. I prayed really hard on it." I nodded my head for lack of a response. "So, Khalil, what made you come today?"

"I don't know why today. I just wanted to share something with you. There's something that I need to say in order to move on before I get married."

"You're getting married?" she asked with a huge smile appearing on her face coupled with the misty eyes again. "God is good."

"Yes. Honey and I are going to Hawaii next week to be married."

"I've been once. Which island?"

"Oahu."

"That's going to be beautiful. Are her parents going?"

"Her mother is deceased and she doesn't know her father." Her face showed a quick hint of regret for asking. "She and I have a lot in common when it comes to bad parental backgrounds."

She held her head down. "I'm sorry," Frannie said. I looked into her eyes and saw the same woman I loved so much when I was a child. The only differences in her now were the beginnings of crow's-feet in the corners of her eyes and the gray strands in her thick, black hair.

"Frannie, I came here today to let you know that I forgive you. I've been to therapy to overcome the things that happened to me when I was growing up. I blocked so many things out but it wasn't until recently that I remembered what you did . . ." I cleared my throat. "I remembered what you did to me."

She tilted her head to the side, looking puzzled. "You went to therapy?"

"Yes. And it took me a long time to get to this point, but I accept that it happened and I forgive you. I forgive you."

"Khalil, you don't know how long I waited to hear you say that to me. I haven't ever forgiven myself. I don't know why I did it." She broke down and began to sob. "I'm soooo sorry," she cried out as her chest began to heave.

I sat there unsure of what to say. The best I came up with was "Did you ever think about getting some help?"

"Help? What can I do about it now? I knew that I shouldn't have left you, that I should have stayed or taken you with me. I should have protected you."

"Say what?"

"I should have taken you with me. I shouldn't have left you. It has haunted me all these years, the image of you and the look on your face when I took you back to the home."

"Frannie, is that what you are apologizing for?"

"Yes, and I don't know how to let you know how much . . ."

I cut her off. "That's not what I'm talking about. Yeah, that hurt too, but I'm not talking about that when I say I forgive you."

She stopped crying and wiped her eyes and simply stared at me. "Then what?"

"I'm talking about you . . ." I clenched my teeth as the anger seethed. "I'm talking about you molesting me. In my room."

She jumped out of her seat as if her ass had been set afire. "Khalil, I did no such thing. Is that what you remember?" Her tone was so strong without being defensive. She went on. "Is that what you think I did?"

"Yes."

She shook her head and said, "Lord Jesus, help us. Help this child. Khalil, I never did anything to harm you. I would never have done anything like that to you."

"But . . . I remember . . ."

"No, Khalil. You don't remember that. Think back to that

night when I came home late from work and I was looking for your father, the night I walked into your room and caught him . . ." Now it was her turn to lose control. Her hands began to tremble. "Your father molested you. I caught him and we fought all night. He was drunk and he did that to you."

She might as well have driven a sword into my chest as the words she spoke cut deeply into my soul. I looked into her eyes and as she gazed back at me I knew she was telling the truth. I remembered.

"Khalil, there are some things I need to tell you."

I sat on her couch and listened for the next twenty minutes as my life unraveled right before me.

Even though it was pouring down raining, I made it from Philadelphia to the George Washington Bridge in record time. Frannie had tried to calm me as I thanked her and stormed out of her house. She knew where I was headed. I didn't call Honey until I reached my old building.

"Baby, I love you," I said as I cried.

"What's wrong, Khalil?" she asked in a panic. "I knew I should have come. Tell me what's wrong."

"Honey, I'm sorry. But I have to do this. He has to die."

"Who has to die? What are you talking about?"

I was crying. "It wasn't Frannie who did that to me first. It was my father, or let me say the man who I thought was my father. Kevin Graves was not my father. My father and mother were killed in a car accident. Kevin was my uncle and it was his wife that was a drug addict, not my mother. He lied to me, Honey." I was rocking back and forth like Dustin Hoffman did in *Rain Man*. "I have to go."

"Khalil . . ." I heard her calling my name as I hung the phone up. I stepped out of the truck into the rain. In my mind I visualized the murder. I was going to drag him from the house and toss him down the steps, or I'd strangle him. I knew that Rikers was in my near future, but as much as I loved Honey, I couldn't control the anger that had become my entire spirit.

I banged on the door like the NYPD. Perhaps I could get a temporary insanity. I banged some more until a "Who is it?" came from the other side.

"It's Khalil."

"Khalil who?"

I banged again and a woman opened up. "Where is Kevin?"

The woman looked familiar but I couldn't place her. She said, "I know you. You Kevin's boy. I recognize you. I used to live up the hall. Daaaamn, baby. The last time I saw you, you was a little thing. Look at you now all grown up and shit."

My recollection became clear. It was Tenille's lover from up the hall. I felt sick on my stomach. "I'm looking for Kevin."

"Are you serious? You ain't on no drugs or nothing, are you?"

"Do I look like I'm on drugs?"

"Hell no. You look fine as hell, but looks can be deceiving."

"Well, no. I'm not on anything. I just want to see Kevin." My tone was low and I'm sure threatening.

"Sugar, I don't know how to say this, but you about three months too late. Kevin passed away in June. I took over this apartment and he didn't leave much of anything."

I backed away from the door, wanting to punch a hole in the wall, but as mad as I was, I knew that I would have broken every bone in my hand.

She began to speak but I turned and walked away. With the

knowledge that I had escaped a twenty-year sentence, my rage melted as I walked slowly through the pouring rain back to my vehicle.

I drove home, listening to an oldies CD as I tried to digest everything that had happened to me during the course of the day. By the time I got off of the turnpike I'd all but figured out that my life had been cursed. I had so many questions but no strength to seek the answers.

I crossed the Delaware Memorial Bridge and cruised back into Maryland before I even decided to call Honey and let her know that I was okay. When I picked my phone up, there were thirty missed calls from her phone and Frannie's number.

When I called her phone she answered, "Baby, please tell me you're okay."

"Yes, I'm okay. I'm headed home." Then I heard a voice in the background. "Who is that?"

"Baby, I'm at Frannie's house. She and I were headed to New York. I called her and she told me what happened. I raced up here. I was so scared you were going to do something that . . ."

"Well, I guess God beat me to it. Kevin died a few months ago."

"Oh my goodness," she cried out.

"The whole thing is like a sick joke."

"I'm coming home. I'm going to get in the car and I'll meet you at the house. Are you okay?"

"I don't know. I just don't know if I can take much more. I just want to go bury my head under a pillow. Can we talk about it when you get home?"

"Yes, we can. I'll see you in a little while. I love you. Drive safe."

"I will. You too."

I needed a drink and fast, so I slammed on the pedal in an attempt to bend time and make it home in a matter of minutes.

The last forty minutes were the longest but finally I pulled up to the gate and hit the remote. I prepared to turn into the driveway, only to be cut off by a strange vehicle. The car had come from thirty yards down the street. I wasn't scared, only curious as to why the car pulled slowly up to me. We were adjacent to the drive, so I couldn't pull around them and into the gate. I stood still and waited; our windows both now down as we locked eyes.

"I know we haven't met formally, but I feel like I already know you. Khalil, there are some things that you need to know about Honey. After you hear them, trust me, brother, marriage will be the last thing you'll want to do with her."

31

HONEY

When I picked up the letter I almost had a heart attack. I had driven home to support Khalil. Now here I was sitting on the floor of the foyer on my knees, crying as I read the words over and over again.

Honey,

I left because I feared what I would do if I saw you. Today I was in the mood to confront my demons. Then a mood to kill one. The day ends with me finding out that I was about to marry one.

How could you do this to me? A prostitute. Never mind how much money you made or that you probably want to call yourself an escort. The word for what you do is called "whoring." The word for what you've done to me is "destroyed."

I guess you made an enemy out of the wrong person. What made you think that I wouldn't find out?

I'll be back next Saturday at noon to get my things. I'll
leave the key when I come. Please don't be here as I never
want to see you again. Never. As for the baby, I trust you'll
do the right thing and end the pregnancy.
Khalil

Next to the letter, his cell phone was shattered in thirty pieces. I read his words once more, emotion took control of me, and I began screaming "no, no" at the top of my lungs. As I cried on the floor it was a battle for me not to hyperventilate. My head was spinning as the temperature in the room felt like it went up to one hundred and ten degrees. Without warning I leaned forward and began to vomit. My world had unraveled just when I believed that I had put it all together so tightly that I'd never have a care. When I believed that I'd never be alone.

I barely made it up the steps to the bed as I clutched the letter in one hand. I called his phone to leave a message but I got nothing. He'd turned off his answering service.

I lost track of how many times I called his phone as the thought of sleeping never even crossed my mind. When the sunlight began to burst through the windows of the bedroom I realized that I was close to losing my mind.

I don't know when it happened but eventually I passed out from the exhaustion. When I woke up it was late in the afternoon. I tried every number that I had for Khalil's friends. It was a short list. As I expected, no one had seen or heard from him. He had called Frannie and told her that when I called to let me know that I was not to call the police or his friends looking for him. He also sent word to please respect his wishes and not to be home when he came to get his things.

Frannie was extremely short with me. As if she was a mother protecting her child.

I sat in the kitchen all day and waited for him to change his mind. By the time the sun set, I'd driven past his house only to see the tenants coming out of the door. Another sleepless night was waiting for me as my pain began to give way to the rage and confusion. Priest had gone too far. No one else would have done it.

He would pay with everything he had. This was the last time that anyone would screw me over.

For three nights straight I tossed and turned as I teetered on the brink of a breakdown every time I breathed. *"Khalil please come home to me. Please,"* I begged him in my dreams. He cursed me out and called me out of name, but at least he was there. Waking up and finding out that I was alone was the real nightmare.

At seven A.M. I walked into my closet and grabbed my safe from underneath the carpet. I pulled out the portable hard-drive storage key and uploaded the contents into my computer.

Then I logged on to the computer and got the numbers to the *Enquirer* and the *Star*. What I did next, I did for free. I outed Priest Alexander and e-mailed the photos to Wendy Williams. After that I called the Miami Police Department and gave them an anonymous tip regarding information on both of the Bobbsey Twins and shared the theory of possible foul play on Priest's part.

By noon I'd set the wheels in motion to destroy his life just as he'd destroyed mine. I didn't leave the house, I didn't make another phone call, nor did I bother to shower. I sat on the sofa until the sun set again, waiting for my nightmare to end. I imagined how Priest was feeling now that I'd struck back. But even the revenge didn't do much to abate the pain that I felt without Khalil.

I had to find him. I had to make him understand why I'd done the things I had. He had to know how much I loved him.

At around eleven I climbed off of the couch, forced to the re-frigerator by the hunger pains. I thought about the baby growing inside of me and how Khalil requested that I abort. There was no way I would do that. If nothing else I believed that his child might be the only way I'd keep him in my life. I had to eat to take care of the baby.

I turned on the television as I prepared an egg sandwich and out of curiosity I flipped on ESPN. I nearly dropped the frying pan as the headline story was about Priest. "Scandal Rocks the League as Priest Alexander Is Wanted in Miami for Questioning in Connection with the Deaths of Two Women" was the opening headline.

I watched as the sportscaster burst in with "Not since Kobe's rape charge have we seen such a wildfire brewing in profes-sional basketball. Anonymous tips to the police, mysterious photos allegedly depicting Priest Alexander in a compromising position with a longtime friend and bodyguard surfacing on the Internet ... We're all wondering right now how all of this ties in together. But at the moment, things look awfully dim for the two-time All-Star. Awfully dim. So far Mr. Alexander has not is-sued a statement. We're still waiting."

As I watched more, I remembered Priest's words: *"Your man? Bitch, you're a fucking whore. A high-class one, but still a whore nonetheless. Any man who's claiming you has got to be some pussy-whipped idiot."*

I felt no remorse.

32

KHALIL

I hadn't answered the phone in my hotel room all day, so when Cameron knocked on the door I wasn't surprised. I'd been holed up in the Greenbelt Marriott for three days straight. She banged incessantly and I knew that she wasn't going to give up.

I climbed out of the bed and opened the door to see her standing there looking the part of a concerned ally. "I brought you some Boston Market. Let me by."

"I'm not hungry. I told you that and I also told you that I don't want company."

"Khalil, you can't just stay up in here and shut the world off. You have to keep on moving. She's not worth this. Nobody is."

Hearing her speak negatively about Honey angered me. Even with all that I'd learned, I still loved her, though I wouldn't admit it to anyone. Cameron insisted that I eat and I had to admit for the first time in days that the thought of shoving a meal down my throat didn't make me want to throw up.

Before I knew it a couple of hours had passed and Cameron

and I were talking the way we used to in her office. She was off the record and insisted that I respond the same way. It was like a free session. We talked about the pain of my discovery in regards to my parents and about my desire to kill Kevin, which I was glad to learn was normal.

"This was a really bad time for you to find out about Honey, I know. Just dealing with your other issues has to be incredibly tough, but you *were* about to marry her. So in essence, this may have been the best time."

I digested her words and accepted that she may have been right. "So what do I do?"

"What do you want to do?" she asked in response. "I mean if you love her and you think you can get past it maybe you should call her."

"I could never forgive her. Our whole relationship was built on lies."

"Perhaps, but let me ask you this. Do you feel like you know why she didn't tell you the truth from the beginning?"

I thought about it and the answer was so easy that I imagined that Cameron was trying to set me up. "She lied so that I wouldn't know that she was a call girl."

She smiled. "No, she lied so that you wouldn't judge her for her past. You see as humans we all have secrets, things we do that we wouldn't want to share with anyone else in the world. As time goes on, we find acceptance from ourselves and that is often so incredibly difficult. Sometimes we beat ourselves up daily over these things. Naturally we reason that if we have so much trouble accepting ourselves that there's no way in the world someone else will accept us for who we really are or in certain cases who we were."

"So are you saying that I should forgive her?"

"I'm not telling you anything except for what I'm telling you."

"Which is?"

"Do you have ears?" She laughed. She stood up and said, "Khalil, I have to go. It's getting late. I'm in a hotel room with a man who I'm slightly attracted to and who I know deep down inside is somewhat attracted to me. The thing is I know that that man is in love with someone else. Someone who has secrets just like everyone else in the world."

"Even you?"

"Especially me." She headed for the door and before she turned the handle she said, "Khalil, call me if you need me. Don't sit in this room too much longer, it won't help the pain, and most of all be true to yourself." I was listening attentively. "Always remember, you can't choose who you love. When you find that the person is bad for you, usually it's gonna hurt. As a matter of fact, it always hurts."

With that she walked out of the room.

Hours after Cameron left I stood in the shower, replaying the entire scene in my mind. The car pulling up, the window going down. *"I know we haven't met formally, but I feel like I already know you. Khalil, there are some things that you need to know about Honey. After you hear them, trust me, brother, marriage will be the last thing you want to do with her."*

Cheron had gone on: "I told Honey that she couldn't build a future on a lie, and that you deserved to know the truth. As much as I don't want to admit it, Honey is evil and I know you've been through so much already that you don't need to be with someone else who would deceive you about something so important."

I hated to admit that I had become all ears as Cheron poured out hateful gossip that was more lethal than acid. Each word destroying a piece of the love and trust that I felt for Honey.

I questioned her motives at first but she never made an advance. It was like she was playing the role of my guardian angel.

"I thought you were her friend. Her best friend," was the only thing I had responded with.

"I was. But right is right and wrong is wrong."

I climbed out of the shower and got dressed. My heart ached and felt as though it might stop beating at any second. I needed to see Honey. I picked up the phone to let her know that I was coming home. I got halfway through dialing the number when I heard a knock at the door.

I hung it up and walked to the door. "Who is it?"

"Cheron."

When I opened it up she walked in. "What are you doing?" I asked, shocked with her boldness.

"I came to check on you." I'd made the mistake of calling her from the hotel the next day for more details. She'd seemed to take pleasure in delivering as much detail as I was willing to listen to.

"I'm okay."

"Really? I brought you something to help you out." She lifted a bag of liquor and put it on the dresser. "I thought you could probably use a drink."

"I don't think . . ." She was already popping the top and pouring the XO into a cup.

"Plus there are some things I wanted to talk to you about." She was talking really fast. "First I need to use the bathroom."

As she headed into the bathroom I realized that I wasn't wearing anything but a towel and I needed a pair of underwear. I began digging through my bag, searching to no avail, when the door swung open. I looked at the door and she was standing there in nothing but her bra and panties.

Cheron had to be at least five or six years older than me but her body took my breath away. She looked like one of the girls you see in *King* or *Smooth* magazine. I knew what time it was as I scanned the black-and-pink bra-and-panties set. "Cheron, what are you doing?"

"You know exactly what I'm doing."

"So is this why you told me about Honey? So you could steal me from her?"

"No, that's not it at all," she said as she moved toward me, hands-out. She touched my shoulders and as the sensations trickled through my body I lost my temper.

I yelled at the top of my lungs: "Cheron, get the fuck out of my room before I kill you." I was so angry. She had ruined my life. In that instant I wished that she'd never told me anything about Honey. For the first time I realized that staying in the dark about Honey's secrets wouldn't have been so bad. She'd taken an HIV test at the prenatal appointment, which came out negative, so it was a case where what I didn't know wouldn't have hurt me. My anger persisted. I shoved Cheron into the wall and told her for the second time to leave.

She yelled back but sounded fearful: "I'm trying to help you out. All I did was try to look out for you. Nigga, you crazy."

"Nah, your ass is crazy." Like Martin Lawrence sending Cole,

Pam, or Tommy out of his crib I yelled, "Now get to stepping." I grabbed her clothes and opened the door. I tossed them into the hall along with the liquor bottle. "Your ass ain't a friend to anyone. You're a snake."

She scrambled out into the hall and grabbed her clothes. Ten minutes later I was on my way to Honey.

33

HONEY

The sound of footsteps startled me but didn't wake me. I wasn't asleep. I sat up in the bed as soon as I heard the sound of feet moving through the house. I reached for the light on the nightstand. I knew he'd come. I hadn't turned the alarm on all week, anticipating seeing him again.

When the light hit the room I saw the surprised look on his face. If it weren't for the baby inside of me things might have gone differently. I might not have held out the hope of survival. Maybe I wouldn't have prepared myself to go to these lengths.

Once he saw me he began to cry. "How could you do this to me? You took everything from me. My life is over. I kept my end of the deal. I left you alone," Priest said.

"You told my fiancé everything. You told him what I did and he left me."

"What are you talking about? I did not," he said, almost whining.

"Why lie about it Priest? You've done enough lying to last a lifetime I'd think."

"I'm not lying. If I was going to tell I would have done it the day I saw you downtown. I've been overseas since the day after that. I was in town to take pictures at the Capitol with the other players who were on the U.S. National Team. We left the next day. I just came home this morning. I couldn't have done it."

I was puzzled at what he was saying. I did remember the sportscaster saying that he was unavailable for comment. He went on, "I was playing in a tournament when the story broke. Then I come home to this." His voice was trailing off. "I come home to you ruining my life, my marriage, my career."

My body began to get cold. I believed him. I had always been good at reading someone's body language and Priest was being straightforward. I sucked in air and tried to stay calm. He was sweating as he began to ramble on and on about his family and his career.

Speaking just below a yell he said, "What am I supposed to do now? You tell me that." He began to ramble. This made me nervous in light of the fact that he'd come to kill me. The gun he held in his hand and the black gloves he wore were a dead give-away of his intentions.

"Stay calm and don't lift that," I said. "I swear I will use this." The Smith & Wesson that I had been aiming at his face since the second he walked into my bedroom had kept him steady up to that point. I'd purchased the gun years back and I knew how to use it. I'd learned a long time ago that there were some situations where pepper spray just wouldn't get the job done.

"So you gonna kill me?" he chuckled in a tone of disbelief. I don't think he doubted for a second that I would pull the trigger. I did think that he was having a hard time accepting that his revenge would not come to pass.

"I don't want to but . . ." I stopped when we both heard the front door shut. "Who's with you? Is your boyfriend with you?"

"I'm alone," he said in a panicked tone. When I heard the voice my heart began to beat again.

I heard the familiar pattern of Khalil's feet moving quickly up the stairs. I couldn't believe that he had come home. He turned the corner and saw Priest standing there with the gun in his hand.

I wanted to scream out that I had it under control but Khalil's eyes lit up with anger and he rushed toward Priest. He didn't move quickly enough and I watched as Priest lifted the weapon and fired three shots. They all hit Khalil.

I wanted to scream; instead I aimed for Priest, who looked surprised at what he'd done. By the time he faced me I was squeezing the trigger. I lost track of how many times I fired, but I didn't stop until he slid down the wall as the crimson blood began to pour from the holes I'd put in him.

"Oh God no," I yelled out. I ran and stepped over Priest to Khalil. "Baby, please. Don't die. Don't die," I kept repeating.

I was a flash as I ran for the phone to call 911. As I ran down to unlock the door and the gate, he was still breathing. When I got back to him, he wasn't.

One Year Later

FROM HONEY TO HAILEY

On a lovely spring morning I delivered a beautiful and healthy, seven-pound four-ounce baby boy. I named him Khalil after his father. The only sad thing about the birth of my child was that I was forced to deliver him alone in a small town in West Virginia. It was just one of those things. After a tear in the lining of my uterus, I'd begun bleeding heavily and had been transported from Alderson Federal Prison Camp to Greenbrier Valley Medical Center.

Fortunately, I hadn't been charged for Priest's death, but the people at Mark-One International did their best to have me charged with blackmail. It turned out that they were paper gangsters, because the only muscle they sent after me was their lawyers. They also seemed reluctant to reveal which account they'd paid me from. I suspected that they had done a few shady things as well, because they quickly let the issue go. After wasting time and money, they found out that they had no way of tracking the money I'd received, finding it, or retrieving it. They'd wired the money to an account that no longer existed, even in Antigua, where it had been formed. At the direction of my banker on the island, I'd done like the rest of the white-collar criminals and moved the money thirty times across four continents.

I wound up taking a plea to tax evasion, since I admitted to accepting hush money that I didn't report. I laughed at the one-hundred-thousand-dollar fine, but I didn't laugh at the one-year sentence I received. Nor did I find anything funny about having to go back to "Camp Cupcake," as the women's prison was called, while my baby went home with his father.

Khalil survived the bullets that Priest fired into him and he stood by my side every day after that. He also put his career on hold to take care of the baby while he waited for me to come home.

We sold the house in Annapolis after the shooting, of course. Believe it or not, people lined up to buy the house that Priest Alexander died in. I loved Khalil more each day as he would come to West Virginia and stay for a few days at a time.

Everything seemed to work out beautifully as he was able to persuade Frannie to move temporarily to Fort Washington, into our new house. Frannie and Khalil were like new, as she got used to being a grandmother.

In federal prison, the best anyone does with early release is doing eighty percent of whatever they're sentenced to. With this in mind I counted down the days. Even in the worst case I'd be home by Christmas. Of course I was hoping for September.

As was customary, Khalil and I were on the phone. "So what's he doing?"

"He's about to fall asleep, it looks like. Before that he was eating and in a little while he'll be taking a crap in his Pamper. That's all he does." Khalil laughed.

"I would do anything to be there to change one of those. To be able to help you."

"You will soon."

My heart ached for my man and my baby. "I love you. I love you both so much," I said with tears in my eyes, as usual. I talked to Khalil every day and every day I cried. Next he did the usual and prepared to put the phone to the baby's ear.

"Go ahead baby and sing to him." As he placed the phone to K.J.'s ear, I began singing the words to an old-school song that one of the inmates had taught me, called "Sukiyaki":

> If only you were here,
> you'd wash away my tears.

Khalil said, "Keep singing. He's smiling."

It was a rough beginning for our son, having to break out of jail just to bust out of his mother's womb. But even though it'd started like this, I swore K.J. would have everything that both his father and I didn't. I promised to myself. Most important, he'd have love and he'd be protected.

Even though I wasn't there with him every day, I gave all that I could, and that would have to hold him over until I made it home. I didn't stop singing for three or four minutes. By the time I stopped, Khalil whispered, "He's asleep, Honey. I'm going to go put him in the crib."

"Okay."

"Khalil," I said in a whisper. "Thank you for giving me another chance. Thank you for saving my life. You might not know it, but you save my life every single day."

"You're welcome, Hailey."

We hung up and I went to my bunk, where I drifted off to sleep for the first time daring to dream about a happy ending.

ACKNOWLEDGMENTS

First I want to thank my readers and fans, old and new. Your support and e-mails mean the world to me. I don't know about other authors, but I am truly humbled by all the love.

Next I want to thank the entire Amistad staff, especially Dawn Davis and Christina Morgan, for your patience and dedication. Also, Gilda Squire, Laura Klynstra, Bryan Christian, Michael Morrison, and all the other members of the Harper family who helped bring my books to fruition.

A few special friends have been instrumental in all of my projects. First off, Rockelle Henderson; I'll miss you as a colleague but I'll have you as a friend for life. You have been a godsend from day one. Kelli Martin, you never forget your first . . . editor. Again, Joy King, love you for life. Enid Pinner, Chad Cunningham, Derek Lowe, Sheryl Hicks, test readers from the past, I credit you with helping me get to the present. Gina Blake, thanks for your help and for all the good energy. You popped into my life just when I needed you. Stick around.

To all my friends, family, and readers who've lent a hand in promoting my work, I thank you. If I named you all, the acknowledgments would be longer than the book. Please . . . you know who you are. Some of you I can't get anything done without: Tressa Smallwood, Yolanda Johnson, Lynn Thomas, Tamara Cooke, and Tracye Stafford. Shaka, get ready for one more run! A heartfelt thanks to DeWright Johnson Jr. We may have lost the connection, but the love remains. I always hear you, even when you think I don't. I'll be back, but until then, I wish you nothing but the best. To my man, Eyone Williams, just keep doing what you're doing and you'll get where you're trying to go. Dannette Majette, so full of energy, you are one of a kind. Much success to you.

To Karibu Books, my family and my home from the very beginning, thank you for the support. Shout out to my special deejays, Justine Love and Todd B on WPGC. Also much love to Michel Wright and Natalie Case. Thanks to all the black-owned bookstores fighting the good fight across the nation. I also have to acknowledge the African-American buyers at the chains, who have supported me from day one. At the top of the list, Sean Bentley, thank you.

As always, I have to thank my mother for her support and help with my most precious commodity, my son. Thanks for letting me get those sixteen-hour days in. I needed them.

Although this book is not an exercise in my spirituality as far as the content goes, still, I must thank God for the air I breathe, this gift of life, and allowing me to complete this task. Many people will write me and tell me that they love my work or that they think I'm great—not being conceited, just being real. For those thoughts I truly am thankful, but I'll take no glory for the stories I create, this career, or for even becoming published. My life has been just as much a miracle as a work in progress. I am nothing without HIM.

READERS GUIDE QUESTIONS

1. Was there any excuse for Honey's transformation or behavior?

2. Both Honey and Khalil faced tragic circumstances during their critical teen years, but unquestionably Khalil fought through his better. Why do you think this is so?

3. Do you think that people use their baggage as an excuse to do what it is that they really want to do all the time?

4. Is it possible that life deals certain people hands that they have no control over, and when that happens is it okay to do what you need to in order to survive?

5. How realistic do you think it is that people in Priest's position have secrets like his?

6. Do you think that Honey was justified in any of the things she did to retaliate against people who she felt wronged her?

7. What was it about Honey that caused Khalil to fall so hard for her? Was it sex, the challenge, or could they have been soul mates?

8. What is your understanding, if any, of the impact of mo-

lestation or engaging in sex at too young of an age on the mental development of young men? Do you think that Khalil showed the effects of this?

9. What percentage of men do you believe will engage in sex for hire?

10. As a woman, do you feel that a man owes a woman anything—monetary, material, or commitment-wise—for engaging in a consensual experience?

11. What do you think was the author's purpose for writing this?

12. Who was your favorite character? Least favorite?

13. What did you enjoy most or least about the book?

14. Ultimately, do you think a man could really forgive a woman with a past if it was sordid?

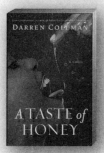

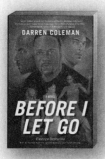

NVISION PUBLISHING ORDER FORM
Buy any Nvision Publishing title or Darren Coleman book from Nvision Publishing!

DO OR DIE
$15.00

LOST & TURNED OUT
$15.00

BEFORE I LET GO
(Amistad Edition)
$14.95

DON'T EVER WONDER
(Amistad Edition)
$14.95

LADIES LISTEN UP
(Amistad Edition)
$14.95

A TASTE OF HONEY
(Amistad Edition)
$14.95

PURCHASER INFORMATION

Name _____

Register # _____
(Applies if incarcerated)

Address _____

_____

City _____

State/Zip _____

Which Book _____

# of books _____

Total enclosed $ _____

Send to
Nvision Publishing/Order
P.O. Box 274
Lanham Severn Road
Lanham, MD 20703

Make check or money order payable to
Nvision Publishing. Checks must clear before
orders are sent. (Not advisable to send cash.)

Add $4.00 for shipping via U.S. Priority Mail for
a total cost per book of $19.00

Nvision Publishing deducts 25% from orders
shipped directly to prisons. Cost is $11.25 plus
$4.00 shipping for a total cost per book
of $15.25